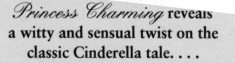

Princess Charming reveals
a witty and sensual twist on the
classic Cinderella tale. . . .

Thanks to the mischievous meddling of his match-making sister, Ashton Wilde meets a damsel in distress during the midnight magic of a lavish ball. But Maura Collyer isn't looking for a prince—or an intimate pairing with any member of the scandalous noble Wilde family.

Intrigued by Maura's beauty and daring, Ash is determined to aid in the rescue of her beloved stallion, sold by her wicked stepmother to an evil viscount. As his adventure with Maura becomes rife with peril and passion, Ash suspects he's found his heart's desire.

Even though her dearest friend may be her self-proclaimed fairy godmother, Maura is mortified at being pushed into a romance with a notorious rake such as Ash. Dashing and charming, he comes to Maura's rescue just in time to help her steal back her precious horse. As they flee across the countryside, she can't resist his sweet seduction. But is her prince playing a role in a fairy tale to test an improbable theory, or is the love awakening in her heart proof of her own happily ever after?

❧

By Nicole Jordan

Legendary Lovers
Princess Charming

The Courtship Wars
To Pleasure a Lady
To Bed a Beauty
To Seduce a Bride
To Romance a Charming Rogue
To Tame a Dangerous Lord
To Desire a Wicked Duke

Paradise Series
Master of Temptation
Lord of Seduction
Wicked Fantasy
Fever Dreams

Notorious Series
The Seduction
The Passion
Desire
Ecstasy
The Prince of Pleasure

Other Novels
The Lover
The Warrior
Touch Me With Fire

Princess Charming

A Legendary Lovers Novel

NICOLE JORDAN

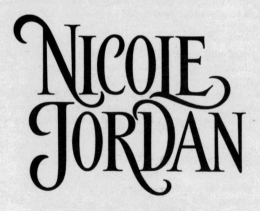

BALLANTINE BOOKS • NEW YORK

Princess Charming is a work of fiction. Names, characters, places, and incidents are the products of the author's imagination or are used fictitiously. Any resemblance to actual events, locales, or persons, living or dead, is entirely coincidental.

A Ballantine Books Mass Market Original

Copyright © 2012 by Anne Bushyhead

Published in the United States by Ballantine Books, an imprint of The Random House Publishing Group, a division of Random House, Inc., New York.

BALLANTINE and colophon are registered trademarks of Random House, Inc.

This book contains an excerpt from Book Two of the Legendary Lovers series by Nicole Jordan. This excerpt has been set for this edition only and may not reflect the final content of the forthcoming edition.

ISBN 978-0-345-52527-7
eBook ISBN 978-0-345-52528-4

Cover design: Lynn Andreozzi
Cover illustration: Alan Ayers

Printed in the United States of America

www.ballantinebooks.com

9 8 7 6 5 4 3 2 1

Ballantine Books mass market edition: February 2012

To my newest dear friends and co-conspirators,
RaeAnne Thayne and Victoria Dahl.
Thank you for helping me bring my passionate,
pleasure-loving Wilde cousins to life!

Prologue

Kent, England, August 1804

Pausing hip deep in water, Ashton Wilde watched protectively as his four younger siblings and cousins frolicked in the lake at Beauvoir, the ancestral seat of the Marquises of Beaufort. Shrieks and squeals and peals of laughter filled the air when their game of water tag devolved into a pitched battle.

It was nearing summer's end, but this was the first time in many months that Ash could remember feeling totally carefree.

He'd carefully arranged the outing—riding and fishing and swimming with an alfresco picnic in between—partly because the day was too glorious to spend indoors, but mainly because he wanted to re-create a sense of normalcy for his family, especially the two girls, who were much younger than the three boys.

A smile curved Ash's lips at the tableau: Eleven-year-old Skye pushing seventeen-year-old Jack's head underwater and Jack magnanimously permitting her victory. Katharine, age twelve, joining in the fray, pelting eighteen-year-old Quinn with scoops of lake water. Quinn pretending to sputter and beg for mercy before turning for his revenge, which sent Kate racing out of reach, her mirth echoing around the shoreline.

They deserved to feel joyous again, Ash thought with satisfaction. In the past hour, two different servants had come to summon them home for tea, but he wouldn't allow anyone to spoil this golden afternoon. For a short while at least, he was determined to restore the innocence of childhood that had been wrenched from them with the devastating deaths of all their parents in a shipwreck the previous winter.

Ash, who was almost a year senior to Quinn, had the heavy responsibility of being the eldest orphaned Wilde cousin, in addition to prematurely inheriting the illustrious Beaufort title and fortune.

Just now his own heart felt immensely lighter than at any time since the tragedy. Grief still remained a strong undercurrent in their lives, but for now it had been banished by cool water and hot sunshine.

Ash knew Quinn felt a similar bitterness toward the cruelties of fate after becoming the Earl of Traherne far too soon. The Beaufort and Traherne estates were situated in adjoining neighborhoods in Kent, so that even though Quinn and Skye hailed from a separate branch of the Wilde family, the distant cousins had grown up together as close as siblings. The proximity had also eased the merging of their two households under the legal guardianship of their middle-aged bachelor uncle, Lord Cornelius Wilde.

The anguishing loss of both sets of their parents had turned Quinn into a cynic at an early age, yet even he had gone along with Ash's plan to provide some much-needed moments of happiness for the girls, and Jack as well. Jack's familial status was the oddity in the bunch—a first cousin to Ash and Katharine, but also their adopted brother.

"Take care, Ash! Quinn is coming for you!"

The screeched warning from young Skye interrupted Ash's reverie just as he felt a hard tug on one leg and realized that a submerged Quinn had snuck up on him.

His balance upended, Ash went down with a mighty splash while swallowing a mouthful of lake water. When he surfaced, hacking, Quinn flashed him a wicked grin of triumph, which only provoked Ash into launching his own counterassault.

The two of them wrestled in the shallow water for a time, their flailing arms trying to find purchase on slippery bare torsos. Rather than bathing costumes, the boys were shirtless and garbed only in breeches, while the two girls wore sleeveless smocks and leggings.

When eventually Quinn broke free and dove for the deeper middle of the lake, the other Wildes set out after him in hot pursuit, shouting gleeful cries of "Catch him, catch him!"

Some twenty minutes of hard play later, the five of them clambered up the grassy bank and collapsed upon their picnic blankets, where they lay spent and panting beneath the blue summer sky.

Sprawled there with his siblings and cousins, the healing sunlight beating down on his wet skin, Ash felt almost content. Admittedly, his need to protect his family had become a compulsion for him, like a fire burning in his chest. He would die before letting any further harm come to them—and yet he wanted more than mere survival for his family. He wanted them to *flourish,* which meant contriving special days such as today to dull the pain.

His feeling of lazy warmth and contentment, however, was soon dashed by Kate's unexpected musings.

"I have been thinking, Ash," she announced in a dreamy voice. "You need to marry and bring us home a mama."

His eyes flying open at the startling comment, Ash somehow managed to choke again, even though he was a good distance from the lake.

"*Marry?*" he repeated when his fit of coughing subsided. "Just what put that maggoty notion into your head, minx?"

"If you wed, we would have a mother to raise us, and then we would not have to go away to boarding school in a fortnight."

Skye's ears perked up. "That would be famous, Ash. I don't want to be sent away to school."

At least he understood Katharine's rationale for wanting a new mother: She hoped to prevent the breakup of their close-knit family. Throughout their privileged childhood, the Wilde cousins had been given superior educations with the best tutors and governesses, but that would soon end. Ash was to return to Cambridge shortly, having sat out the last term in an attempt to help the younger Wildes rebuild the shattered pieces of their lives.

Quinn, whose razor-sharp mind needed a challenge that no normal tutor could provide, would accompany Ash to university this autumn, and reckless, roguish Jack would follow a year later. As for the girls, they were to attend an elite academy for young ladies, against their heartfelt objections.

"Attending school is not the end of the world," Ash tried to reassure them.

"It will be the end of *our* world," Katharine insisted. "You have to save us by finding us a mama, Ash."

Wincing at her ardent tone, he raised himself on one elbow. "I am barely nineteen. That is too young to marry."

"Well, Uncle Cornelius is too *old* to marry," his sister countered, "so that leaves you."

"Uncle is only one and fifty," Ash replied, although knowing a half century would seem ancient from her perspective.

"But he does not want to raise us any longer," Kate complained.

"That isn't so. He merely believes you deserve better than to be brought up under the guidance of a reclusive scholar."

Ash was certain their uncle's motives were quite selfless, although granted, Cornelius wished to return to his intellectual pursuits. He'd given up his studies completely these past eight months to care for his late relations' unruly offspring.

Skye interjected a heavy sigh. "Uncle Cornelius says when we are older we will thank him for broadening our horizons, but I don't want broad horizons. I cannot bear to leave our home for so long."

"Nor can I," Kate said, pushing herself up to a sitting position.

At their lament, Ash glanced at Quinn for assistance. In response, his cousin reached over and tugged on Kate's red-brown braid. "Uncle fears we are turning into a pack of savages, Katie-love, and savagery is inappropriate for a young lady of your high station. You and Skye have run wild with us boys this entire summer."

Kate shook her head, evidently not willing to accept his logic. "If Uncle thinks a boarding academy will improve my conduct," she muttered, "he is greatly mistaken."

Then, like a dog gnawing a bone, she returned to her previous argument. "Why can you not simply find someone to marry and fall in love, Ash? It should not be too difficult for you. We Wildes are always lucky in love, everyone says so. Mama and Papa were madly in love, and so were Aunt Angelique and Uncle Lionel."

"*I* will never marry," Skye declared to no one in particular, "unless I find my one true love."

Bolstered by that loyal show of support, Kate warmed to her theme. "Mama always said someone special is waiting out there in the world for me— indeed, an ideal match is waiting for each of us."

Jack rolled his eyes at Katharine's claim. "You have been reading too many romantic fairy tales, bratling."

Kate made a face at him. "Perhaps, but Uncle Cornelius says that reading of any kind will strengthen my mind, even fairy tales. And at least," she added defensively, eyeing the small book of Greek myths she had brought with her, "fairy tales usually have happy endings, unlike those violent Greeks and Romans in literature—"

Ash held up his hand to cut off their dispute, knowing his headstrong sister wouldn't let go of her romantic notions or cease her desire to problem-solve without a firm rebuff. "I've vowed to look after you all, Kate, but marriage is out of the question just now."

"If not now, then when?"

"Someday."

Clearly disappointed, Kate flopped back down and gazed up at the sky overhead. "I wish it would happen soon. You could find us a mama in a trice if you would only bother to look, Ash. We know how all the ladies swoon over you."

"She does have a point," Quinn offered, amusement lacing his drawl. Quinn was smirking, enjoying his discomfort, Ash realized.

He skewered his cousin with a piercing look. "If you think bringing home a mother for the girls is such a capital idea, why don't *you* volunteer to find a wife? You could marry just as easily."

"No, I couldn't. I haven't sown enough wild oats yet."

"Why would you want to sow oats?" Skye asked.

Jack let out a snort of laughter. "Never mind, puss."

"You are clutching at straws, Katie," Ash said finally, although softening his tone. "I love you more than life, but I won't wear leg shackles simply to spare you boarding school."

Additionally, he was convinced the girls would benefit from a new environment, where they wouldn't be so isolated and insulated as they were here at Beauvoir or Tallis Court, the nearby Traherne family seat.

"You will meet new friends at school," Ash added consolingly. "And of course you can come home for the summers and every holiday. We will all be together again before you know it. And I mean to visit you frequently at your new school—"

"You had better, or I will never forgive you," Kate threatened before glancing away. "Even so, it will never be the same ag-gain. . . ."

On that last note, her voice broke, a show of weakness that Ash knew was anathema to her.

With a huff of self-disgust, Katharine climbed to her feet and stalked off a short distance to stand with her back to them, trying to control her sniffling.

Feeling inadequate, Ash rose and followed her. When he touched her shoulder comfortingly, she suddenly turned and flung her arms around his waist in a fierce hug. "I will m-miss you so t-terribly, Ash. . . ."

"I will miss you too, love," he said, returning her embrace with the same ferocity.

When a sob escaped her, Ash glanced behind him. The two boys were both staring at them somberly, while Skye was struggling to fight back tears also.

Longing to ease their sadness, Ash bent down and flung Kate over his shoulder, then carried her down to the lake, where despite her pleas of protest, he tossed her in.

To his vast relief, she came up spitting water and grinning. "I know very well that you are trying to distract me!" she yelled, pushing wet tresses from her eyes. "But I am not ever giving up!"

"No," Ash yelled back with a dry chuckle. "I would expect nothing less of you."

It was then that he recognized the tall, lithe form of his Uncle Cornelius in the distance, approaching them on foot. Most likely when the servants hadn't been able to corral them home, the long-suffering gentleman had come himself to rescue the girls, even though they would not want rescuing.

When Lord Cornelius finally reached their picnic blankets, he looked exasperated and frustrated. It wasn't that his discipline was nonexistent; it was merely not very effective. At least Ash could control the youngsters *most* of the time.

Cornelius halted with his arms crossed, his foot tapping, and let his gaze slowly sweep over the lot of them before focusing sternly on Ash.

"I warned you about the intensity of the sun at this time of afternoon, Master Ashton." He then pointed to Skye's face, which was flushed pink.

Upon realizing his cousin's fair skin was burning, Ash instantly swallowed his rebuttal. "We are coming at once, Uncle," he said, sending Skye a rueful glance and nodding at the others.

At his pronouncement, they all began gathering their belongings and loading down the horses.

Then as a group, they turned and reluctantly trudged home toward the manor. Kate cradled her collection of Greek myths in one arm and fell into step with Uncle Cornelius. Quinn and Jack followed, leading the horses, while Ash and Skye brought up the rear.

As they left the sparkling lake behind, Ash glanced around them, committing the special moment to memory. Not only was this the end of their golden summer afternoon, but soon they would be going their separate ways, and like his young sister, he badly wished to delay their inevitable parting.

He suspected Skye was feeling a similar poignancy, for she tucked her smaller hand in his.

"I don't want a new mama, Ash," she said in a low voice.

"No one can ever replace our mothers, love," he

tried to reassure her not for the first time. Yet evidently he had misjudged her reasoning.

"No, I meant that you needn't find us a mama and marry for *our sakes*. You should only marry for love, Ash."

To his surprise, her chin no longer quivered with her effort to hold back tears. Instead, Skye looked up at him with a quiet, trusting smile.

At her obvious desire to comfort him, Ash smiled in return and squeezed her hand. "Thank you, sweetheart."

After another moment, he swallowed the ache in his throat and slid his arm around her delicate shoulders.

"Everything will be all right, Skye," he murmured . . . and for the first time in many, many months, he could actually believe his own empty promise.

Chapter One

London, May 1816

The flash of amber silk intrigued him, although not as much as the lovely woman wearing it.

Lounging negligently against a column in his crowded ballroom, Ashton Wilde, eighth Marquis of Beaufort, narrowed his gaze in speculation. The blond beauty had followed one of his noble male guests through the French doors onto the terrace beyond.

Maura Collyer, his sister's bosom friend. What the devil was she up to?

Curiosity warred with odd disappointment as Ash considered her intent. It appeared that Miss Collyer was trysting with Viscount Deering.

For all her beauty, he would never have taken Maura for the scarlet woman sort. As far as he knew, she didn't even *like* most men, and at four-and-twenty she was long on the shelf. And yet she had accompanied Lord Deering onto a moonlit terrace in the middle of a grand ball for what looked like an assignation.

His boredom suddenly evaporating, Ash pushed

away from the column and forged a path through the glittering, bejeweled sea of company. He had expected better of Miss Collyer—

Wry amusement twisted his mouth at the quaint thought. That the leading member of the passionate Wilde clan could condemn a lady for flouting propriety with a lovers' tryst was the height of irony. The Wildes had long been legendary for their scandalous exploits, their surname synonymous with a blatant disregard for the rules governing the *Beau Monde,* and Ash himself was currently his family's worst offender.

Still, he couldn't banish his contrary stab of displeasure at the notion of Katharine's closest friend taking Deering as a lover.

The terrace doors had been flung open to alleviate the heat from the chandeliers and the crush of perfumed bodies. Upon reaching the threshold, Ash paused to let his eyes adjust to the dimmer light on the terrace and focus on the couple near the stone balustrade.

Although not embracing, they were standing close together—or rather the lady was standing before the gentleman. Her position offered Ash a view of her profile, so he could see that her delicate jaw was set while her hands were tightly clenched.

It did not appear to be a romantic tryst but a confrontation, he decided. He could overhear her low, impassioned voice imploring the viscount, although the noise from the chattering, dancing throng behind him drowned out most of her words.

Ash moved a step closer just as a momentary lull in

the music brought Miss Collyer's urgent declaration to him.

"Emperor did not belong to her, I tell you! She had no right to sell him to you."

"I have a legal deed of sale that says otherwise," Deering responded in an arrogant drawl that evidently grated on the beauty's nerves.

She inhaled a deep breath, as if striving to maintain control of her emotions. "Then allow me to buy him back . . . *Please*."

"You cannot afford my price, Miss Collyer."

"I can raise the funds somehow. I will sell the entire stables if I must."

When Deering laughed in that supercilious way of his, Ash felt the same grating irritation.

He knew Rupert Firth, Viscount Deering, fairly well. Of similar age—a year past thirty—they had attended Cambridge at the same time. Like Ash, Deering had dark curling hair, a noble title, and a significant fortune. But there the similarities ended. Most notably, the viscount was a head shorter, with a body that was turning to flab from an overindulgence of fine port wine.

Ash had never liked Deering, mainly because of his attitude of snide superiority. That dislike only increased as the discussion continued:

"I might be persuaded . . . for a price," Deering said with a smirk that made Ash itch to intervene.

"What price?" Miss Collyer asked warily.

In answer, the nobleman reached out and trailed a languid finger along her bare throat to the low neckline of her gown.

When she visibly gritted her teeth, Ash felt some satisfaction that she wasn't soliciting the viscount's advances, far from it. Yet he was surprised by his own violent reaction: The urge to wrap his hands around the lecher's throat speared through him.

Then Deering gave a low, seductive laugh that raised his ire even further.

"I see you take my meaning, Miss Collyer. If you are truly interested in regaining your property, you will accommodate my wishes. You are quite lovely. I find I want you almost as much as I coveted your magnificent stallion."

Flinching, she took a step backward, out of reach, distaste written in every line of her face. "I regret I must decline your proposition, Lord Deering."

"You should realize that beggars cannot be choosers."

"I am not a beggar quite yet."

The viscount moved closer, but she stood her ground. When his fingers covered her breast and squeezed, Ash took a reflexive step toward them.

But Maura Collyer evidently did not need defending, for she brought her heel down hard on the viscount's instep, forcing him to release her. Even with her soft evening slippers, the impact must have hurt.

It did, if the viscount's pained growl was any indication.

"Your stubbornness reminds me of your damned father!" Deering ground out through his teeth. "I could not persuade him to sell, but I found a way to win in the end. Your stepmother was far more accommodating."

For a moment Miss Collyer froze, her expression one of devastation. Only then did Ash recall the bad blood between her family and the viscount. Deering had accused her father of cheating at cards two years ago, but Noah Collyer had died before the matter could be resolved.

When Deering reached for her breast again, she broke out of her paralysis with ferocity. Uttering an audible curse, she brought her knee up to contact with the viscount's satin breeches at an especially vulnerable point.

Deering gave a harsh groan and doubled over, clutching his bollocks. Then Maura stamped down on his other instep for good measure.

Ash didn't know which of his emotions was strongest just then—amusement, admiration, or anger.

Amusement because he'd wanted to do the same thing to Deering for years.

Admiration because very few females outside those in his own family had the spirit or courage to engage in a physical brawl with a significantly larger man.

And anger because a genteel young lady had been accosted in his own home. Specifically this young lady, who was Katharine's friend and therefore deserved his protection.

Deering was clearly angry also; in fact, he was in a fury. "You . . . will regret this . . . you damned vixen!" he panted, still bent over.

"The only thing I regret," retorted Miss Collyer, "is thinking you were honorable enough to let me plead my case! I was fully prepared to purchase my horse back, not sell myself to you!"

She was panting as much as her suffering adversary, but her breathlessness stemmed from outrage instead of pain. Even at a distance, Ash could practically see sparks flashing from her eyes. When she balled her fists as if she might strike a blow at the viscount's sneering face, Ash decided it was time to intervene.

"It is time you took your leave, Deering," he declared, striding across the terrace toward them.

At his sudden appearance, Miss Collyer gave a start, while the viscount straightened painfully.

"This is none of your affair, Beaufort!" Deering snapped.

"It is very much my affair. You assaulted one of my guests."

"*I* assaulted *her*?" he sputtered. "That she-devil is the one who assaulted me!"

Ash bit back a smile. "I would not advertise that fact if I were you, Rupert. You will only invite scorn and make yourself a target for the cartoonists. Do you need assistance calling for your carriage?"

"Bloody hell . . . no, I can summon my own infernal carriage."

"Then pray do so. You are no longer welcome here."

The viscount shot Ash a look of extreme dislike. "This is no way to treat a peer, Beaufort, ordering me to leave while taking that witch's side."

"Spare me your protests. You got exactly what you deserved. I would have hurt you myself if she had not."

Deering's expression only darkened. After another fierce glare at Miss Collyer, though, he limped off in the direction of the ballroom.

Alone on the terrace with her, Ash turned and found

his gaze arrested by the enchanting picture she made. Maura stood with her fists still clenched, her cheeks flushed with anger, her bosom heaving softly. In the candle glow spilling from the ballroom windows, she looked fiery and beautiful, her honey-colored hair only a few shades lighter than the gold-embroidered amber silk gracing her tall, lithe figure.

He was not accustomed to seeing Miss Collyer so stylishly garbed. Her ball gown was an elegant confection, with short puffed sleeves and a low décolletage that offered meager coverage for the ripe swells of her breasts. Usually she wore plain muslin or kerseymere or—since her father's unexpected death from heart failure two years ago—the black bombazine of mourning.

Her long white kid gloves shielded her arms from the cool night air, but she was still shaking, no doubt in the aftermath of rage rather than from the chill.

Seeing all that trembling intensity, Ash could imagine her in his bed, shuddering in the throes of passion.

Aware of the primal surge of lust streaking through him, he tamped down on his inappropriate urges at the same time he noticed that one sleeve of her gown had been pulled down to bare her pale white shoulder.

Stepping close to Maura, he straightened her sleeve, trying to make his helpful gesture appear casual and brotherly.

Her flush deepened, as if she suddenly recognized that he'd witnessed the entire event, including the viscount's ignoble sexual advances.

When Ash finished repositioning her sleeve, she turned quickly toward the French doors. But he stayed her with a light touch on her gloved arm. "You should remain here for a moment. You cannot return to the ballroom looking so disheveled and distraught."

"I am not distraught! I am furious."

"Don't quibble," he said humorously. "It amounts to the same thing. You are breathing fire. You will frighten all my guests."

She grimaced in frustration, but apparently agreed with him, for after a short hesitation, she went to stand at the balustrade, her gloved fingers clutching at the gray stone. "Why are you even out here, Lord Beaufort? You are supposed to be hosting your sister's ball."

Joining her at the railing, Ash answered honestly. "You roused my curiosity when you followed Deering here. I thought you might be having a liaison with your lover."

"With *Lord Deering*?" She sounded appalled, disgusted. "I would sooner take a snake as a lover—not that I would ever take a lover of any kind," she hastened to add. "Or that it would be your concern if I did."

Ash let her intriguing denial go unremarked. "I realized your dislike of him when I overheard your conversation."

"Did no one ever teach you that it is impolite to eavesdrop?" she muttered.

He smiled at her question. "Any number of people have tried to teach me polite manners, but I fear little of their instruction took hold. In your case, however, it was not rudeness that led me to eavesdrop."

"No?"

"No. I relish a mystery, and I was suffering a near

fatal case of ennui. When you slipped away, I was delighted that finally something interesting was happening this evening. And then I remained here on the terrace because I thought you might need my protection."

She shot him an irritated glance. "I did not need your protection. I can defend myself."

"Obviously," Ash said with dry amusement. Her hazel eyes were still shooting daggers. "If looks could kill, Deering would be six feet underground by now. As it was, you temporarily unmanned him."

"I wish it could have been permanent," Maura said through gritted teeth.

Her agitation was still visible, and she seemed intent on shredding her kid gloves against the rough stone.

Just then, voices from the ballroom grew louder, wafting through the open doors behind them. Not wanting an audience, Ash reached out on impulse and peeled Miss Collyer's fingers away from the balustrade.

"Come with me," he ordered, catching her hand in his. Turning toward the terrace steps, he tugged her behind him.

"Where are you taking me?" she demanded, trying to pull back.

"Only down to the garden so you can cool off. You need time to recover your composure."

She accompanied him then, although rather unwillingly.

As he led her down the wide marble steps, Ash tried to analyze why he felt so protective of Maura, and more inexplicably, why he felt this unexpected possessiveness toward her.

Her statement moments ago about not wanting a lover of any kind gave him a strange satisfaction. He'd never heard of Miss Collyer engaging in any romantic affairs, yet that didn't mean she hadn't indulged discreetly.

He supposed his protectiveness was a result of her close connection to his sister Katharine and his cousin Skye. The three girls had become fast friends years ago at their elite boarding academy.

Like Katharine, Maura was unique in that she enjoyed more masculine pursuits than was typical of their peers. Breeding racehorses was most assuredly not a ladylike profession either. After losing her father so unexpectedly, Maura had retired to the country and thrown herself into improving the breeding stables she'd inherited so that she could support herself.

Ash had always been impressed by her fire and spirit. Yet he'd kept his hands off her because he considered her off-limits.

Unquestionably he had noticed her, though. From the time she had turned sixteen, in fact, during one of her visits to Beauvoir. What red-blooded male wouldn't? He'd have to be dead not to feel the rush of attraction for a beauty like Maura. But a gentleman—even a Wilde—did not go around seducing innocent schoolgirls, particularly a classmate of his sister's.

Maura was clearly no longer a girl. Ash was intently aware of her graceful, ripe body as they reached the gardens below the terrace. She was also out of mourning for her father now, which made her fair game if he chose to pursue her. . . .

The notion intrigued him, yet he set it aside for now as he guided Maura along a path illuminated by the occasional Chinese lantern.

"Perhaps you should sit down," he advised, leading her to a stone bench shadowed by a lilac tree.

She took no notice of his suggestion, but pulled her hand from his grasp and began to pace back and forth along the flagstone path.

Amusement tugged at Ash's mouth as he settled on the bench in her place. Prepared to indulge her, he stretched his long legs out before him and crossed his ankles. Despite his pleasure in watching her, though, he knew it would be more gallant if he attempted to divert her from her agitation.

Consequently, he broke the silence after a moment. "Allow me to offer you my apologies, Miss Collyer."

"For what?" she asked absently.

"I regret that you had to suffer Deering's lechery."

"You are not to blame for his disgusting behavior."

"No, but this is my home, and I am responsible for the actions of my guests."

"Perhaps, but Deering is as far from a gentleman as it is possible to be. The gall of him," she muttered under her breath, "thinking I would have any interest in selling myself to him."

"You handled him well. I am all admiration. Where did you learn that trick of incapacitating a man?"

"From my steward, Gandy. There are some unsavory characters in the racing world, and Gandy wanted me to be prepared should I encounter any."

"I thought Katharine and Skye were the only gently-bred females who were skilled in self-defense. I taught Kate that move myself."

When that brought no response, Ash continued casually. "I should thank you. Your altercation spiced up my evening and saved me from excruciating boredom."

His admission seemed to gain her attention for a moment, or at least she paused to glance at him. "Why did you even hold a ball if you are so jaded by them?"

"You know why. Because Katharine asked it of me."

"And you can never refuse her?"

"Oh, I regularly refuse her, but in this instance, I was doing my duty as her elder brother. She claimed she was finally ready to look for a husband, much to my surprise."

"It surprised me also," Maura allowed, resuming her pacing.

Frankly, it had startled Ash two weeks ago when Katharine suddenly announced her desire to find a husband and requested a ball to aid her search for eligible candidates.

But he was not interested in his sister's matrimonial prospects just now. Instead, he wanted to know what had led to her closest friend's confrontation with one of his noble guests. Most particularly, why Deering would assume that Maura Collyer's charms were for sale. . . .

"Why don't you tell me what prompted your encounter with Deering?" Ash suggested. When she didn't immediately answer, he prodded further. "What led him to proposition you?"

"He believes he has leverage over me," she said in a

low voice. "He illegally gained possession of something very precious to me."

"Your stallion, Bold Emperor, I take it?"

"Yes."

Precious, indeed, Ash mused. He'd had the privilege of seeing the famous stallion race on past occasions. A descendant of the Byerley Turk—one of three official sires of the Thoroughbred line—and more recently, of the champion Noble, Emperor possessed blistering speed and remarkable stamina and had obliterated the competition in numerous prestigious races during his spectacular career. At ten years of age, the horse now no longer raced, but stood at stud at Maura's farm near Newmarket and had sired a dozen winners thus far.

Indeed, the Collyer Stud was becoming known as one of the premiere breeding stables in England, due primarily to the stallion's superior bloodlines in combination with the canny expertise of the aging stable master, George Gandy.

"I hadn't heard that Emperor's ownership had changed hands," Ash remarked.

"My stepmother sold him to Deering three weeks ago, even though I am his rightful owner." The bitterness in Maura's voice was unmistakable. "Emperor has always belonged to me. My father gave him to me the night of his birth, and I helped raise him from a foal."

"Then how did your stepmother manage to sell him to Deering?"

The story came spilling out then, perhaps because she was too enraged to hold her tongue. "Lord Deering has his own racing stables and has long wanted the prestige of having a prize stallion. He succeeded in gaining Priscilla's allegiance by promising his patronage for her daughters' society debuts."

The assertion matched what Ash knew about Maura's family situation. At a young age she had lost her mother to a fever, and her father had remarried again some dozen years ago, to a widowed lady who already had two young daughters of her own; girls who were now of marriageable age, but whose chances of making even modest matches had been scotched by the disgrace attached to their family name during a cheating scandal. Reportedly, Maura shared an uneasy relationship with her stepmother, in large part due to maternal envy. It had never set well with Priscilla Collyer that Maura outshone her rather plain stepsisters so markedly.

"I thought your father provided Mrs. Collyer an adequate fortune, but left the stud to you," Ash probed.

"He did," Maura acknowledged. "When my father died, our house in London went to Priscilla, but his will left the farm and breeding stables to me, including all the horses. The deed of birth for Emperor, however, was in my father's name, not mine, and Priscilla exploited that fact. When she visited my farm a few weeks ago, she took the deed from my files, then sold Emperor to Viscount Deering for a significant sum. I didn't even realize what she had done until Deering came with the sheriff to collect Emperor. I was away from home that afternoon, so Gandy had to let my horse go."

"And you have no proof of ownership?"

"No, none. I have little recourse, either. I could try to sue in court, but I might not win. And by the time the legalities are sorted out, Emperor could suffer irreparable harm." Maura's hands curled into fists, betraying her anxiety. "Deering brought him to London, of all places, and is stabling him in a cramped mews with no place to run. And according to Gandy's connections, Deering has taken a whip to Emperor more than once. I cannot bear to think of him being beaten and abused."

"So you decided to try and buy the stallion back rather than fight a legal battle you may lose?"

Maura nodded. "I don't have such a huge sum at my disposal just now, since I put my entire inheritance into building up the Collyer Stud, but the bloodstock is worth a great deal, and I am willing to sell my two other stallions and all the broodmares if need be. In fact, I immediately came to London for that very purpose—to make my offer to Deering in person. But he refused to receive me every time I called. Then Katharine hit on a plan to aid me."

"What sort of plan?"

"When she learned what happened, she promised to ensure that Deering attended her ball this evening so that I would have a chance to speak to him."

Ash felt himself frown slightly. "When was this?"

"A fortnight ago."

About the time Katharine had asked him to throw her a grand ball, he realized. The timing seemed curious. In truth, he could almost recognize his sister's fine hand at work here. Katharine frequently plotted to bend fate to her will. He wouldn't be surprised if she had contrived the entire ball merely to help her bosom friend.

"But all our careful planning was for naught," Maura muttered.

"Because Deering refused your offer outright?" Ash asked.

"Yes. You heard his odious reply. I swore I would control my temper when I confronted him, but I couldn't manage it." She bit her lower lip. "I suppose I should never have hurt him like that, even if his proposition was utterly revolting."

"Probably not," Ash murmured wryly, his mouth curving at the memory of the viscount getting his comeuppance.

When Maura stopped her pacing to glare at him, however, he stifled his smile. "That was not a criticism of your courage, sweeting. I only meant that Deering cannot bear being bested. You clearly earned his enmity by savaging his pride. 'She-devil,' 'witch,' 'vixen' . . . what other names did he call you just now?"

Her voice vibrated with irritation. "I have a few choice names for that conniving villain as well. And yet I have likely ruined any chance to persuade him to sell Emperor back to me." Suddenly Maura brought a hand to her temple as if just now realizing the ramifications of her actions.

To Ash's surprise, she trudged over to the bench and sank down beside him. Her elegantly-clad shoulders slumped as she gazed unseeingly at the ground.

"I would not put it past Deering to punish an innocent animal," she lamented, "but I will never forgive myself if he takes out his anger at me on my horse."

Ash didn't much like that note of despair in her voice, or her look of defeat either. He would rather have Maura spitting fire than surrendering to frustration and disappointment.

When she shivered and rubbed her gloved arms, Ash knew that she'd finally become cognizant of her surroundings, now that her ire had eased somewhat. The spring night air was cooler here in the gardens and held a dampness that raised goose bumps on her exposed skin.

Reflexively, Ash slid his arm around her shoulders and drew her close. His gesture, although intended to be benevolent, was not exactly proper, and she stiffened accordingly.

"Hold your protests, Miss Collyer," he advised lightly. "You need warmth, and I can provide it. I would do the same for my sister and cousin."

Rather than argue, Maura accepted his offer of warmth and let his arm remain around her.

"I could loan you my coat," Ash added in further explanation, "but it would do your reputation no good to be seen wearing my clothing when we return to the ball."

"I confess surprise, my lord," she rejoined with a hint of her usual spirit. "I thought you didn't give a fig about propriety."

"Ordinarily I don't, but you are my guest after all."

A short silence ensued while he held her, sharing his body heat. Despite his avowal of innocent motives, though, Ash realized that he wasn't fooling himself; he was not feeling the *least* brotherly toward Maura.

Not when he was so aware of her deliciously soft form pressing against his side.

He cleared his throat. "Perhaps I can assist you in dealing with Deering," he suggested, as much to focus his attention elsewhere as from any conscious plan to aid her.

Glancing up with a look of surprise, Maura searched his face before answering. "Thank you, Lord Beaufort, but I believe in solving my own problems. Besides, Katharine has already put herself out enough on my behalf."

Even though he admired her pluckiness in taking on the viscount, he wasn't convinced she could handle the problem on her own. "What do you intend to do then?"

"I will think of something. I have no intention of leaving Emperor in his hands for long. But my body is too high a price to pay—" She broke off with a grimace and looked away again. "Here I am, going on and on about my private affairs that can be no concern of yours. Pray forgive me."

She seemed rather embarrassed by her loosened tongue, Ash noticed. He doubted Maura was accustomed to sharing her intimate confidences in such detail. Moreover, she was correct; her affairs were none of his concern. And yet some chivalrous part of him balked at leaving her to face a lecher like Deering alone.

"You ought not reject my offer of assistance out of hand," he advised. "As a peer, I have resources at my command that you do not."

Evidently he had struck a nerve, for Maura went

rigid again. "How well I know it," she grated under her breath. "Wealthy, powerful noblemen can literally get away with murder. It *galls* me to have to beg the man who killed my father."

Her wild claim voiced in that fierce tone took Ash aback, but he returned a measured reply. "That is a serious charge, my sweet witch. How do you know he was complicit in your father's death?"

She gave a hard shrug. "Oh, I know he didn't murder Papa *directly*. Just drove him into an early grave with his accusations of cheating. Papa's heart gave way before he could clear his name, and the doctors believe the scandal was the prime cause."

"I don't think I ever heard the entire story," Ash said leadingly.

"It is quite simple. Deering has coveted Emperor forever and frequently offered to purchase him, but Papa would never sell him. So in order to win our stallion, two years ago his lordship tried to force my father's hand at the gaming tables. He lured Papa into a gambling den and then claimed he was playing with marked cards. Of course it was a brazen lie, but who would believe a commoner accused by a prominent nobleman?"

From the tense vibrations of her body, Ash knew she was getting angry all over again.

"And then to hear Deering boast tonight about his success . . ." Maura whispered. "It was like a knife to my chest. How I despise that contemptible man! It was all I could do to force myself to speak to him civilly." She made a growling sound deep in her throat. "But I don't know whether I am more furious at him or at my own impotence in fighting him."

She hardly seemed helpless, Ash mused to himself, but he now understood her anger better. Maura not only blamed Deering for her father's death, but the viscount's underhanded appropriation of her stallion several weeks ago had only added insult to injury.

She was tense with fury now. When Ash felt another shudder of anger and loathing ripple through her body, he resolved to distract her from her wrath. Granted, his chosen method of distraction would probably unsettle her, but it was the most effective way he knew to jolt Maura out of her despondency and bring back her usual spirited temperament.

Yet it was only fair to give her proper warning, he decided.

"You need to take a deep breath, love."

After a moment, she did as he bid, inhaling deeply and exhaling in a controlled rush.

"Again," he ordered, waiting until she complied twice more. "Are you calm yet?"

"No, why?"

"Because I want to know if you will respond in the same way when I kiss you."

Giving a start, Maura peered up at him. "You cannot kiss me, Beaufort."

Ash raised an eyebrow. That sort of bald challenge was irresistible to a Wilde. "Certainly I can—and I will. Your anger still needs soothing."

She stared at him in mute disbelief. When he tightened his arm around her, she drew a hushed breath upon realizing he was serious.

Her beauty was alluring in the golden lanternlight,

her lips intensely inviting, Ash reflected as he bent closer.

It was outrageous of him, provocative in the extreme, and might earn him the same response his predecessor had received. But he was acting again on impulse, following his instincts as he lowered his head to capture her ripe mouth. . . .

Chapter Two

Evidently he had startled Maura enough to catch her off guard, for she went utterly still in his arms.

Her lips were just as delectable as he'd imagined, Ash thought, relishing their softness. Driven to explore further, he parted the seam of her mouth and slipped his tongue inside to tangle with hers.

When she remained frozen, he took advantage of her momentary paralysis to deepen his kiss, sliding one hand behind her nape and holding her head so that he could drink more fully of her. Maura opened for his penetration, her response tentative, curious, as if she were contemplating his taste.

The experience made heat rise inside Ash. His loins stirring to life, he trailed his free hand downward, along her throat to the swell of her breasts. Maura reacted with a small indrawn gasp. Yet instead of pulling away, she leaned into him and raised one slender arm to twine it about his neck.

Her involuntary surrender only increased Ash's craving for her. Painfully aroused now, he felt a primal male urge to take what he wanted—and an even stronger need to heighten her desire.

Still savoring her mouth, he slipped his fingertips below the edge of her bodice, delving under her chemise and corset, gliding against bare, silken skin.

Her resulting shiver filled him with satisfaction. Lightly brushing her hardened nipples with the back of his knuckles, Ash freed one luscious breast from her confining garments and bent down to taste her. When he flicked the taut rose-hued bud with his tongue, she gave a soft moan—an unmistakable pleasure-sound that made Ash suddenly recall their surroundings. . . .

Sweet hell. He was getting so carried away that he was about to undress Maura Collyer right there in the garden, within shouting distance of three hundred ball guests.

Breathing heavily, Ash forced himself to draw back. In the rasping silence, Maura blinked up at him, looking dazed and dreamy-eyed.

"That is quite far enough, my lovely witch," he murmured, his voice huskier than he would have liked.

His comment apparently broke the spell she was under, for her entire body gave a start. Yet Ash was forewarned and thus prepared for her next instinctive action. When Maura drew her fist back, he caught it and locked his fingers around her wrist to prevent her blow from landing painfully on his jaw.

"I should have known you would try to plant me a facer," Ash said with a rueful smile. "And perhaps I deserved it."

"No doubt you did." Breathing hard herself, she jumped up from the bench and retreated a safe distance, looking both disconcerted and disgruntled as she awkwardly covered her bosom. "I *told* you not to kiss me, Lord Beaufort," she complained.

"No, you said I *cannot* kiss you, which is not at all the same thing. Telling a Wilde he cannot do something is like taunting a bull with a red cape."

"How well I know it," Maura admitted with a huff of annoyance. "Katharine is the same way. But I was not challenging you to prove your manhood, I promise you."

"Perhaps I just couldn't help myself," he said with more honesty than was wise.

She raised her fingers to her lips, then shook her head in bewilderment. "Not for a moment do I believe you lacked self-control."

"You should. I could not resist kissing you, Miss Collyer. You look very beautiful when you are in a towering rage. But I also wished to provide you a diversion and take your mind off Deering."

"Now *that* I might credit."

"My tactic worked, did it not?"

His question made her pause. "As a matter of fact, it did." For a moment, Maura offered him a wondering, if fleeting, smile. Then she shook her head in exasperation. "You are utterly outrageous, Lord Beaufort."

"So I have been told."

"I always knew you were an infamous rogue, but I never suspected you to be as lecherous as Deering."

"Good God, I should hope not." Ash gave a mock shudder. Although he'd enjoyed his share of scandalous liaisons, he was hardly the libertine that Deering was.

Maura shook her head again, as if trying to corral her wits. "I suppose I should thank you. You were right—

I needed to remain out here in the gardens to cool off. But I am calm enough now. You needn't concern yourself with me any further," she added as she turned back toward the house.

"Where are you going?" he was surprised into asking.

"To find Katharine and take my leave of her."

Ash was hard-pressed to explain his disappointment. "The night is still young. The ball has barely begun."

Maura halted to glance over her shoulder at him. "I only came this evening so I could speak to my nemesis and implore him to sell my horse back to me. But since my attempt was an utter failure, there is no point in my remaining. I dislike balls almost as much as you do."

She might have left him then, but when Ash remained seated, she hesitated. "Don't you intend to return to the ball?"

"In a moment. Kissing you had an unfortunate effect on my anatomy. I need to cool off myself."

Reflexively Maura glanced down at his loins, where the thick bulge in his satin knee breeches proclaimed his state of arousal. A becoming flush stained her cheeks as she evidently understood his meaning.

She opened her mouth to retort, but then apparently thought better of engaging him in a duel of words on such a subject as male arousal. Turning away again, she hurried along the path toward the terrace steps.

With a half-amused, half-pained grin, Ash braced his hands behind him on the bench. Tilting his head back, he gazed up at the dark sky in bemusement, contemplating the powerful effect Maura Collyer had on him.

He was immensely attracted to the deliciously spirited beauty. In fact, he hadn't experienced so fierce a sexual attraction in years. He probably should not have kissed her, however, for now he knew exactly how she tasted.

Well, he'd wanted to enliven his evening, and his wish had been granted in spades. What intrigued him most, though, was why Maura had allowed him to embrace her so brazenly, even for those few short moments. He supposed he should be gratified by her reaction when he'd stroked her lovely breasts. When Deering had tried to fondle her, she'd fended off his advances by kneeing him in the groin.

Ash winced with wry amusement, realizing it was a good thing that she had been sitting down when he was driven to caress her.

Almost as intriguing as Maura's momentary surrender was her admission that Katharine was a confederate in her battle against the viscount. Ash wanted to know exactly what role his sister was playing in the affair. If he knew Kate, she was cheerfully engaged in machinations.

One thing was for certain, he ruminated as he stood and readjusted his clothing to make himself presentable to his guests: He intended to have a serious discussion with his meddlesome younger sibling as soon as her tiresome ball ended.

Fearing that her heated flush still showed, Maura bypassed the crowded ballroom with its resplendent denizens of the ton and went directly to the entrance hall, where she requested that Lady Katharine's carriage be brought around and that a footman be sent to summon her friend.

Then Maura waited impatiently at one side of the entryway, pondering the inexplicable question of why she had allowed Lord Beaufort to sweep her away as she had. Even though he had warned her in advance of his audacious intentions, she'd sat frozen with disbelief at his sensual assault, unable to utter a protest, much less extricate herself.

Unconsciously Maura raised her fingers to her still tingling lips as she relived the marquis's stunning kiss. *He tastes like sin* had been her first dazed thought. Enticing, wicked sin.

He had devastated her senses, to the point that she had practically melted in his arms. No wonder women whispered with awe about Beaufort's skills as a lover. She had never understood the word *desire* until that moment.

He'd rendered her dizzy, weak with yearning, making her breasts feel heavy and swollen while kindling a strange ache between her thighs. And then the sensual caress of his tongue on her nipple had shocked her with pleasure. . . .

Thank heaven he had stopped before she'd surrendered completely to his brazen lovemaking!

Maura found herself wincing in memory of her idiocy. It should not have surprised her, though, that Katharine's dashing older brother knew how to seduce with breathtaking effect. The Marquis of Beaufort was a favorite of the ton, admired by both sexes, the darling of matchmaking mamas despite his scandalous behavior and his well-founded reputation as a captivating Lothario.

Handsome did not begin to describe him . . . roughly chiseled features, dark unruly hair, eyes that were the vivid color of emeralds. All five cousins in the extraordinary Wilde family were notorious for their bewitching charm, but as aristocratic rogues went, Ashton was the acknowledged champion.

Yet Maura couldn't help wondering why Lord Beaufort had bothered kissing her this evening. He'd claimed his motives were altruistic, that he merely wanted to help release her pent-up anger, but he had never looked twice at her before tonight.

His impact on *her* had been overwhelming. One moment she was seething with frustration, railing on about her nemesis; the next she was speechless with desire.

She'd been kissed twice in her life—several years ago during her comeout Season, in fact—and neither occasion had been particularly memorable. Certainly not enthralling, as tonight's episode had been. Moreover, she couldn't comprehend why she had craved Beaufort's touch so desperately when Lord Deering's had only repulsed her.

And why had she permitted the marquis to drag her pitiful tale of woe from her? Normally she would never dream of spilling her intimate secrets to a nobleman she knew more from his wicked reputation than his female relatives' rare confidences. It was mortifying enough that he had witnessed her altercation with Deering.

Maura was highly vexed at herself for finding Lord Beaufort so irresistibly attractive. She ought to be worrying about how to retrieve her cherished stallion from the clutches of a devious viscount instead of dwelling on a spellbinding kiss like a dazzled widgeon. She wished Katharine would come—

No sooner had the thought formed when her friend appeared in the entrance hall, obviously searching for her.

Garbed in a ball gown of emerald green to match her sparkling eyes and highlight her shining auburn hair, Lady Katharine Wilde was the picture of vibrant beauty.

Breathing a sigh of relief, Maura stepped forward.

"How did your meeting go with Deering?" Katharine asked at once, which made Maura grimace.

"Truthfully, it was a disaster . . ." Quickly she recounted the viscount's ignominious proposition and her own wrathful response.

Kate looked outraged on her behalf, but immediately protested Maura's decision to quit the ball early.

"But you cannot leave just yet!" she insisted.

"There is no point in my remaining," Maura repeated the argument she'd made to Katharine's provocative older brother. "But you know I am immensely grateful for all you have done, dearest Kate. I will return your lovely dress tomorrow."

Katharine had loaned her the ball gown of amber silk, since she had nothing fine enough to wear to a grand ball and little money to waste on fashion in any case. Additionally, Katharine had sent her own carriage to collect Maura from her stepmother's house, since Maura only had a gig in London and no coachman. She loved Katharine dearly, like a sister, but she still felt uncomfortable having to accept her generosity. No doubt it was pride that made her want to be independent and stand on her own two feet.

At the mention of the ball gown, Kate gave a dismissive shrug, then suddenly changed the subject. "What about Ash?"

"What about him?" Maura responded warily.

"I saw him follow you outside onto the terrace. And you remained out there with him for aeons. What happened between the two of you?"

"Nothing happened," she lied.

"Then why is your face so flushed? Come now, Maura. I know you too well."

She sighed, knowing her friend would never give up until her curiosity was appeased. "Your brother kissed me, if you must know," she confided in a low voice.

Rather than look startled, however, Katharine smiled slowly in satisfaction. "And how did you like it?"

"What does that matter?" Maura asked in exasperation.

"Because I want to know."

The heat in her cheeks increased. "I liked kissing him very well," she finally admitted, although not even under pain of death would she confess that she'd been far more intimate with the marquis than a mere kiss.

"You don't say." Kate clasped her hands together in delight. "This is even better than I hoped."

Maura's gaze narrowed on her best friend. "Katharine Wilde, what in deuces are you talking about? Please tell me you did not invite me here to throw me in your brother's path. You did not, *did you*?"

"Well, perhaps I did, a little."

"That is perfectly *ridiculous*—"

"I disagree, darling Maura. I think you and Ash may be meant for each other." Before Maura could sputter an objection, Katharine hurried to add, "In any event, Ash is the very man to help you get your horse back."

"No, he is *not*. I can manage on my own."

"No doubt, but you should not have to. You know Skye and I are your family. You claimed us years ago."

That much was true, Maura allowed. Upon being sent off to boarding school by her stepmother when she was twelve, she'd arrived at the Ingram Academy for Young Ladies shortly before Katharine and her cousin, Lady Skye Wilde, who was a year younger. The Wilde girls had been orphaned by then, having lost both sets of beloved parents in a tragic accident at sea, and Maura had befriended them at once.

At that point in her young life, she was feeling terribly alone and lonely herself, and when she'd heard Skye crying softly in her bed late one night, grieving her loss and missing her remaining family—her older brother Quinn and her cousins Jack and Ashton—Maura had promptly declared that *she* would be Skye and Katharine's family. The three girls had made a pact then and there, a bond that had only grown stronger over the following years as they shared the tribulations and joys of school days and holidays together; then as young ladies negotiating the uncertain waters of society debuts; and afterward, as they moved into full-fledged womanhood, which fostered new dreams and aspirations for each of them.

When Maura made no reply, Katharine pressed her. "Promise me you will at least discuss the matter with Ash when he calls on you tomorrow."

"How do you know he will call on me?"

"Because I intend to make him."

Maura raised her eyes to the gilded ceiling. "Katharine, you know I love you like a sister—"

"Then trust me, Maura. You know I only have your best interests at heart." Hearing a swell in the music, Kate glanced over her shoulder. "I should return to the ball. I have a great deal of convincing to do tonight."

After planting a swift kiss on Maura's cheek, Katharine spun around and hurried off, leaving Maura shaking her head in dismay and fond exasperation. Yet she should be accustomed to Kate's outrageous schemes by now and knew they were usually wellmeant.

The fiery, passionate Wilde cousins had always proudly lived up to their name, rousing the secret envy of the ton with their adventures and exploits and derring-do. No doubt their recklessness came from being raised primarily by their uncle, Lord Cornelius Wilde, a scholarly bachelor who was much happier with his nose buried in a Greek tome than when trying to discipline his unruly nieces and nephews.

Reportedly the cousins' vivacious, pleasure-loving parents had generated even more tales of scandal and passion during their day. The elder Wildes had lived enchanted lives, ruling the lavish, wealthy world of the British aristocracy until their ship sank crossing the Channel from France during a lull in international hostilities. The tragedy had combined the two separate branches of the noble Wilde family—the Marquises of Beaufort and the Earls of Traherne. The five orphans had moved in together under the nominal supervision of Lord Cornelius.

As they grew to adulthood, the cousins often skirted the edge of scandal, even the two girls. Lady Katharine and Lady Skye, however, were partially sheltered by rank and fortune and thus allowed much more license than other unattached young ladies. Certainly more license than plain Miss Maura Collyer, whose commoner father had died under a cloud of dishonor.

Maura couldn't help but envy the Wildes for their freedom. *She* had to deal with a stepmother who slavishly followed the stringent rules of the *Beau Monde*.

When her borrowed carriage finally was announced, Maura gladly made her escape from the ball, although she was not eager to return to her temporary lodgings. While in London, she stayed with her stepmother on Clarges Street, in the same home that her mother had lovingly presided over so many years ago.

She hoped she wouldn't encounter Priscilla tonight. There had always been discord in their relationship, beginning with their first encounter. Maura believed Priscilla had wed Noah Collyer mainly for his fortune, and Priscilla deplored her lack of ladylike manners and thought her a complete hoyden. Shipping Maura off to boarding school was intended to cure her of her hellion ways, as well as reduce the competition with her new young stepsisters for her doting father's affections.

After Noah's passing, Priscilla had distanced herself from Maura as much as possible, except to argue frequently about finances. Pris maintained that because of the scandal, her widow's portion wasn't nearly large enough to launch her daughters into society, and that she should receive a much larger income from the farm and breeding stables to compensate for the additional obstacles they faced.

"Seasons are enormously expensive, you know," Priscilla had complained countless times. "But the notoriety staining our name makes it immeasurably more difficult to find suitable husbands for your stepsisters. It is only right that you help us out, Maura."

Priscilla's chief goal at present was to marry off her two daughters, Hannah and Lucy. Their comeouts had been postponed while they were in mourning, but more critically, the ignominy that haunted Noah Collyer's death had severely damaged their chances of making good matches.

Maura did feel a responsibility to help her stepsisters. They were sweet girls and she loved them both, even if they were unrelated by blood and shared few interests with her. But their London Seasons ought not to have come at so exorbitant a price as her beloved stallion.

She'd had a major row with Priscilla over her deceit three weeks ago. Pris claimed she had sold Emperor not simply for the funds, but to cultivate Lord Deering's much-needed good graces. Given that he had made the accusations of cheating against Noah Collyer in the first place, Priscilla was convinced that Deering could mitigate the scandal if he chose, perhaps even erase the blot from their family name entirely. And with his aristocratic connections and the outsized power he wielded in society, the viscount's active support could surely smooth the path for her daughters' matrimonial prospects.

In truth, Pris did sincerely care about her daughters' welfare and would go to great lengths to see them properly married, including conspiring to appropriate a celebrated racing stallion from the Collyer Stud and win Deering's favor.

Maura would never forgive her stepmother's betrayal, however. She stood to lose the thing she loved most in the world. Emperor was like her own child, as well as friend and pet.

After Priscilla's defection, Maura considered her horse and her steward her only close family, other than her dear friends Katharine and Skye, who had stood by her during those horrible, dark days of grief and scandal. If not for them, she would have had to fight the world alone for the past two years. She was immensely grateful, of course, but if Kate had some reckless matchmaking scheme in mind . . .

Well, Maura thought as she was handed into the waiting carriage, she had no time for such foolish distractions.

It might take an immense amount of willpower, but she intended to forget the stunning kiss Lord Beaufort had given her. She was determined not to be sidetracked by a seductive marquis or his well-meaning sister from her mission to rescue her precious stallion.

Chapter Three

To Ash's surprise, he did not have to search at any length for his sister. Katharine found him shortly after he returned to the ballroom.

"I cannot believe you let Maura leave," was her preemptive comment. "You should have stopped her."

Ash arched an eyebrow. Kate was taking *him* to task for her friend's abrupt departure? "And just why should I have been responsible for stopping her?"

"Because someone has to save her from that villain, Lord Deering, of course. At the very least you could have asked Maura to stand up with you for a set of dances, so everyone could see that she is under our family's protection."

His response was interrupted when one of Katharine's many beaus approached to claim her for the next set. Ash forestalled the gentleman with an upraised hand, then caught Kate's arm and bent to murmur in her ear. "We have some serious issues to discuss when your ball is over, minx."

While her partner waited politely at a distance, she

glanced boldly up at Ash. "Indeed, we do, dearest brother. In fact, I mean to call a meeting of the entire family tonight."

The determined gleam in her green eyes sparked Ash's suspicions even more than her announcement about an impromptu family gathering. "Why?"

"Because we have a matter of great importance to consider—something that could affect all of us. We should meet in the library. I suspect Uncle Cornelius has already taken refuge there, given that I've seen nothing of him since the receiving line disbanded."

She started to break away, but Ash tightened his hold. "You fabricated your need for this ball, didn't you, love?"

"Only slightly," Katharine admitted with no remorse whatsoever.

Annoyance speared through him. Although he considered balls the most boring of entertainments, he had spared no expense for Katharine's grand evening. He would do anything for his family. Yet he disliked being duped, even by his endearing spitfire of a sister.

"Did you ever intend to search for a husband as you claimed?" Ash demanded.

Katharine smiled sweetly. "Well, yes, some day I will. Just not at this precise moment. I am more concerned about rescuing Maura. She is far too proud to ask for help, and arranging a ball was the best I could do on short notice."

His audibly muttered oath held irritation but also a telltale hint of exasperated amusement.

Surprisingly, though, Kate's expression turned intent to the point of graveness. "You *must* help her, Ash."

He raised a hand. "Oh, no, sweetheart, you won't fish me into your intrigues. I've done my duty by hosting your damned ball."

"But I need you. *Maura* needs you. You cannot say no until you hear me out. *Please. . . .*"

Just then the music began anew, and Katharine turned away to join her partner while calling over her shoulder, "I will explain everything later in the library, Ash, I promise."

"Yes, you will, dear sister," he said under his breath as his troublesome youngest sibling fled his proximity for the relative safety of the ballroom floor.

Admittedly, Ash's curiosity was piqued, however.

At the conclusion of the ball, when the last of the carriages had rumbled away from his Grosvenor Square mansion, and his household staff had begun clearing the remnants of the late supper and extinguishing the flames in the crystal chandeliers overhead, Ash escorted a cheerfully secretive Katharine to the library.

It was three o'clock in the morning, and not surprisingly, they found their Uncle Cornelius in his favorite haunt, slumped in a stuffed-leather armchair near the hearth fire, sound asleep and snoring softly, his spectacles sliding down his nose. The elderly gentleman loathed social gatherings, especially balls, and always hid in the library as soon as he could politely escape.

The other Wilde family members were waiting with various degrees of anticipation. Skye, with her deep blue eyes and pale gold hair, looked bright and fresh as a rose, as if she hadn't just spent the entire night wearing out her dancing slippers.

Her elder brother Quinn, the Earl of Traherne, was also blue-eyed and fair-haired, but of a darker gold hue. Quinn's appearance of a bored, jaded aristocrat was highly deceptive, since in addition to being the most adventurous of the five cousins, he had the sharpest mind and a wicked wit that could slice opponents to ribbons.

Currently Quinn lounged in an armchair, looking slightly amused but willing to tolerate a family gathering for curiosity's sake, if nothing else.

Lord Jack Wilde, Ash's raven-haired first cousin and adopted brother—who was not quite thirty years of age—was sprawled irreverently on the sofa, his eyes closed.

Without opening his eyes, Jack spoke upon their entrance. "Do edify us, Kate. What was so urgent that it couldn't wait till morning? You are interfering with my beauty sleep."

She laughed lightly. "Pardon me for disturbing your rest, but we have a crucial situation at hand."

Bestirring himself to sit up, Jack swung his long legs over the edge of the sofa. "Very well, but pray, make it fast. I have a curricle race early tomorrow. . . . In less than five hours, in fact."

With a glance at the sleeping Lord Cornelius, Katharine moved over to the large library table where they'd held many a Wilde family conference in the years since their parents' tragic demise. Ash sat at one end, at the head of the table, Quinn at the other, with Kate and Skye between them. Jack joined the council but declined a chair, instead resting one hip on the tabletop itself, facing Katharine.

All the Wilde cousins regularly came to London each Season, but they were not often together as a family anymore. Katharine still resided with Ash and their Uncle Cornelius, either at the London house in Grosvenor Square or the magnificent Beaufort family seat in Kent. Jack had his own house nearby in town, since as a bachelor he'd wanted his own abode so he could come and go as he pleased. And Quinn and Skye resided together at the Traherne mansion in Berkeley Square when they weren't at their palatial country manor in Kent.

Both noble estates were situated some forty miles east of London, within an easy drive of each other. Being raised in the same district had fostered a tight-knit kinship that was unusual among distant cousins, even before their households had been combined under Lord Cornelius's guardianship.

"So what is afoot?" Ash asked, breaking the silence.

Katharine clasped her fingers together, looking uncharacteristically hesitant all of a sudden. "You may be wondering why I called you together. . . ."

Quinn gave a chuckle. "Out with it, love. You are trying our patience."

"Very well. I suppose I should start by reminding you of our family lore. You know that we Wildes only marry for love—"

"What does it matter, why we marry?" Jack interrupted.

Katharine frowned at him. "I will tell you if you give me the chance."

Guessing where the conversation was headed, Ash hid a wince. In the past dozen years, Kate's romantic notions had been a source of both amusement and discomfort for the family, particularly him, since he was often the target of her matchmaking. But he'd learned to deflect her schemes, so he was prepared to indulge her now.

Clearing her throat, she continued. "According to family legend, we Wildes never lose our hearts readily, but when we find our one true mate, we love passionately and for life. Quite a number of our ancestors were celebrated lovers, including all of our parents. But none of *us* has found true love yet."

Ash saw her glance around the table as if expecting an objection, but no one disputed her claim. Thus far, none of the current generation of Wildes had been struck by love, despite having ample advantages and multiple opportunities.

"And why haven't we fallen in love?" Katharine asked rhetorically. "Because we have not met our true mates yet. The thing is, I think I have hit upon a way to solve our problem."

"I wasn't aware we had a problem," Ash said.

"Certainly we do. Life is passing us by, Ash, and we are very likely missing our chance at happiness."

"Go on," he directed noncommittally.

"We have only to look to legendary lovers in history," Katharine explained. "Literature is filled with classic, timeless tales of love that can lead us to find our own matches. In short, I am proposing that we attempt to follow in the footsteps of the world's greatest lovers."

The silence that greeted her suggestion was accompanied by blank stares and several pairs of raised eyebrows.

"I have researched very carefully," Katharine went on doggedly, "and have spent countless hours quizzing Uncle Cornelius about various possibilities to fit our needs. His vast store of knowledge has proved invaluable."

"What classic tales are you speaking of?" Skye asked.

Katharine answered readily. "Oh, you know—from Greek mythology, renowned authors such as Shakespeare, even fairy tales. In fact, based on my research, I believe I can identify several possible ideal matches for us right here and now."

In response, the differing expressions from her family members ranged from amusement to scorn. Ash felt his own mouth curl in a wry smile. Leave it to Kate to still astonish them in unexpected ways.

"Of all the bird-witted notions," Jack commented, "that takes the ultimate prize."

Katharine fixed a scowl on her dubious adopted brother. "I *knew* I would have difficulty convincing you all of my theory, especially the first time—"

"I should say so," he drawled.

She held up a hand. "Just pray hear me out."

With an exaggerated sigh, Jack left his perch on the table and slid into an empty chair while crossing his arms over his broad chest. Quinn leaned back, observing her from under half-lowered eyelids, his skepticism obvious.

Only Skye seemed willing to encourage Katharine's romantic flights of fancy. "I think your theory sounds very intriguing, Kate. I should like to hear more."

"Thank you," she said with a look of gratitude. "Now where was I?"

"You said you have identified possible matches for us."

"Yes, based on legendary lovers." Her gaze shifted to Ash. "I think your match is Maura Collyer."

After an incredulous pause, he laughed outright at that. "I suppose you mean to tell me why you specifically chose her."

Katharine nodded eagerly. "You are aware of Perrault's tale of Cinderella? Well, Cinderella had a wicked stepmother and two stepsisters, just as Maura does. In truth, the moment Uncle Cornelius mentioned Perrault, I immediately thought of her. When we were at school together, I sometimes roasted Maura about her family situation. But I never thought it would prove the perfect sign of her compatibility with you."

"I gather that you are acting as her fairy godmother?" Ash asked sardonically, a guess that was confirmed when Kate nodded again. "At least that explains why you requested your ball under false pretenses. That was your underhanded way of contriving an encounter between me and Miss Collyer."

Kate had the grace to look a trifle guilty then. "Yes, but I knew better than to tell you of my plan beforehand, Ash. You would have scoffed and told me to go to the devil."

"Which is exactly what I mean to do now. You can't seriously expect me to play the role of prince to her Cinderella."

"I only want you to keep an open mind. . . ."

When he didn't immediately respond, Kate's tone turned imploring. "Truly, Ash, she could be your perfect mate. You know Maura is nothing at all like the young misses who drive you to distraction with their witless chatter. She has brains and beauty and spirit, and she can ride like a centaur," Kate added, singing her friend's praises. "She is far ahead of her time, managing a breeding stable, and independent enough that she would never chase after you for your fortune and title."

Nothing like other young ladies indeed, Ash thought, remembering Maura's unconventional actions earlier tonight.

"Moreover, she is an orphan, like we are."

"Is that supposed to arouse my sympathy?"

"Yes, of course. We Wildes know how painful it is to lose our dearest loved ones."

In self-defense, Ash tried a different tack. "If you are so convinced of the brilliance of your theory, Kate, why don't *you* go first?"

"Because your tale presented itself first. It is staring us right in the face. Besides, you are the eldest. You have more than fulfilled your duty as head of the family, Ash. You've taken care of all of us for years, and it is time you looked out for yourself."

"I *am* looking out for myself."

"Not well enough. You have never given love a chance, but you need to do so now."

"So says the spinster."

Despite being the wealthy daughter of a marquis, Katharine was considered practically on the shelf, having turned down countless offers of marriage because, she claimed, she had never found the man who could prove her match and she wouldn't settle for anything less than true love.

"Yes," she countered, "but it is not for my lack of trying. I simply have never met the right candidate. And you haven't either. I know you will never agree to look for a bride from among this Season's crop of insipid debutantes. You would certainly never have to worry about Maura being insipid."

Ash glanced at the others. Quinn had relaxed upon realizing he wasn't the immediate target of Katharine's madcap schemes, and amusement wreathed his mouth. Jack also appeared more sanguine and seemed to be enjoying seeing his elder brother under the gun.

Skye spoke again, giving Ash a reprieve. "You said you have tales in mind for the rest of us, Katharine. What is your legend to be?"

Katharine made a face, followed by a self-deprecating smile. "I expect I will have to settle for Shakespeare's comedy, *The Taming of the Shrew.* You know my temperament. And my name is even spelled like the Bard's Katharine."

Jack leaned over and pulled a lock of her flame-dark hair from her elegant coiffure. "And whom do I get for my match?"

"Oh, I have the perfect candidate in mind for you, *mon frère, Jacques.* But you probably won't like it," Katharine warned.

"I expect I won't. I know you too well. But enlighten me anyway."

"Well, then, it is *Romeo and Juliet.*"

"The devil I will," Jack responded roundly. "I'm not playing the role of the tragic lover who dies."

Katharine gave a short laugh. "Of course you won't die in your ending. What kind of ideal romance would that be? But trust me on this, Jack, you will reconsider once you meet your Juliet. She is quite beautiful."

"Who is it?"

"No, I am not telling you. Not when you are so mulishly determined to be closed-minded."

"What about me, Katharine?" Skye asked curiously.

Kate looked to her cousin. "I haven't determined your tale yet, Skye, but I am working on it. But Quinn, I think you will have Pygmalion and Galatea. You know, the Greek myth depicted in Ovid's *Metamorphoses,* where a sculptor comes to love his ivory creation so deeply that the gods take pity on him and bring her to life."

Quinn inclined his head while eyeing her narrowly. "I know the tale, but you have gone stark raving mad if you think I will fall in love with a statue."

While Ash chuckled, Jack chimed in. "Yes, it's clear our dear Kate is suffering from a brain fever. I hope it isn't catching."

"I cannot believe my own flesh and blood is so craven," Kate retorted. "You are not behaving like Wildes at all. You know that we prefer to take fate into our own hands rather than have it act upon us. It is up to *us* to shape our own destinies. I am willing to help, but I can only do so much. For my theory to work, you each have to be responsible for meeting your match and making your particular tale come true."

When no one replied to her suggestion, she gave a huff of exasperation. "What do you have to lose? Treat my mad idea as a game, if you like. Or a challenge. You have always relished a challenge, Ash. All I am asking is that each of you have one significant encounter with your possible match. Then you can decide whether to pursue your legend further."

Ash wouldn't mention that he'd already had a significant encounter with Maura this evening . . . one that had led to a heated embrace and roused his primal male instincts with a vengeance. He'd unwittingly played right into Kate's hands, and he wasn't inclined to continue any further, out of sheer stubbornness if nothing else.

Before he could refuse, however, Quinn claimed Katharine's attention by rising and planting a light kiss on her temple. "If we are quite done . . . I shall leave it to Ash to be your test subject. Like Jack, I have an early morning."

Jack also got to his feet, but he patted Kate's shoulder in an avuncular way meant to provoke her. "If you expect me to play along, sweet shrew, you will have to come up with a better tale for me." He looked to Ash. "Let us know what you discover, brother."

The two men excused themselves, with Quinn striding out purposefully and Jack strolling more slowly while shaking his head in disbelief.

Skye sent Kate an apologetic smile. "I, for one, am very curious to see if your theory works." True to form, Skye was the only one who was remotely interested in following Kate's lead.

Across the library, Lord Cornelius gave a sudden snort and stirred, then settled back down in his chair.

"Uncle Cornelius needs to go to bed," Skye said softly.

Skye was most tenderhearted of all the Wilde cousins, although more than capable of stirring up her own lively brand of mischief. She rose and crossed to the hearth, where she gently woke their slumbering relative.

Cornelius sat up, blinking and fumbling for his spectacles. Now over sixty, with thinning hair that was turning silver, he had the tall, refined build and high-boned features of an aristocrat, but a vague, unfocused air that belied the fact that he was actually a brilliant scholar.

Cornelius was the only one of the Wildes in his generation who had never known a passionate love, as his cousins and brothers and only sister—Jack's mother, Lady Clara—had done. It was ironic that even though Cornelius had never married, he had wound up raising their five orphaned children.

When he caught sight of Katharine, he offered sheepishly, "Forgive me for sleeping through your ball, my dear, but I know you and Ashton had it well in hand."

"You are forgiven, Uncle," she said sweetly. "Especially since you were the inspiration behind my plan to find our perfect matches. I was just telling Ash about his legendary tale."

"Well . . . yes, very good . . ." Cornelius said awkwardly, looking around for the nearest door. He might have provided the literary framework for Kate's plotting, but he clearly wanted no part of the execution.

"Good night, my dears," he mumbled, climbing to his feet and eagerly escorting Skye from the room.

Ash realized he would not be so lucky as to escape, though. The entire time, Katharine had been studying him, and as soon as they were alone, she resumed her argument. "You have always told us that we should make our own destinies, Ash. Well, you need to go out and make yours. Maura Collyer could be your destiny, if only you will claim her."

Ash cut her off just as quickly. "I can't imagine that she is willing to go along with your mad scheme," he stated bluntly.

Katharine paused. "Not quite yet. I suspect she will require some persuading. Maura isn't interested in love or romance or balls or anything so mundane. She is still grieving her father's loss, and now she is fighting to save her stallion."

"Which is a prime reason to forget all about your absurd plot."

To his surprise, Katharine threw up her hands and sank back in her chair with an aggrieved sigh. "Very well, forget all about my idea. But even if you won't consider courting Maura, the very least you could do is use your power and influence to help her reclaim her rightful property from Viscount Deering. Her circumstances have become rather desperate."

With that exhortation, Ash felt on more solid ground. "I didn't say I wouldn't help her. In fact, I already offered my assistance earlier this evening, and she refused."

"I told you she is proud," Katharine replied, making a face. "She won't like playing the role of damsel in distress. Maura is accustomed to being the rescuer, not the other way around. You should have seen her at school. She always stood up to the girls who tried to bully and torment the younger ones. But Lord Deering is too powerful for her. You simply have to make her accept our help, Ash."

At his silence, Katharine played her final trump card. "If you do this for me—if you agree to help Maura—I promise I will do my utmost to find my own match next."

He eyed her skeptically.

"I mean it," Katharine insisted. "I want to prove to you all that my theory works."

"I intend to hold you to that promise, love. I am eager to get you off my hands."

She responded to his teasing declaration with a faint laugh. "So you will help Maura?" she asked more earnestly.

"Yes, on one condition. That I never hear another word from you about Cinderella or princes or wicked stepmothers."

"You have a deal." Her profound relief evident in her brilliant smile, Kate stood and threw her arms around his neck. "I knew I could count on you, dearest Ashton."

He suffered her embrace in ill-humored silence, but could tell that her quick mind was already racing ahead.

"We have no time to waste, Ash. You must call on Maura first thing in the morning, before eight o'clock if you hope to catch her before she leaves the house. She rides early whenever she gets the chance—"

"Why don't you leave the tactics to me?" he warned.

"As you wish. I am just thankful that you mean to help her. And who knows? You may find some merit in my theory after all. This could be the chance of a lifetime—"

When he held up a hand to ward off any more arguments, Katharine grinned in understanding. "Very well, I won't press. But I can hope, can't I?"

With that lighthearted shot, she exited the library, leaving Ash alone to contemplate what he had just agreed to.

He had to give his sister credit. Her proposal that the Wilde cousins imitate classic lovers in literature was her most novel invention to date. One argument of Katharine's, however, had decisively captured his attention: *It is up to us to shape our own destinies.*

Admittedly, the power to shape his destiny held a strong appeal for Ash. After fate had dealt his family such a devastating blow, he'd felt driven to control his future and that of his clan.

He would never forget the moment he learned the terrible news: Seeing Uncle Cornelius's face drain of blood at the letter of notification . . . reading the letter for himself. The shock and anguish as comprehension sank in. The days and weeks afterward when he'd railed impotently at life's cruelties.

Ash's overwhelming grief was underscored by panic at realizing that he'd inherited the title of marquis and so had to attempt to fill his father's shoes.

Granted, he'd overreacted in the beginning. He was too harsh with the boys and overly protective of the girls. But as the eldest cousin, Ash was their leader, accountable for their welfare and their happiness. They had endured enough sorrow, and he'd vowed to spare them any more.

The five of them had vastly differing personalities and interests. His younger brother Jack, who'd been born the bastard son of a European prince, seemed a fun-loving rogue, yet there was a dark streak inside Jack stemming from his early childhood when he'd lived alone on the streets of Paris after Lady Clara's death during the Revolution. Jack's foreign upbringing had often left him feeling like an outsider, despite the fact that he'd been legally adopted by Ash's and Katharine's father.

Sweet, lovely Skye—the youngest and probably the heart of the family—somehow always managed to get her own way, effortlessly wrapping them all around any finger she chose. Despite her deceptively innocent demeanor, Skye possessed an innate curiosity that frequently led her into trouble. That, combined with her mischievous streak, had caused their Uncle Cornelius many a gray hair.

Quinn had inherited Cornelius's intellectual brilliance, but he hid it under a lust for danger and adventure.

And fiery Katharine was the spirit of the Wilde family. As such, she claimed the role of social director in addition to being an unabashed romantic at heart . . . which had led to Ash's current predicament.

Searching for his ideal mate with the goal of finding love was not his preferred method of shaping his destiny. No doubt his reluctance to form any deep attachments stemmed from losing so many loved ones when he was younger. His entire world had been shattered, and he wasn't certain he wanted to risk that kind of pain again. Nor was he eager to upend his life by marrying. He had his family, and he'd never felt the need for more.

The five of them had closed ranks when they'd lost

their beloved parents. In fact, their tragedy had brought them much closer together and made them fiercely loyal to one another. It was the Wilde cousins against the world. . . . And yet at the same time, they were resolved to fulfill the family legacy and carry on the legendary Wilde joie de vivre. They lived life to the fullest, since they knew how short their time on earth could be.

Even so, the questions his sister raised intrigued him. Could Maura Collyer be his ideal match? Ash wondered.

Undeniably, he was fascinated by her fire and passion. And he couldn't help believing she would bring that same kind of passion to her lovemaking. He wanted Maura in his bed, without question. And there was no way to get her there short of marriage, since he was not that much of a rake to seduce her out of wedlock.

Either way, he had no choice but to involve himself in her trials and tribulations. Maura deserved his support, given her long history with Katharine and Skye. Besides, he was sympathetic to Maura's cause and admired her courage in fighting against long odds. Undoubtedly he could improve her chance of winning her battle against a powerful nobleman like Deering.

Still, it was one thing to help Maura. It was quite another to be swept headlong into a situation that could lead to matrimony. Finding himself shackled in wedlock would hardly be controlling his own fate, Ash thought with an ironic smile.

His smile faded as he made up his mind. Standing, he crossed to the hearth and spent a moment banking the fire. If he wanted to get any sleep and yet rise early enough to meet with Maura before she left on her morning ride, he needed to retire now.

But he wouldn't allow himself to be drawn into his sister's absurd theory about playing Cinderella's prince, Ash vowed. He would help Maura Collyer recover her cherished stallion and that would be the end of it.

Chapter Four

Maura woke at her usual early hour the next morning, feeling groggy and bleary-eyed. She'd spent a mostly sleepless night tossing and turning and stewing over her course of action regarding her beloved horse.

After last evening's disaster with the odious Lord Deering, she knew she had to regroup. More aggravatingly, when she'd finally managed to doze off, she couldn't prevent herself from dreaming about a much more appealing nobleman. Even now, she found herself dwelling on the stunning kisses Lord Beaufort had given her, remembering the bewitching taste of him, the sensuality of his illicit caresses—

With a groan, Maura cut off the seditious memory and buried her face in her pillow, highly vexed with herself. Deciding she might as well rise, she climbed out of bed and performed her ablutions, then began donning her riding habit. A brisk ride before breakfast should help to clear her mind. And with luck, she might encounter Lord Deering. She had it on good authority that he rode Emperor in the park on some

mornings, although her two previous efforts to inter-
cept him there had failed.

She was attempting to button the back of her shirt-
waist when her bedchamber was invaded by her two
smiling stepsisters, no doubt eager to hear about the
ball.

Hannah and Lucy were both garbed in frilly pink
dressing gowns that unfortunately did nothing to flat-
ter their somewhat plump figures. Both girls, Maura
surmised, must have inherited their straight brown
hair, brown eyes, and round features from their father, since their mother was a raven-haired, blue-eyed
beauty. Indeed, Priscilla's beguiling loveliness was the
prime attraction that had lured Maura's own father
into matrimony.

The girls also lacked their mother's refinement and
social skills. Lucy, the youngest at seventeen, was a
pert chatterbox, while the shier nineteen-year-old
Hannah had a generous nature, which she promptly
exhibited when she noted Maura's struggle with the
buttons.

"Here, let me help you," Hannah offered kindly,
while Lucy launched into a spate of questions.

"Was the ball very grand, Maura? How many guests
attended? How many times did you dance? Did you
waltz? What was Lady Katharine wearing? Was her
gown as beautiful as your amber one?" Lucy paused
her prattle to take a breath. "I vow that gown you
wore last night was the most beautiful one I have ever
seen in my whole life."

Maura sighed inwardly. She had little desire to be
dragged into evaluating last night's fashions or her
scarcity of dance partners. But her stepsisters were like

puppies seeking affection, and she couldn't turn them away.

They perched on her bed while she did her best to report on the details that would interest them. And when she had tied the laces of her half boots and slipped on her riding jacket, they followed her downstairs to the breakfast room, where a light repast awaited her, supplied by the cook who had worked faithfully in the Collyer household since Maura was a child, and who knew exactly how to tempt her appetite when she was so preoccupied with her precious horses that she would have forgotten to eat.

At least she needn't worry about encountering her stepmother just now. Priscilla rarely rose before ten o'clock, especially after a late evening, which evidently had been the case last night. Thankfully, Pris had still been out when Maura arrived home from the ball, and so had avoided any more bitter rows regarding the cost of Seasons and unlawful sales of stallions.

At the conclusion of Maura's recount of the ball, Lucy gave a dreamy sigh. "I should have loved to attend," she confessed. "Mama was angry that you were invited and we were not, even if Lady Katharine *is* your bosom friend and we claim no acquaintance with her. And Mama was pea green with envy over that splendid gown you wore."

Maura refrained from mentioning that it was business, not pleasure, that had compelled her to attend the ball, and that the "splendid gown" had not even belonged to her.

"I cannot say the same," Hannah admitted. "I would have been terrified to face all those imposing people."

"You are terrified of everything," Lucy stated frankly.

"I am not!" the elder girl defended herself. "Maura helped me overcome my fear of horses."

"Yes, well, you ought not boast about it. An attachment to horses is not something that sits well with Mama." Lucy surveyed Maura's forest green riding habit. "You know Mama will not be pleased that you are riding this morning, Maura?"

Very familiar with her stepmother's stance on the subject, Maura made no reply. Priscilla had long feared that her deplorable hoydenish tendencies would rub off on her stepsisters.

She could just hear Pris's habitual protests: "I cannot for the life of me understand why you insist on wallowing in dirt and manure with the stablehands, Maura. You attended the best finishing schools in the country, so you know perfectly well what is required of a lady."

Since Priscilla truly was the epitome of grace and elegance, she particularly lamented Maura's current profession. No lady of quality would deign to operate a horse stud!

To be fair, Pris had lived under the strain of scandal for two years now, and worried that not only would her daughters be further tarnished by maintaining a close association with Maura, but that their marital chances would be completely ruined. Without question, Priscilla preferred that her shockingly unconventional stepdaughter remain hidden away in the country. When Noah Collyer was still alive, the family had made their home primarily at the farm manor in Suffolk, but upon his unexpected death, Priscilla had hastened to remove her daughters to London, gladly leaving the breeding stables and Maura behind.

Hannah and Lucy, on the other hand, professed to regret that their stepsister was no longer an intimate part of their family. They seemed particularly delighted to have Maura in London now, no doubt because she was willing to stand up to their exacting mother.

To say that the girls were intimidated by Priscilla was a vast understatement, in part because she was always criticizing their unladylike conduct. "Stop slouching!" was Pris's favorite phrase.

Maura, though, did not mind overly much being excluded from her stepfamily's lives if it meant avoiding Priscilla's frequent rebukes. Granted, the first year alone after Papa's death had been painfully hard, but her grief had eased somewhat with the passing of time. If there were still occasions when she felt lonely and alone . . . well, she was usually far too busy to dwell on it.

And now she had even greater problems to deal with. She had hoped to conclude her business with Lord Deering as soon as possible and return home to help Gandy with the new spring foals, but to her dismay, it appeared she would have to remain in town a good while longer—

Her thoughts were interrupted just then by a footman, who announced that the Marquis of Beaufort had called for Miss Collyer.

Caught off guard, Maura grimaced at the news, while Hannah's eyes grew wide. "Can it be true, Maura? The *marquis* has come to call on you?"

Lucy clapped her hands in excitement. "Oh, famous!"

She was clearly delighted at the prospect of so prestigious a visitor, yet Hannah frowned with uneasiness.

"Mama will be unhappy if she is not here to receive him, Maura. If you can delay his lordship, we can wake her and allow her time to dress."

Just then Beaufort strolled into the breakfast room. Clearly he hadn't waited to be invited, but at least he had the manners to offer her a polite bow.

When his gaze locked with hers, Maura felt her heartbeat quicken at the impact of those vivid green eyes. Indeed, Beaufort's mere presence had the power to unnerve her. Then her gaze dropped to his mouth, and she shivered, remembering her dreams about his sensual kisses.

Quickly, she cleared her throat. "My lord, what brings you here at this early hour?"

He raised an eyebrow. "Have you forgotten our engagement this morning?"

"Engagement?"

"To ride."

They had made no such appointment, but he gave her no time to argue as he shifted his attention to her stepsisters. The fact that the girls were still in their dressing gowns must have dawned on them both at the same time; Lucy giggled, while Hannah turned red in the face.

Beaufort did not seem to notice their dishabille, though. No doubt because he was accustomed to seeing females in various stages of undress.

"Will you introduce me to these lovely young ladies, Miss Collyer?"

She complied. "These are my stepsisters, Hannah and Lucy Collyer."

He offered them a bow and a charming smile. "A pleasure to meet you, ladies."

Both girls were clearly awestruck by his attentions and by his stylish elegance. He wore a burgundy riding coat, buff breeches, and shining black boots, attire that molded his broad shoulders and long legs to perfection.

Hannah sat staring at him, tongue-tied, while Lucy giggled again.

It *was* rather disturbing, Maura thought in sympathy, having a noble rake of his caliber in their breakfast room. Even so, she was a fool to let Lord Beaufort affect her so. She didn't even know why he was there. On second thought . . .

I think you and Ash may be meant for each other.

Remembering Katharine's declaration last night, Maura pressed her lips together. The suspicion that her friend was bent on matchmaking filled her with dismay. As if she didn't have enough to worry about just now.

Her first inclination was to be rid of the marquis as soon as possible, but apparently he had other ideas.

"Pray, do not rush yourself, Miss Collyer," Beaufort said easily as he pulled out a chair across from her and settled in it. "It is a lady's prerogative to keep a gentleman waiting. However, you could offer me breakfast. The ball ran so late, I didn't rise in time to dine this morning before our ride."

Maura's eyebrows shot up at his boldness in inviting himself to eat at their table, but while she debated how to answer, Lucy broke in.

"Yes, please do join us, my lord," the girl implored. "Our mama will be enraptured to meet you."

That reminder settled the issue for Maura. She had no desire to have Beaufort's escort on her morning ride, but she urgently wanted to get him out of the house before her stepmother appeared and made him a captive audience.

Setting down her napkin, Maura rose with alacrity. "His lordship will have to meet Mrs. Collyer at some other time, Lucy. We should go, my lord. You won't want to keep your horse standing."

He had provoked her into letting him accompany her, and the smile in his eyes suggested he knew it. When she stood waiting impatiently for him, Beaufort rose also and snagged an apple from the bowl of fruit on the table before following Maura from the room.

She held her tongue as she hastened to collect her gloves and hat from the footman at the front door, not wanting to argue in front of Priscilla's servants. Then she quickly led the marquis outside and down the steps to the street, where her mount was being held by a groom.

Yet when Beaufort asked in that amused tone of his, "What is the hurry, Miss Collyer?" Maura explained in a low undervoice. "Even if you are an unwanted guest, you don't deserve to be subjected to my stepmother. She would toady you to death."

"Your effort to spare me is much appreciated," he murmured in return, "although it wounds me to be considered unwanted."

Refraining from replying, Maura allowed the groom to aid her into her sidesaddle while Beaufort mounted his own horse, a splendid bay gelding. When she urged her mount down the street, he fell in step beside her.

"But you *are* unwanted, Lord Beaufort," she continued when they were out of earshot. "I am only letting you come along because it will save me having to take one of Priscilla's grooms. I would rather not have her know my business, and her servants usually report back to her."

His mouth curved wryly. "Even more wounding, being relegated to the role of servant." When that got no rise out of her, he commented further. "Surely, you can venture out of the house on your own, Miss Collyer. I would not have expected you to fear for your reputation."

"I don't fear for mine," Maura said honestly. "But I have my stepsisters' reputations to think of. Besides, my stepmother may not like having to spare a groom, but she dislikes even more having me ride about London without one. And since I am living in her home at present, I try to accede to her wishes."

She said nothing further as she turned the corner onto a busier street.

"Where are we riding?" Beaufort asked after a moment of negotiating various carriages and wagons and pedestrians.

"Don't you know?" Maura countered archly. "You concocted this pretense of a prior appointment."

"I thought to leave the choice to you."

"How magnanimous of you."

"Indeed, it was."

When he offered her a winning smile, Maura's defenses went on full alert. Lord Beaufort was as charming as the very devil, but she couldn't afford the distraction of an irresistible rake just now.

Still, she couldn't keep her eyes off him, noting his tall, muscular elegance as he sat his powerful mount with ease. She knew he was a bruising rider from summers and holidays visiting Katharine and Skye at their family estates, and undeniably his accomplishments as a horseman impressed her. Yet she felt far too self-conscious around Beaufort, no doubt because of those disturbing kisses of his . . . and because of his sister, too.

Reminded of Katharine's threat to throw them together, Maura felt a renewed surge of mortification. She was not one to shrink from a conflict, however, and so decided to be frank. "You have not explained why you invited yourself to ride with me, Lord Beaufort. You are here in order to placate Katharine, are you not? She said last night that she would convince you to help me, but I told her I didn't need your help."

"I did not need convincing. I planned to intervene even before she pleaded with me."

"I do *not* want her dragging you into my affairs," Maura declared in frustration.

"Are you always a termagant at this hour of the morning?" he asked, surveying her.

His simple question brought her up short. Whatever Beaufort's faults, he did not deserve to be treated rudely.

Maura sighed. "Not always. I did not sleep well last night."

"That is understandable. Let me guess. You spent much of the night fretting and plotting a new course of action to save your stallion."

She had plotted, yes, although she had not come up with any concrete ideas to rescue Emperor from the viscount's clutches.

"Fortunately, I am here to discuss a plan," Beaufort announced amiably.

"You needn't go to such trouble."

"I expected that exact response from you. According to Kate, you are too proud to ask for help."

Maura shot him an exasperated look. "And here I thought she was supposed to be my friend."

"Oh, she is. She is merely concerned for you, and rightly so."

"Perhaps, but you have no reason to concern yourself with me."

He gave her a long, considering look. "Why are you so resistant to my involvement? Other than your pride, that is."

Maura managed a shrug. "It is embarrassing, having a man who is practically a stranger privy to my private affairs."

"Why, because you care for my good opinion?"

His unexpected query surprised a fleeting smile from her. "Surely you can understand why last night was mortifying for me."

"Because you don't like being in a position of weakness."

"Well, yes. I imagine you would not either."

"True. If Deering had propositioned me as he did you, we would be meeting over pistols at dawn."

Maura could well believe it. Even though dueling was illegal, the Wildes were known to use pistols to settle their controversies, which had resulted in more than one blood feud to enliven their family history.

"I don't intend to shoot him," she muttered, "much as I would like to."

"Yet you are obviously not thinking clearly, Miss Collyer," Beaufort pressed. "If you allow me to join forces with you, it will strengthen your position.

Deering will think twice if he knows he has to deal with me."

Her gaze fixed intently on him. "Will your involvement make him return my horse to me?"

"Not alone, no. But I can help you develop a strategy to fight him, one that is not so haphazard as the vague plan you are pursuing to buy back your stallion."

When Maura remained mute, Beaufort prodded her further. "I gather you mean to approach Deering this morning."

"If I can find him."

"Is that wise so soon after the contretemps last night?"

"Perhaps not," she conceded.

"Have you arranged to meet him?"

"No."

"So you intend to attempt an ambush. You aren't worried he will repeat his offer to make you his mistress?"

"Hyde Park is a public enough place. I doubt he would proposition me again in front of witnesses. And I won't allow myself to be caught alone with him again."

"But what do you hope to accomplish?"

Realizing Beaufort would not give up his questioning until his curiosity was satisfied, Maura gave in. "As galling as it would be, I may have to apologize for unmanning him last night."

She saw Beaufort's lips twitch. "I didn't think you fancied eating crow for breakfast."

Her own lips twisted in an unwilling smile. "I don't, but I am willing to swallow my pride for the sake of my horse. I mean to try one more time to persuade Deering to sell Emperor. Barring that, I will ask him to return Emperor to my farm, or at least to one of his own estates in the country. It is a reasonable request. Emperor is highly nervous in London traffic, and Deering is known as a ham-handed rider. He is treating a champion racehorse like a common hack, riding him in a busy park. Any idiot would know better."

"True, but you underestimate Deering if you think him a complete idiot. He is merely excessively vain. No doubt he hopes to increase his prestige by showing off his new prize possession before the ton."

Maura found herself grinding her teeth again, and her voice dropped to a low growl. "I suspect he also wants to broadcast his victory over me. He enjoys rubbing salt in my wounds," she added with a touch of bitterness.

Beaufort thought about that for a moment before asking another question. "Just how do you know what Deering's riding customs are?"

"I told you, my steward Gandy has connections."

"Ah, you have a spy in his stables."

Maura blushed to have her underhanded methods exposed, but she'd deemed it necessary to fight fire with fire. "Something like that. Emperor is stabled in the mews behind Deering's home, and some of the grooms there are former colleagues of Gandy's, and so are willing to keep him informed."

"I am surprised Gandy is not here to help you deal with the problem."

"He originally came with me to London, but he couldn't remain long because it is prime foaling season."

"Then you have all the more reason to welcome my support."

Maura bit back a sigh. Beaufort's forceful personality was much like his sister's; opposing him would be like trying to resist a powerful storm.

Her conclusion was proved right with his next words.

"Regardless of your stubborn pride, Miss Collyer, I intend to offer my unwanted advice. You are letting anger and grief cloud your judgment. You need someone with a cooler head to help you formulate a new plan."

He sounded eminently logical and rational, drat him.

"If you have half the intelligence I credit you with," he added for good measure, "you will allow me to help."

Maura fell silent, acknowledging the truth of his observation. She would be foolish not to at least consider his offer.

"What did you have in mind?" she asked cautiously.

"Your best course is to gain some leverage over Deering, something that will force him to sell."

She didn't reply, and Beaufort said nothing more, doubtless deciding to let her think about his advice. They reached the entrance to Hyde Park a short while later. Maura kept her eyes peeled for Deering, but there was no sign of him.

She and Beaufort cantered their horses along Rotten Row, the wide thoroughfare beside the Serpentine Lake, which was flanked by trees that had leafed the lovely green of spring. After a time, though, Maura began to fret with impatience and frustration. Where was Deering? Would he even come? And would he be riding Emperor?

She had just dropped back into a walk when she drew a sudden breath, having spied her beloved horse in the distance.

She would recognize that powerfully muscled form anywhere, but Emperor was unique in other ways: the elegant head, the kind eye, the sleek black coat that held no trace of white except for a small star on his forehead, and most of all the lively, mischievous temperament. Her horse had a vivid personality all his own.

His rider was indeed Lord Deering, Maura saw as she moved closer. She quickened her pace, even though realizing the viscount had paused beside a landau to speak to the occupant. Her heart sank when she spied the long whip Deering carried and the sharp spurs he wore.

The stallion obviously recognized Maura in return, for he abruptly lifted his head and let out a piercing whinny before breaking into a trot and heading in her direction. In response, Deering hauled on the reins, sawing the bit against Emperor's tender mouth and digging those wicked spurs into his flanks. Not surprisingly, the horse laid back his ears, resenting the savage treatment.

Then the nobleman raised the whip. Maura went cold, watching helplessly as the leather weapon came down hard on the stallion's rump again and again. Giving a small cry, she spurred her own mount forward, but after two more blows, Emperor began combating the beating, rounding his back and giving a violent buck that sent the viscount flying.

Free of his tormentor, the stallion raced toward Maura, seeking her protection. When she pulled up, breathing erratically, he came to a skidding halt before her and stood trembling.

Clamping down on her fury in order to croon soft words to him, she reached down and caught the reins, then stroked the stallion's sleek neck, trying to calm him with her touch and her voice.

By now Deering had picked himself up off the ground and was stalking toward them. His hat was missing, but he still held the whip and his face was livid. He was clearly enraged that the stallion had made him look foolish and inept in front of his riding colleagues and the Marquis of Beaufort, who had ridden up beside Maura.

When Deering reached them, he raised the whip again, brandishing it at the stallion, who shied in fear.

Appalled, Maura sputtered a fierce command to stop. "Don't you dare hit him again!"

Deering turned his rage on her. "I have every right to punish my own horse!"

Holding the whip high, he moved in for another assault, but Maura intervened, desperately stretching down and snatching the whip from his gloved hands.

Deering was not deterred, however, but drew back his fist, aiming for the stallion's defenseless face.

With another cry, Maura brought the whip down across the nobleman's shoulders, making him flinch in startled pain.

She might have continued, but suddenly felt herself being lifted completely out of her sidesaddle. Beaufort had hauled her off her horse and set her before him on his own mount, to prevent her from attacking the viscount further.

Breathing heavily, she sat glaring at Deering, who had spun to face her and was glaring back.

"You bloody she-devil," he gritted out. "How dare you strike me!"

"I was only giving you a taste of your own medicine!" she retorted. "How do *you* like being beaten and abused, your lordship?"

When he took a threatening step toward her, Beaufort's sharp command rang out. "That is quite enough, Deering."

Heeding the warning in the marquis's tone, the viscount stopped. Then he looked around him, realizing they had a shocked audience. Activity in the entire park had come to a halt, with all the nearby occupants avidly watching the spectacle.

Just then the viscount's acquaintance in the landau drove up to join them. Taking stock, the distinguished elderly gentleman voiced disapproval. "I say, Deering, there was no call to hit the horse so savagely. Especially such a magnificent animal."

At the rebuke, the viscount's face turned a different shade of red, this one resembling embarrassment rather than rage.

Maura agreed wholeheartedly with the reprimand. She wanted to dismount and comfort her still-frightened horse, but Beaufort's arm was wrapped firmly around her, pinning her against him.

He evidently knew the elderly gentleman, for he spoke with familiarity. "Lord Pelham, perhaps you can help relieve this awkward situation by letting us borrow your tiger for a short while."

Maura turned her head to eye the lad perched at the rear of the landau, noting his ornate livery.

When Pelham raised quizzical eyebrows, Beaufort explained his suggestion. "If you are amenable, your lad can lead the stallion back to his stables while you take Deering up in your carriage."

"Yes, of course," Pelham agreed. "An excellent notion."

When Maura would have protested this Solomon-like judgment, Beaufort's arm tightened about her, keeping her still as he addressed the viscount. "As soon as I return home, I will send one of my grooms to check on the stallion, to be certain he has suffered no ill effects."

"That will not be necessary," Deering said tightly.

"Even so, I should like to relieve Miss Collyer's mind, and my own as well."

The hard warning note in Beaufort's voice was back, and Deering must have heard it, for he nodded once, resentfully signaling his acquiescence.

In short order, the plan was put into effect. To Maura's relief, Lord Pelham's tiger approached the stallion quietly and calmed him with a gentle touch before drawing the reins over his head to lead him toward the park entrance.

Neither of the main combatants was satisfied, however. Deering, Maura knew, had again been humiliated before witnesses in a brawl with her, while she was forced to watch impotently as her precious horse was taken away.

With one final glare at her, Deering climbed into Pelham's landau and drove off. The spectators eventually disbanded, but Maura sat with her fists clenched as despair and guilt welled up to join her fury. *She* was at fault for this latest explosion with Deering. She had wanted to save her horse, not expose him to more suffering. Innocent animal that he was, Emperor had only been trying to greet her and had received a vicious beating for his pains.

Remembering the blows he had endured, Maura felt the burn of tears sting her eyes.

Beaufort evidently sensed her distress, for he reached up to touch her chin and turn her face up to his. "Why are you crying?"

"I am *not* crying!" she muttered.

"I have a sister and a female cousin, remember? When a woman protests so vehemently, the opposite is usually true."

She dashed her tears away and swallowed hard. "You are insufferable, Lord Beaufort."

"So Katharine and Skye tell me. But that doesn't explain your tears. I expected better of you."

His jibe made Maura's spine stiffen. "I am upset because I meant to hold my temper and address Deering diplomatically when I encountered him."

"And instead you only made matters worse by striking him and berating him in front of his peers."

"Yes," she mumbled, hanging her head. "I should have been able to protect Emperor."

"You will." Beaufort's tone had become softer, genuinely reassuring, and so were his eyes, she discovered when she looked up again. For a moment she found herself caught in those emerald depths . . .

Realizing suddenly that she was sitting on his lap with his arm locked around her, Maura shifted uneasily. "You can release me now, my lord."

"I intend to, once you are calmer."

"I *am* calm."

He looked dubious and hesitated to do as she asked.

"Set me down, I say," Maura said more sternly. "You are causing a spectacle."

Beaufort's mouth curved. "You dare to accuse *me* of causing a spectacle after that little drama you just enacted? You could be an honorary Wilde." When she failed to appreciate the compliment, his smile faded. "I am preventing you from doing something you will regret, my little hothead. You would do better to use your wits. You need to be cool and unemotional whenever you confront Deering."

"I cannot possibly be unemotional with him."

"My point exactly."

She didn't want to hear Beaufort's logical arguments, but she couldn't ignore them either. "Will you truly send your groom to look after Emperor?"

"I said so, did I not? I am a man of my word."

That was some consolation at least.

Meeting his level gaze, Maura gave in with reluctance. Fighting the Marquis of Beaufort in public would only result in another scene that could be detrimental to her cause of rescuing her horse, and to her stepsisters as well. As it was, she would have a lot to make up for. Priscilla would be livid when she heard about this morning's confrontation with Deering.

When Maura nodded, Beaufort set her on her own horse, but appropriated her reins before she gathered her wits enough to realize what he was doing.

"Where are you taking me?" she protested as he led her from the park.

"Somewhere you can expend some of your anger."

"This is becoming a vexing habit of yours, Lord Beaufort."

"You don't say."

"Let me have my reins," she insisted.

"Not yet. I don't trust you not to do something idiotic."

"What is this, an abduction?" Her voice turned exasperated as well as frustrated. "Do you mean to constrain me against my will?"

"If I must." When he glanced back at her, his green eyes held amusement. "I intend to save you from yourself, sweet vixen. Now hush and behave long enough for us to leave the park."

He sounded every inch the imperious nobleman, expecting instant obedience; he was a marquis, after all. And he was clearly giving her no choice but to accompany him.

His dispassionate behavior was one small consolation, Maura supposed. His sister might be trying to matchmake for him, but thankfully Beaufort did not seem interested in romance in the least.

With a sigh of resignation scraping past her tight throat, she allowed herself to be led away while trying to ignore the interested stares of the nearby park-goers.

Chapter Five

Ash led a silent, brooding Miss Collyer out of the city, heading southwest toward Richmond. Once they reached the countryside, he returned her reins to her, since she seemed to have regained control of her militant emotions.

Ash maintained a similar silence during the ride, contemplating the odd amalgam of his own emotions. Upon watching Maura come to her horse's defense, he'd felt a fierce anger on her behalf, as well as an outsized protectiveness. And now that the physical threat was past, he could only shake his head in amusement and admiration.

She was indeed one of a kind. He doubted even his feisty, headstrong sister would have assaulted a nobleman in a public park with his own riding whip, despite the sore provocation.

If he hadn't been eager to champion Maura's cause before, her actions just now would have convinced him. She was fearless, a tenacious fighter, but she badly needed a pacifying influence to curb her reckless impulses before her fiery passions landed her in even deeper trouble.

Ash's mouth curved as he glanced at the beautiful hellion riding beside him. To think that *he* would be bent on keeping anyone *out* of trouble.

His ironical smile faded just as suddenly when he recalled the Wilde family conference last night, when Katharine had claimed to have found his perfect match. It was a jolt for Ash to realize that she had a point: Maura Collyer could indeed prove a compatible mate for him.

She was passionate, opinionated, tart-tongued, and prone to violence—just the sort of spirited female who most appealed to him. The kind who either fascinated or frightened men. And he was wholly fascinated.

That didn't necessarily mean he wanted her for his bride, Ash rationalized. He wasn't *that* smitten as to offer for her hand in marriage on so tenuous an acquaintance. But as much as he hated to admit it, perhaps his sister was right. He ought to at least *explore* the possibility that Maura Collyer could be his ideal match.

Seeing her glance wistfully at the fields flanking the road, Ash corralled his distracted thoughts.

"Shall we ride cross-country?" he asked.

When she quickly nodded in agreement, they left the main road and turned onto a country lane. As soon as they reached a grassy meadow, Maura guided her horse over a ditch and broke into a full gallop. Ash had to urge his bay for a burst of speed just to keep up with her.

Eventually they slowed, then dropped to a walk to cool off their mounts. Maura seemed reluctant to turn back, however, for the verdant meadow where they rode now was covered with spring wildflowers, and the warm sunshine beating down upon them seemed to soothe her.

After a time they stopped beside a stream to let their horses drink. No doubt they were trespassing on some farmer's property, for they'd passed occasional barns and cottages and pastures populated by grazing livestock, but they were shielded from civilization now by a copse of sun-dappled willows.

To Ash's surprise, Maura dismounted without his help and pulled off her gloves. Then, unpinning her feathered shako hat, she knelt beside the stream and splashed water on her face, perhaps to erase any remaining sign of tears.

When she was done, she didn't rise. Instead she sank back upon the grassy slope and sat with her arms wrapped around her updrawn knees, staring at the bubbling stream.

Ash swung down also and left his horse to graze as he joined her on the grass. Her face was still wet, he noted, while damp tendrils of honey-blond hair that had escaped her chignon clung to her forehead and cheeks. When silently he handed her his handkerchief, she took it without comment.

"Why are you being so nice?" she finally asked in a low voice. "You should be scolding me for not heeding your advice."

"I expect you are scolding yourself enough for the both of us."

"I am," she said despairingly. "I have certainly ruined any chance of buying back my horse, and much worse, put him in actual danger. Deering may very well take his vindictiveness out on Emperor."

"I doubt he would seriously hurt so valuable an animal," Ash said reassuringly, although he wasn't wholly convinced himself. "But you have indeed complicated matters."

Heaving a sigh, Maura lay back on the grass and covered her eyes with her arm. "I have no excuse for letting my temper get the best of me, especially not when it could result in harm to my horse. It's just that my best intentions always go awry when it comes to dealing with that detestable man."

"It's understandable why you would hate him if you believe he murdered your father," Ash offered.

"I suppose he isn't solely to blame for my father's death," she said with great reluctance. "It was partly my fault also."

Ash frowned as he glanced down at her. "Why would you say so?"

"If I hadn't loved Emperor so much, Papa would not have been so adamant about refusing to sell him. And if he'd been willing to sell, Deering never would have accused him of cheating. That is my lifelong regret . . . that my father died with a cloud of dishonor hanging over him. The doctors said the distress and humiliation strained his already weak heart. . . ." She paused, as if struggling against tears, and beneath her concealing arm, he could see her lower lip trembling. "Papa's heart broke from shame, and I might have prevented it."

Anguish vibrated in her voice, making Ash's heart twist in sympathy. The memory was obviously deeply emotional for her, not only because of grief, but because of the guilt she bore, however unjustified.

"You are not to blame for Deering's attempt at blackmail," he reminded her gently.

"No, but perhaps Papa would not have died had he not suffered that vile stain on his good name. Even facing disgrace, he was determined to retain possession of Emperor for me. If he had given in, Deering would have withdrawn his spurious accusations. And now my father is gone with no chance to absolve his name."

Ash understood her grief at losing her father, since he'd experienced the same grief. His own most ardent regret was losing his beloved, vivacious, larger-than-life parents long before their time. But Maura's guilt was misplaced; she had not killed her father simply because she had dearly loved her horse.

Ash's first impulse was to comfort her, yet he knew she was unlikely to accept comfort from him. Thus, he settled for repeating his offer.

"I trust now you will allow me to help you fight Deering."

She exhaled another heavy sigh. "I am sure it is too late now to make any difference."

"I never expected you to take such a defeatist attitude."

Despite his deliberately provoking tone, Maura didn't reply. Ash couldn't tell if her silence was due to despondency or merely a return of her usual stubbornness. He would much prefer stubbornness.

Reaching down to catch her wrist, he drew her arm away from her face.

Her eyes were shut, but with the golden sunlight

warming her ivory skin, her beauty struck him anew. She had pulled her hair back into a tight chignon, but there were damp wisps framing her face. Gently he pushed a tendril back from her temple.

At his first touch, her eyes fluttered open. She gazed up at him until he traced her lips with his fingertips. Then she went still, staring at his mouth, as if she'd forgotten to breathe.

A moment later she swallowed hard, and her voice dropped a husky octave when she spoke. "I know what you are about, Lord Beaufort. You mean to seduce me into accepting your help."

Ash could have truthfully denied the accusation just then. There was really nothing so calculated in his motives. Moreover, actual seduction would not have been honorable. But since logic hadn't worked, perhaps a bit of sensual coercion was in order. He was highly confident of his persuasive talents when he exerted his charm, even with unwilling females like Maura Collyer.

Curiosity was also driving him. He wanted to know if the fire he'd felt between them last night had been an aberration or a trick of his senses because of the unusual circumstances.

And then there was the intriguing question about her possibly being his ideal mate.

But most of all, he couldn't ignore the simple fact that he wanted her.

"I hadn't thought so far ahead as seduction," he murmured in reply. "But now that you mention it . . ." Bracing his hands on either side of her head, he bent closer.

At his nearness, her eyes flared, accentuating the gold

flecks in the hazel depths. When he lowered his head the final distance to kiss her, Ash heard Maura draw a sharp breath. Yet she didn't fight him when he captured her mouth. She merely hesitated a heartbeat before parting her lips beneath his—if not in welcome, then without resistance.

At the delectable contact, the familiar fiery sparks shimmered through Ash; the same lightning-in-the-blood sizzle as during their first embrace. This kiss was sheer heat, a heady sensation that went straight to his loins and only magnified his urge to stake his claim to Maura.

He hadn't imagined his fierce sexual attraction for her, he concluded; it had only been tamped down. If anything, the primal lust he'd felt last night had deepened. Especially when she yielded to him more fully, returning his kiss with untutored skill.

He forced himself, though, to keep the pace unhurried as he savored her soft lips, her tantalizing, womanly warmth. Angling his head to permit his tongue greater access, Ash eased down beside Maura on the grass and gathered her against him.

The kiss stretched for an enchanted interval. Time seemed to slow, while pleasure welled and surged between them with the rhythm of their shared breaths.

Lost in the moment, Ash slid one hand to her throat, then lower, caressing her lightly. He felt her thudding heartbeat even through her riding habit and the stays of her corset.

There were too many restrictive layers of clothing between them, he thought with increasing frustration, yet he could remember the warm swells of her bare breasts from the previous evening, the sweet taste of her nipples. . . . In response, his rising maleness swelled and throbbed painfully inside his breeches.

It was all Ash could do to stave off the burgeoning ache as he slipped one knee into the cradle of her thighs. Their bodies fit together perfectly, as he'd suspected they would. Maura might have felt a similar rightness, for she murmured incoherently—an alluring sound—and reached up to twist her fingers in his hair.

The craving to possess her only intensified inside Ash. His lips plied hers more urgently as his hand splayed over her stomach and trailed down over her skirts. She was hot and restless now, arching against him, making soft whimpering sounds in her throat as she clung to him and returned his devouring kiss.

Desire rode Ash hard, spurring aching hunger and sharp need. He could imagine taking Maura on the warm grass just now, could almost feel himself sinking into her hot, welcoming flesh. . . .

When he cupped her woman's mound through the skirts of her riding habit, she gave a moan and rocked her hips, pressing against his hand. Seeking to heighten her pleasure, he stroked slowly between her thighs, arousing her with deliberate provocation.

Yet it wasn't enough. He wanted more, much more.

All his senses inflamed, he continued feasting on her mouth as he drew her skirts up to her hips, baring her feminine flesh to his touch.

When his hand dipped between her legs to find the wetness there, Maura shivered at his first caress. It was only when his exploring fingers probed her slick folds, searching for the sensitive bud of her sex, that she suddenly pulled back with a gasp of shock.

Sitting up abruptly, she pushed her skirts down over her bare legs, then scrambled backward, far away from him.

"Can you not even go two minutes without trying to ravish me?" she asked hoarsely.

It took a moment for Ash to gather his wits enough to realize that he'd carried his lust too far. He had indeed wanted to ravish her.

His smile was more grimace than humor as he raised himself up on his elbows. "Apparently not in your case," he replied dryly.

Desire had roughened his voice, while his cock ached. Even with the pain, however, he was grateful that Maura had been the one to end their embrace this time, for he wouldn't have had the willpower.

Her willpower was not much stronger, he decided, surveying her lovely flushed face. She had averted her gaze, yet he could tell she was still shaken by the passion she'd felt, as was he. He throbbed with the primitive need to claim her for his own.

Once again Ash marveled at her extraordinary effect on him. It wasn't unusual that he would be captivated by a woman with Maura's enchanting face and tempting body. But she had made him burn, despite her innocence and inexperience.

"I won't allow you to seduce me, Lord Beaufort," she murmured as if to convince herself as much as him. "I am not so easily manipulated."

"I was not attempting to manipulate you, sweetheart," he insisted truthfully.

She cast him a skeptical glance. "No? Then I suppose you were intent on getting your way. I dared reject your offer of assistance, and you cannot bear to lose an argument. Either that, or you are merely amusing yourself with me."

He raised an eyebrow in puzzlement. "Why would you think so?"

"Because you are a renowned rake who cares for nothing but his own pleasure."

The accusation was largely unfounded and prompted a swift denial from Ash. "I assure you, your pleasure is of much greater importance to me—as I could very easily show you."

That silenced her just as swiftly. Her blush deepening, Maura struggled to her feet and pointedly turned her back to him.

Ash looked up at the sky, pondering the irony with self-deprecating amusement. Women had always eagerly welcomed his attentions, nearly swooning at the promise of becoming his lover. So why was he interested in pursuing the one woman who didn't?

His feeling of possessiveness with Maura was singular. He had no claim to her—not yet, at any rate. But in a very short time, he'd become allied to her cause.

Reminded of the major issue between them, Ash resumed their earlier conversation. "I am involved in your fight now, whether you like it or not, Maura. In fact, I am determined to defeat Deering now, not merely for your own sake but just on general principle. He needs to be taught a lesson."

She remained silent as she went to her horse. After gathering her reins, Maura glanced back at him. "So what do you advise me to do?" she asked quite unexpectedly. "I mean, given this morning's fresh disaster, how am I to prevail over him?"

"I haven't decided yet," Ash answered candidly. "I need some time to think on it."

She took a deep breath. "Very well, then. You win."

His gaze arrested. "What have I won?" he asked cautiously.

"You may help me fight Deering."

Her apparent capitulation more than surprised Ash. "What brought about this sudden change of heart?"

Maura shrugged. "I realized that you are right. There is no use in crying over what cannot be changed. I have to move forward. Indeed, I should be thanking you for your help, my lord. I promise I will listen if you think of a plan. But for now, I need to return home. My stepmother will be livid about this morning's spectacle in the park. Will you please give me a leg up?"

She stood patiently waiting as Ash got to his feet and dusted off his breeches. And when he joined her, she gave him back the handkerchief he had loaned her. She seemed quite calm, but he was leery of her odd reaction, for she had given in much too easily. When he eyed Maura suspiciously, though, she gave him a wan smile.

The uneasy feeling in his gut continued as he set her on her horse and mounted his own. Even so, Ash argued with himself, the fact that Maura rarely acted as expected was a large part of her appeal, and precisely why she might make him a good match. She would forever keep him intrigued.

She could also hold her own with him, when most women couldn't. In that respect, she was like all the females in the Wilde clan—strong, independent, and sharp-witted. She would be a handful to deal with, but a fascinating challenge for the right man.

And he could be that right man.

Perhaps Katharine was not completely mad in urging him to pursue his classic lover's tale, Ash decided thoughtfully. Legend had it that every Wilde had his one true mate, and he now wanted to see if Maura Collyer was his.

Chapter Six

Maura did indeed have to feign nonchalance as Lord Beaufort escorted her back to London. Her body still throbbed from his scandalous touch, her mind felt dazed.

Casting the marquis a surreptitious glance, she was keenly conscious of the tender ache in her breasts and between her thighs—

Maura gave a mental moan at her weakness. Once again she'd fallen victim to her traitorous senses and failed to put up even the slightest measure of resistance. She should have learned her lesson by now: She couldn't be near Beaufort without succumbing to temptation.

Frankly, she was disgusted with herself for letting him distract her from her mission to save her stallion, even temporarily. But at least now she had settled on her course of action.

She had no choice now but to take drastic steps. Deering would never forgive her for humiliating him twice in as many days, Maura knew.

Yet it was clear she would have to act on her own. Lord Beaufort had no immediate solution to her problem, he'd said so himself, and she couldn't afford to wait for him to develop a fresh strategy. Not when she feared for her horse's welfare, perhaps his very life. She couldn't stop fretting over Emperor, worrying about how he was being mistreated right this very moment. She would not—could not—leave him in that villain's hands any longer.

Nor could she confide her plan to Beaufort, since undoubtedly he would try to stop her. Which is why she had pretended to accept his counsel a short while ago.

It had required her best acting skills, and she could tell that he didn't quite believe her sudden acquiescence. And she still had to convince him of her benign intentions. Therefore, Maura spoke little on the return ride and replied vaguely to any comment he made.

When they reached the Collyer residence on Clarges Street, he started to dismount, but Maura stopped him. "No, pray don't trouble yourself to help me down. I can manage on my own."

Unhooking her leg over the sidesaddle, she dropped lightly to the ground just as a footman exited the house to take possession of her mount.

"Good day to you, my lord," she said politely, looking up at Beaufort. "Thank you for the pleasant ride."

Maura was glad that he seemed to accept his dismissal for now, although not happy with his promise of future conversation. "I will call on you tomorrow morning, Miss Collyer, if that is agreeable. We can discuss a new plan while we ride."

"Yes," she murmured, "that is quite agreeable."

He surveyed her for a long moment, as if distrustful of her amiability. Finally he tipped his hat to her and turned his bay gelding down the street.

Maura breathed a sigh of relief as the marquis rode away. She would be very pleased to see the last of him, for her own self-preservation.

She handed her mount over to the footman, to be returned to the nearby livery stable where the Collyer horses and vehicles were kept. Additionally, she asked to have her gig delivered at one o'clock that afternoon. "And please make certain that it is drawn by my chestnut, Fripon. The livery will know which horse I mean."

"Very good, Miss Collyer," the footman replied. "Also, Mrs. Collyer bade me tell you that she wishes to speak to you as soon as you returned."

"Thank you, John."

Maura ran up the steps, thinking ahead. She had a great deal to accomplish if she hoped to pull off her plan, yet for the first time in days, she felt almost calm because she knew exactly what she had to do.

First, however, she would have to face her stepmother, who would surely ring a peal over her head upon hearing the news of her public brawl.

Not surprisingly, Priscilla was alone in her favorite parlor, an elegant room done in shades of rose and cream that complimented her ivory complexion, raven hair, and blue eyes. Pris looked up from her needlework when Maura entered, and as expected, her beautiful features tightened with disapproval, confirming that the ton's network of gossips had already struck.

"How *could* you, Maura?" she demanded at once. "I have had two reports from friends in the space of an hour. It is bad enough that your father left us mired in scandal. You have to go and make it even worse by humiliating a peer of the realm before all of London."

Maura pressed her lips together at the unfair charge against her father. It was a huge point of contention between them. She believed utterly in her father's innocence, but her stepmother seemed to have doubts. Certainly she had never refuted Deering's false accusations with any vehemence, as Maura had. It was almost as if she blamed Papa for leaving her to deal with the disgrace. And now, even worse, she was taking his accuser's side.

"Your outrageous behavior is shaming us all," Pris continued scolding. "And honestly, can you not see that making an enemy of Lord Deering will only hurt your stepsisters? But I suppose you don't care about Hannah and Lucy one whit."

"Of course I care about them," Maura said stiffly.

"Well, it will surely be your fault if they fail to make decent matches."

Maura bit her tongue to hold back her retort, not wanting to say something she would regret.

Priscilla had no such qualms, however. "You are living under my roof. You at least owe me the courtesy of restraining your hellion ways while you are here."

"You are right, Priscilla," Maura agreed with effort, refraining from pointing out that this house used to be *her* roof before Pris had worked her wiles on Noah Collyer. "But you needn't fear that I will disgrace you again in the immediate future. I am returning home to Suffolk this very afternoon."

Her announcement clearly caught Pris by surprise. "You are leaving London?"

"Yes, I would not want to inconvenience you any longer," murmured Maura, unable to repress an edge of sarcasm in her voice. "I only came to London to try and retrieve my horse, and that has proved impossible."

Priscilla lowered her gaze, looking almost contrite. She understood perfectly well that she had wronged Maura by delivering Emperor to the viscount for so many pieces of gold. "I am sorry you lost your pet, my dear," she said in a softer tone, "but I had no other choice if I hoped to provide Seasons for my daughters to improve their chances of marrying."

It was an apology of sorts, one that Priscilla had offered several times before, but Maura was unwilling to accept that excuse.

"As I *told* you," she rejoined, "if you had only waited three months, I could have sold the spring foals to raise the funds you needed."

"But I could *not* wait," Priscilla argued. "Too much time has already been wasted waiting for our period of mourning to be over. It will be difficult enough to find husbands for Hannah and Lucy when they are still young, and the case will be hopeless once they reach spinsterhood as you have. And surely even you can see Lord Deering's patronage is *vital* to their acceptance by the ton. Without his support, their matrimonial prospects are doomed."

"No, I do not see that at all."

Refusing to be drawn further into the familiar, futile dispute, Maura spun on her heel and left the parlor without another word. She went straight up to her bedchamber to pack, her emotions simmering.

She was aware that losing her beloved horse had dredged up old childhood resentments against Priscilla for taking away her father and sending her away from home. But just then Maura couldn't repress the painful reminders.

A half hour later, however, when her stepsisters burst into her room, she had to clamp down on her memories while trying to console them, for they were visibly upset at hearing the news of her impending departure.

"Mama says you are leaving, Maura. Please, won't you stay?" Hannah begged. "How are we to manage without you?"

"I wish I could remain for your sakes," she answered honestly before shading the truth with her next comment. "Gandy needs me at home, with so many foals and yearlings to care for. And there is no point in my remaining in London any longer. Emperor is lost to me."

"It is so unfair that Mama sold Emperor," Hannah said sadly.

"Yes," Lucy seconded her elder sister. "We wish we could help you get him back."

"You know we would do anything for you, Maura," Hannah added. "You have always been so good to us."

Maura was touched by their offer of help. The girls had attended the same academy for young ladies that she had, although not until a year after she had left. But she'd visited them regularly and sent them frequent packages from home to make their lives more bearable. She had also encouraged them to make friends. She hadn't wanted them to suffer the loneliness that she had known before she'd found Katharine and Skye to share her sorrows and hopes and dreams with.

"But what about Lord Beaufort?" Lucy asked unexpectedly.

Maura looked up from the valise she was packing. "What about him?"

"He seems very interested in courting you."

She felt a blush stain her cheeks. "You are mistaken, Lucy. He only called this morning because Katharine thought he could advise me on how to deal with Viscount Deering. But I fear I sabotaged any hope when I lost my temper in the park this morning. Now, if you don't mind, my dears, I need to pack my belongings and write several notes of farewell before I can leave. . . ."

At her strong hint, Hannah and Lucy hugged her earnestly and then trailed out of her bedchamber wearing long faces.

Maura resumed her packing in solitude, but found her thoughts dwelling much too intently on Lord Beaufort and her deplorable weakness for him. She was exceedingly glad to be leaving London just now. If she remained, she would very likely surrender to his wicked allure. She had never met a more irresistible man, Maura admitted. His sensual charm, the laughter in his eyes, his heart-stealing smile, his boldness, his wit, all worked to devastate her defenses.

Which was the height of foolishness.

She knew better than to let herself be dazed by someone's charm and good looks. Her father had been seduced by a pretty face—Priscilla's—so Maura was doubly determined she would never fall into that particular trap. The fact that Noah Collyer had seemed content in his second marriage did not excuse Priscilla's actions either.

Trying to dismiss both her stepmother and the marquis from her mind, Maura spent the rest of the morning carefully preparing, then went to the kitchens to gather supplies and fill a pair of saddlebags.

Her last order of business was to compose a farewell note for Katharine. She wanted to express her thanks and also to return the exquisite ball gown she had borrowed. However, Maura decided, she would wait until the next morning to have both the note and gown delivered. She knew better than to face Katharine directly, for she would have to lie about her intentions, and her bosom friend always knew when she was prevaricating.

This was a secret she couldn't share with anyone, though. And she had to act entirely alone, for what she was planning could be a hanging offense.

Maura was particularly glad that Gandy was safely in Suffolk, so he could deny all knowledge of her scheme. Gandy had helped her devise a contingency plan for rescuing Emperor and they had worked out every minute detail, but she didn't want him implicated in any way.

Finally, Maura dressed carefully in a dark traveling gown and warm woolen cloak. When one o'clock arrived, she descended the stairs with her valise and saddlebags.

Hannah and Lucy were waiting for her at the front door with embraces and kisses, although, thankfully, there was no sign of their mother. Maura promised faithfully that she would write to the girls, and then went outside.

Her one-horse gig had been delivered by the livery stables as requested, and was harnessed to Fripon, a stocky, rather ugly chestnut gelding who happened to be Emperor's favorite equine companion. Maura had driven Frip to London two weeks ago for this very purpose in the event her cause became desperate.

She greeted the horse fondly, then put her valise and saddlebags on the gig's floorboard rather than handing them over to John, since she didn't want him opening the vehicle's boot and finding all the odd items stored there.

A leather trunk had also been strapped to the boot, Maura saw with satisfaction. She dismissed John and the livery groom and was just about to climb into the gig's seat when she heard the sound of carriage wheels.

To Maura's dismay, Katharine drove up in her dashing phaeton and pair, her young tiger perched behind.

Maura pasted a smile on her face, even though she was cursing at her ill luck. Two minutes more and she would have made her escape. Even though she had wanted witnesses to see her leave for home in Suffolk, she knew that Katharine would be much too hard to fool.

With an inward sigh, Maura waited as her friend halted the phaeton expertly. Leaving the young lad in charge of her pair of grays, Katharine climbed down and made her way over to the gig.

"I heard about what happened in the park, Maura," she said in explanation, "and I was worried for you. You do mean to let my brother help you, do you not? You cannot handle the viscount all on your own."

"I know," Maura replied evenly.

"So what do you mean to do now?"

"I will think of something. For now, however, I am going home."

Katharine's raised eyebrows expressed astonishment and skepticism both. "Surely you cannot be serious. You cannot give in to that odious bully."

"I am not giving in. I am merely retreating to fight another day."

Kate's green eyes narrowed. "Why don't I believe you?"

Maura tried to keep her expression neutral, but evidently her pretense didn't work.

"Maura Collyer," Katharine said in a warning tone. "You are plotting something, aren't you?"

"Whyever would you think that?"

"Because I know you too well." Just then Katharine's penetrating gaze swept Maura's traveling attire. "What is this? You were sneaking out of town without even saying good-bye?"

"I said good-bye in a note to you—and I arranged to have your ball gown returned to you also."

"I don't give a fig about the dratted gown! I care about what happens to you." When Maura remained silent, Kate frowned. "I never thought you would keep secrets from me, of all people," she added in an attempt to shame Maura into confessing. "I won't tell anyone, not even Ash. You know I am utterly loyal to you."

"Of course you are."

Kate gave a huff of exasperation. "You could at least let me in on the excitement."

In spite of herself, Maura smiled. Leave it to Katharine to make an adventure out of a dire predicament.

"I appreciate your concern," she said firmly, "but you need to let me deal with this problem in my own way."

Oddly enough, Katharine didn't press her further. "Oh very well. You handle Deering however you wish. But you cannot leave town just now. You will ruin all my plans."

It was Maura's turn to look suspicious. "What plans?"

"I wasn't going to tell you yet, but you leave me no choice. Do you recall that my Uncle Cornelius is a scholar of classic literature? Well, I have developed a theory based on his expert knowledge. . . ."

A confusing minute of explanation ensued regarding Lord Cornelius Wilde's understanding of famous lovers in history. Impatient to get away, Maura heeded with only half an ear, not really caring how similar her family circumstances were to Charles Perrault's French fairy tale of Cinderella written more than a century ago . . . at least not until Katharine concluded with, "So you see, Ashton could be your prince."

Maura blinked. "I beg your pardon? You know that I believe in solving my own problems. I don't need to rely on a prince to save me."

"Of course you don't. But that is not my point. What I meant was, Ash could be your legendary lover."

She stared in disbelief. "Have you gone completely daft?"

Katharine smiled. "No, I am in full possession of all my faculties. You can scoff all you like, Maura, but there could be merit to my theory."

"I very much doubt that!" Grimacing, she shook her head. "And merit or not, it is mortifying that you are trying to push me on your brother. I want nothing to do with your matchmaking."

Turning away, she climbed into her gig and took up the reins.

Naturally, however, Katharine would not countenance her refusal and so reached up to place a delaying hand on her arm. "You cannot pretend you are not attracted to Ash, Maura. You told me yourself that you enjoyed kissing him."

"That doesn't mean I wish to *marry* him." As a thought occurred to her, she gazed narrowly down at Kate. "Does your brother know about your demented theory?"

"Yes, I told him last night."

"Was *that* why he called on me this morning?" *And why he kissed me in the meadow?* Maura added to herself. "Because he was interviewing me as his prospective bride?"

"I don't believe so," Katharine admitted reluctantly. "Ash was just as dismissive of my theory as you are."

"I should think he would be," Maura said with feeling. "What sort of man would marry only to fulfill a fictional legend? He would have to be an idiot, and whatever your brother may be, he is *not* lacking in wits. He would never consider me for his bride."

Katharine's expression turned earnest. "But, Maura, what if Ash were truly serious about marriage? He has to wed sometime to carry on the title. Why shouldn't it be you?"

"Why *should* it be me?" she countered. "No, Kate, the notion of us being legendary lovers is simply ludicrous."

"Don't you want to marry someday?"

The question gave Maura pause. She did indeed want to marry. She had always wanted a family . . . husband, children, love. But given the dishonor staining the Collyer name, her chance for marriage had likely passed her by. No self-respecting gentleman would want a wife whose late father was thought to be a cheat. Even without the scandal, her own unconventional occupation would frighten off any normal suitor, not to mention her advanced age and her distaste for the confining rules of gentility. So despite her profound regrets, Maura had determinedly pushed her yearnings for a husband aside.

"Perhaps I might like to marry someday," she replied, "but if I ever did, it would only be for love. Your brother certainly would never fall in love with me."

"It isn't inconceivable."

"Yes, it is."

Maura was willing to concede that with his dazzling allure, the dashing Marquis of Beaufort could easily fit the fairy-tale role of Cinderella's wealthy, handsome prince. But in her opinion, all the Wildes were pleasure-seekers—most especially rakehell Ashton—and completely unserious about love. She couldn't imagine any circumstance where she would want him for her husband, despite the beguiling possibility of finding a legendary love.

When she saw Maura wasn't swayed, Katharine's mouth curved downward into a pout. "After all we have meant to each other, my ungrateful friend, you could at least *consider* indulging me."

Maura raised her eyes to the gig's roof, striving for

forbearance. Katharine was not above using coercion to gain her way, but that couldn't be allowed to matter just now. She had a much more dire problem to attend to at the moment.

"Dearest Kate, pray forgive me, but I don't have time to discuss my matrimonial aspirations with you just now. I need to be on my way if I am to make it home before midnight."

"Oh, very well, but I am gravely disappointed in you, Maura."

Katharine stepped back, clearing room for the gig to pass.

Hastily, Maura clucked at Frip and snapped the reins at his rump, sending him forward into a brisk trot. She would not be made to feel guilty simply because Katharine had rocks in her head and was bent on testing her nonsensical romantic fantasies on her elder brother.

Maura drove down the street, feeling her friend's green gaze following her until she was out of sight. Relieved to be away, she shook her head once more in disbelief. Escaping Kate's machinations was another excellent reason to leave London.

But the chief reason had nothing to do with matchmaking and everything to do with rescuing Emperor. And just now, Maura reminded herself, she needed to focus her mind and give all her attention to that vital task.

She had intended her contingency plan to be used only as a last resort, in the event she couldn't convince the viscount to sell.

But the odds had always been stacked against her

success, and now she had utterly burned her bridges with him. And since Deering was a wealthy, powerful, conniving adversary, she was unlikely to win against him by challenging him overtly. Therefore, she had only one course left open to her.

She would simply have to steal her stallion back.

Chapter Seven

The waiting was the hardest part.

Maura knew she couldn't enact her plan to rescue Emperor from the viscount's stables until the dead of the night, when his grooms and coachmen would be sleeping. Therefore, she drove to the public livery nearest to Deering's grand Mayfair mansion, where she had already arranged stabling for Frip and storage for her gig.

She had also paid handsomely for the use of a small room above the livery and so settled there for the interim. For the next thirteen hours, she alternately struggled with impatience and nerves.

When darkness fell over London, Maura forced herself to snatch a few hours of sleep, knowing she had a long night ahead of her. She also made herself eat. Even though she had packed provisions enough for a journey of several days, she wanted to keep up her strength for what might be a grueling test of endurance.

It was nearing two o'clock in the morning when she changed out of her gown into the clothing she had brought in her valise, donning leather breeches, sturdy half boots, a shapeless dark shirt, and the fustian jacket of a common laborer. Then she carefully pinned up her long blond hair and hid it under a floppy wide-brimmed hat in an effort to resemble a peddler, the role she had chosen to best disguise her gender and class.

When she descended the stairs, the livery was mostly quiet. The few sleepy lads who were on hand to service the carriages and teams of late-night customers paid her no attention.

Relieved that she fit in with the livery staff, Maura saddled Frip and loaded him down with some of the gear she'd stashed in the gig's boot. She wouldn't need the gelding's services just yet, but she wanted him to be ready to leave at a moment's notice.

Fripon was the French word for rascal, a name that he had earned when he was a foal, but he had matured into a steady, dependable job horse capable of pulling a carriage or carrying a rider untiringly over long distances.

"I am counting on you to help me rescue your friend tonight, my sweet fellow," Maura murmured softly.

Frip snuffled in reply and nodded his head, seeming to understand her urgency.

Leaving him tethered near her gig at the livery, she collected her knapsack, which was filled with an odd assortment of items, including a bridle, and made her way on foot through the dark streets of Mayfair. The half moon above was frequently concealed by clouds and offered barely enough light for her to see, but although she had a tinderbox and candle in her knapsack, she didn't want to risk showing a light. A slight fog also helped to conceal her presence from the occasional carriage that rumbled past her.

Some five minutes later she reached the mews of Seymour Place where Emperor was being kept. The long row of private stables ran behind several great houses and was accessed by a carriage lane.

Maura hugged the shadows of the mews as she inched down the lane. Since Deering's mansion was separated from his stables by extensive gardens, she didn't fear alerting his household servants, but his grooms and coachmen lodged above his stables and might still be awake.

Deering might also have set someone to guard his new prize, although Gandy's careful reconnaissance last week hadn't shown such precautions.

For several long minutes, Maura waited outside the stables, but the continued silence seemed to suggest it was safe to implement the next step of her plan. Her heart thudding, she slowly eased open the side door and crept inside.

There she paused, letting her eyes adjust to the darkness. Thankfully, she encountered no guards or anyone else to impede her progress as she stole down the aisle. With only faint light permeating the windows overhead, she could see little, yet she could hear the quiet sounds of dozing horses, and recognized her own beloved horse's movements coming from the far end.

Emperor was pacing his stall restlessly.

"Damn you, Lord Deering," Maura swore under her breath, knowing the horse would be bursting with energy, no doubt circling and pawing and even kicking out in objection to his imprisonment. If he wasn't to become wild, a stallion needed much more freedom and exercise than mares or geldings, and with so much pent-up force to be unleashed, Emperor could very well hurt himself or others.

She consoled herself by remembering that he only had to endure his maltreatment for a short while longer. After tonight, with very good luck combined with her determination, he would be free of the odious viscount forever.

When she reached Emperor's stall, she realized he had picked up her scent, for he snorted urgently.

"Hush, darling boy," Maura whispered, fumbling with the latch to the door. "I will take you away from here very soon, I promise."

Slipping through the door, she threw her arms around the horse's neck, her heart swelling with love for him. Emperor whickered in return, acknowledging the bond they shared.

Then stepping back, Maura set to work in the dark. Guided mostly by feel, she searched in her knapsack and drew out four folded lengths of cloth.

"Please be still, love. You have to be good and allow me to muffle your hooves."

To her relief, Emperor stood obediently as she tied a cloth around each foot to stifle the sound of steel shoes striking cobblestones. He also allowed her to bridle him without protest and waited while she slung her knapsack over her shoulder. But when she opened his stall door, he pulled against the bit, eager to escape his prison.

"Easy, boy," she murmured, placing a soothing hand on his neck. "You have to trust me, Emp."

At her touch, he seemed to grow calm. Taking a deep breath to gather her courage, Maura silently led the stallion down the aisle and out the side door. When they were free of the stables, she said a mute prayer of thanks, but she couldn't breathe until they reached the end of the lane and turned the corner, so that they were out of view of the mews.

The streets were still chiefly deserted, Maura noted gratefully, yet as they negotiated two more blocks, she couldn't shake the strange sensation of being watched. There was no pursuit, she decided, glancing behind her.

When she reached a hackney station, she veered toward a small park that was set back from the street. She didn't dare take the stallion straight to the livery where Frip waited, for she didn't want to imperil Gandy's cohort, who had helped her orchestrate her desperate rescue plan. Without a disguise, a horse of Emperor's obvious caliber would be too memorable, and she hoped to conceal her trail as much as possible.

Thus, she tethered him to a hitching post beneath an oak tree and dug into her bag of tricks once more. Pulling out a tin of boot blacking, a small jar of white paint, and a leather pouch filled with mud, Maura set about trying to mask his most distinctive features as well as his magnificence, although the final step of turning him into a peddler's nag would have to wait until she reached the livery.

She started by rubbing the blacking into the white star on his forehead. For a moment Emperor stood calmly, his bright eyes alert, but he shortly became impatient and fitful. Even though she murmured soothingly as she worked, he clearly disliked having two white socks and one white stocking painted on his legs.

"Please trust me, Emp," Maura implored in a whisper. "This is for your own good."

She had almost finished slathering his neck and hind-quarters with mud to dull the shine of his coat when the stallion suddenly left off his fidgeting. His head shot up, his nostrils flaring to scent the wind.

When another carriage drove past on the street, Maura decided there was no reason for alarm—until she heard the quiet sound of hoofbeats directly behind her.

She froze, then bit back a scream when a wry male voice broke the silence. "Would you care to explain just what you are up to, sweeting?"

Emperor sensed her fear and whirled nervously, nearly knocking Maura down in the process. Upon regaining her balance, she stared up at the horseman who loomed over her. He was little more than a shadow in the darkness, but she had no trouble recognizing the Marquis of Beaufort. He had crept upon her without warning, the earthen ground having muted his mount's approach.

Torn between relief and dismay, Maura brought a hand to her breast to cover her wildly beating heart. "You frightened me out of my wits," she accused with a scowl.

"I doubt that," he retorted curtly as he sat gazing down at her. "I repeat, what the devil are you doing?"

"What do you think? I am rescuing my horse, of course. I could ask the same of you, my lord," she added. "Why are you here? It is the middle of the night."

"Indeed it is. I suspected you might do something foolish," he muttered, "but nothing this shatterbrained. You should know better than to wander the streets of

London alone at night. It is far too dangerous for a woman."

He was concerned for her safety, Maura realized, hearing the hard edge in his voice. "In the first place, this is Mayfair, not the stews of St. Giles. And in the second, I am dressed as a lad and I am armed. I have a loaded pistol and a knife with me."

"Don't tell me . . . Gandy taught you how to shoot and wield a knife. But you are still taking a huge risk."

"I am not afraid, Lord Beaufort, even if you did startle me half to death."

He drew a long breath, as if striving for patience. "I am not questioning your courage, vixen, only your common sense. Even if you escape harm tonight, you could go to prison or worse. Horse thieves are usually hanged."

Maura studied him warily. "Do you mean to try and stop me?"

"Do I stand a chance in hell of stopping you?"

Despite his withering sarcasm, his rejoinder suggested that he was resigned to her larceny. Relief flooded her, soothing the burning anxiety in her stomach. "Not unless you betray me to Deering."

"I ought to," Beaufort threatened, although with less heat than before. "Or better yet, throw you over my saddle and carry you home."

That last was not an empty boast, Maura realized, recalling how easily he had manhandled her this morning in the park. But she didn't believe he would actually follow through this time.

"I dare you to try it," she said lightly. "I am armed, remember?"

"A pistol will be little protection if your theft is discovered."

"Which is why I am doing my best to keep from being discovered."

His gaze shifted to slide over the stallion. "I've been watching you these past five minutes, wondering what you were about. I see now that you're attempting to disguise your splendid beast to avoid recognition."

"Yes."

Wiping her hand clean of mud in Emperor's mane, Maura closed the pouch and stuffed it back into her knapsack. Then she bent to remove the cloth wrapping his hooves, since it would look strange if she rode into the livery on a horse with muffled feet.

"I have to give you credit," Beaufort remarked grudgingly. "It was clever of you to think of the white markings."

He was very clever himself to have deduced her intentions, she thought.

"How did you know what I planned?" she asked.

"You were too calm this morning after your tirade. The abrupt change made me suspect you were up to something, even before Katharine warned me that all was not quite right with you. She claims it is not like you to simply give up."

"So you followed me?"

"No, I staked out Deering's stables and lay in wait for you. It took you long enough."

"I had to make certain the grooms were asleep."

Another carriage rattled by just then, which recalled Maura to her surroundings. "I cannot stand here arguing with you, Lord Beaufort. I need to be on my way."

"Don't think this discussion is over, sweetheart."

Regrettably, she knew it wasn't. With a sigh, Maura draped the knapsack over her shoulder, untied the reins, grabbed a hunk of mane, and vaulted onto the stallion's bare back.

Much to her exasperation and aggravation, Beaufort fell into step with her as she guided Emperor back to the street. "Where are you taking him?"

"I would rather not say."

"But you plan on stealing him?"

She sent the marquis a sour glance. "I do not call it stealing. Emperor is my rightful property, and I am only reclaiming what is mine."

"The law won't see it that way."

"I know," Maura said bitterly. "So I will have to resort to bending the law. I can't fight Deering by honest means."

"You could if you would allow me to aid you. There is a better way to go about saving your horse."

"Oh, and what might that be, your lordship? Your plan was to *think* about conceiving a plan. Mine actually has a chance of succeeding."

The moonlight was too faint for her to see Beaufort's jaw clench, but she could easily imagine it.

After a moment, he took a different tack. "You obviously have planned your scheme out meticulously, but you must have had help. I presume Gandy is abetting you, but there must be others."

"Even if there were, I could never admit it. I don't want anyone else blamed for what I must do."

"You hope to keep your friends from hanging with you, you mean."

"Exactly. That is why I didn't tell Katharine about my plans—so she could deny any culpability."

Just then they reached the livery, which was dimly lit by lanterns. Before turning into the yard, Maura whispered a precaution. "Please, will you keep your voice down? I don't want to attract any undue attention."

She rode directly to the corner of the yard where Frip waited. The two horses seemed glad to see each other, but she couldn't afford to dally for their reunion. Sliding off the stallion's back, she tethered him to the gig, then opened the boot and began drawing out the peddler's rig.

After securing a harness to Emperor's chest and back, she attached a pliant straw basket to each of his sides.

Beaufort sat watching as she began filling the baskets. "What the devil is all that?" he asked, keeping his voice low.

"His costume," she murmured back. "He needs a more ample disguise than just paint and boot blacking."

She had loaded Frip down with a blanket roll and her saddlebags, including her clothing and food supplies. But she intended to fill Emperor's baskets with the sort of items a peddler would normally sell.

To her surprise, Beaufort dismounted in order to help her. Together they loaded the goods—a few pots and pans, an assortment of knives and scissors and a grinder to sharpen the blades, bottles of elixirs, hair dye, trinkets, copper cups, some cheap jewelry. . . .

Not unexpectedly, the champion stallion objected to such treatment. At first, Emperor merely turned to peer at the strange contraption on his back and snorted as if insulted. But when he began to dance nervously, Maura went to his head and tenderly rubbed his ears and sensitive poll between.

When she had his attention, she put her forehead against his and spoke quietly to him. "I am sorry, love. I understand how humiliating this is for you, being treated like a pack mule, but you must bear it for my sake."

Thankfully, he calmed down enough that she could fasten the lids on the baskets.

"Where do you intend to take him?" Beaufort asked as she finished lashing the final straps.

She gave him a cautious look. "I am not sure I can trust you, even if you are Katharine's brother."

In the lantern light, she could see his expression grow annoyed. "Do you even have a destination in mind?"

"Yes."

Since she was certain Deering would hunt for her untiringly, she'd thought long and hard about where to seek refuge for the stallion. There were scores of livery stables all over London, but she couldn't hope to hide a peerless racehorse among common carriage hacks for long. So obviously she would have to spirit him away from London. She didn't think it wise to tell Beaufort where she meant to go, however.

When her silence dragged out, he muttered a low oath. "I'll be damned if I want to see you hanged."

"I have no intention of being hanged," she assured him quietly. "If I were to be caught, there would be no one to protect Emperor from Lord Deering. Now, I need to be on my way, my lord."

He let her close the gig's boot but then grasped her

arm. "No. It is too dangerous for you to set out alone."

"I cannot let that stop me."

"Maura . . ." His tone was still low, but became more urgent. "You need to think carefully about what you are doing. If you run now, there could be no turning back. This decision could change your life irrevocably."

The deep concern in his voice made a strange emotion twist in her chest. He was right, Maura thought, staring up into his eyes. She was at a major crossroads in her life. Yet she had to do this.

"You don't understand," she replied, her voice unexpectedly quavering with emotion. "I could not save my father from that cursed man, but by heaven, I will save my horse."

To her dismay, she felt her throat suddenly close with tears.

It wasn't like her to be so missish, Maura told herself. No doubt the stress of the past days and hours had frayed her nerves. But she had cried in front of Beaufort once today, and she wouldn't do so again.

Swallowing the aching lump in her throat, Maura resolutely pulled her arm from his grasp and stepped back from him.

Whatever he saw in her face must have convinced him of her unwavering determination, for he held up his hands in a show of defeat and exhaled a sigh. "Very well, then. If you won't abandon your idiotic scheme, I have no choice but to accompany you."

Maura had started to turn away, but froze in her tracks. "That is out of the question."

He went on as if she hadn't spoken at all. "At least

I can give you my protection. If I am with you, perhaps I can save you from prison. In my position, I can get away with endeavors that you cannot."

"I told you, I cannot involve anyone else. I must do this alone. You could be implicated in my crimes, and I don't want that guilt on my conscience."

Beaufort took a step closer. "Let me put it this way," he said slowly, as if explaining to a dimwitted child. "There is no bloody way in hell I am letting you set out alone. I am coming with you, vixen."

She gave him a long, frustrated look. "You realize you are only interfering where you are unwanted?"

"No doubt. But I promised Katharine I would look after you. How do you expect she will react if I return empty-handed? She would hie after you herself."

"Well, you will just have to stop her."

In reply, he reached up to cup Maura's face with both of his hands. His gentle touch caught her off guard and held her immobile, as did the quiet, earnest sound of his voice. "Answer me one question honestly. Do you really want to face this ordeal all alone? A fugitive from your family, your friends?"

The question startled her as much as the answer that instantly sprang to mind: No, she didn't want to be all alone, fleeing in the dark of night, abandoning everyone she knew, a hunted fugitive for God only knew how long—perhaps for the rest of her days.

Maura swallowed again. She had no choice but to risk becoming a fugitive, but she did not have to endure it all by herself.

"No," she whispered. "I don't want to be alone."

"Then it's settled," he said curtly, turning to tend to his horse.

Nothing at all was settled, Maura knew, but she didn't have the willpower to argue. And in any event, protesting would be pointless. The Marquis of Beaufort was accustomed to getting his own way, and he was a Wilde to boot, meaning that he arranged the world to his own liking and expected everyone else to fall in line.

Chapter Eight

Letting Beaufort accompany her was a dreadful idea, Maura told herself, yet she didn't know how she could have stopped him.

They watered the horses in silence, then quietly left the livery. Only when they were on the road did he speak. "Now tell me where we are we going."

"To Scotland," Maura answered. "The Highlands, to be exact."

Beaufort gave her a sharp glance. "That is quite a distance."

"I know, but Gandy has friends there who will hide Emperor and care for him." When Beaufort didn't reply, Maura explained her plan. "Deering will likely search the main thoroughfares first, so we will need to reach Scotland by a circuitous route, traveling cross-country. I thought to head west toward Reading tonight and then veer north to Oxford. And for the first few days at least, I planned to ride at night and hide out during the day."

"Do you have a fixed destination in mind for to-night?"

"Yes. A country farm, which we should reach before dawn. But after that, I have no other resting stops in mind."

"So you will have to improvise," Beaufort said in resignation.

"Yes. But I did not count on your escort. How will I explain your presence?" Maura asked, surveying his elegant attire. His superbly tailored coat and waist-coat, spotless white cravat, buckskin breeches, shining Hessian boots, and tall beaver hat fairly shouted wealth and refinement. "If I am supposed to be a ped-dler, what am I doing in the company of a fancy toff like you?"

Beaufort thought for a moment before offering an impressive array of ideas. "There are any number of excuses we could give out. We could say I'm an eccentric and that I followed you on a lark. Or that when you recently received word that your poor dear papa kicked the bucket, I took pity on you and decided to escort you home. Or possibly I won a wager and claimed your store of worldly goods for myself, and I am making you cart them to my country estate. Or you could even be my groom." His gaze swept down her own attire. "You do resemble a lad in that getup. What have you done to your breasts?"

In the darkness, Maura felt herself flush at his bra-zen query. "I bound them, if you must know."

"That must be uncomfortable."

"Not much more uncomfortable than wearing cor-sets," she said, although that was a lie. The length of linen she had wrapped around her chest was already chafing her skin in several places.

"I don't believe any of those excuses will suffice," she pronounced, returning to the less intimate subject. "We look much too different in class and will call undue attention to ourselves."

"If you insist, I'll buy some coarse clothing at the first village we come to, but I refuse to give up my prime blood to ride a nag."

She smiled. "No, I suppose that sacrifice would be too great for your lordship. Until you find something more suitable to wear, however, we should not be seen together. In fact," Maura said after more consideration, "there is no reason for you to change your appearance at all. You won't be with me for more than a few days. You can help me reach Oxford and then return home."

"Oh, no," Beaufort responded genially. "You are not getting rid of me so easily." He cast her a sideways glance. "I have to admire your gumption, but if you wanted a career as a horse thief, you should have mentioned it sooner. I'm acquainted with all manner of people who might have assisted you, including a few felons. Have you ever stolen anything before?"

"Nothing of consequence."

"What does that mean?"

"I once stole the headmistress's bedroom slippers on a dare. Katharine challenged me, and I couldn't leave my honor undefended."

"So you do have practice as a thief," he commented, amused. "And here I thought you were a relative innocent compared to my madcap sister."

"I was never as madcap as your sister," Maura assured him. "You should have seen the pranks Katharine pulled at school."

"Pray, don't tell me," he said dryly. "I became her guardian the instant I reached my majority, since our Uncle Cornelius no longer wanted the responsibility, so I was supposed to be looking out for her."

"I must say, you did not do a very good job in supervising her," Maura said, still smiling. "Skye was almost as bad as Kate, but from what I hear, they were merely following in your footsteps. They both adore you and think that you can do no wrong, but you set them an atrocious example as the most scandalous member of the Wilde clan."

"*I* could say you deserve some of the blame as well, my lovely hellion. It sounds as if you were quite a threesome."

"We were," she admitted.

He shook his head in consternation, then laughed. "You are going to cause me a lot of trouble, aren't you?"

"I told you not to come with me," Maura pointed out.

Beaufort shrugged. "I am trying to view this journey as an adventure."

Maura couldn't stifle her own laugh at his similarity to Kate. It was just like a Wilde to consider a desperate escape as an adventure.

Even so, her own spirits suddenly felt lighter. Now that she could take a breath, the fear that had burdened her for the past fortnight had eased somewhat, in large part, she acknowledged with reluctance, because Beaufort was with her.

They rode on for several more hours. By then, Maura was growing weary and chilled from the damp air seeping into her bones. When another half hour had passed, she began looking for landmarks from the map Gandy had drawn for her. When she judged that they'd reached the correct turnoff, she guided Frip onto a country lane.

"Gandy has a friend who owns a small farm in this area," she explained to Beaufort. "Unfortunately, his cottage recently burned down, so he temporarily moved his family and livestock to his brother's farm nearby. But the barn is still standing."

A few minutes after she turned onto another lane, they came upon the blackened ruins of a stone cottage. Across the yard was a small barn with a thatched roof.

"This should do until tomorrow evening when it grows dark enough for us to set out again. See, there is a fenced meadow with a stream for the horses to eat and drink. And Emperor's disguise will protect him in this remote area. He will be safe enough there while we sleep in the barn."

Beaufort nodded, but eyed the building without enthusiasm. "How delightful."

Ignoring his ironic tone, Maura dismounted stiffly, aching after so many hours of riding astride, and headed to the barn.

She lit the lantern hanging just inside the door, which provided just enough light to see by as they led the horses inside. The interior was cluttered with tack and farm implements, so there was not much room to maneuver as they removed the saddles and unloaded the peddler's baskets.

When they led the horses back out to the pastures, Emperor immediately galloped away. Just as quickly, he returned to Maura, snorting and prancing until she reassured him that she wasn't abandoning him ever again. Whether or not he understood her words, he calmed enough to lower himself to the ground and roll, clearly delighting in his newfound freedom.

Swallowing the ache of relief in her throat, she returned to the barn with the marquis, who eyed the overhead loft with even less enthusiasm.

"Buck up, my lord," Maura said brightly. "I have spent many a night in foaling barns waiting for mares to give birth, and I can assure you, straw makes a comfortable mattress. And we have a feast for supper, if you can call dining on bread and cheese a feast. Why don't you make yourself useful and draw some water from the well? That is, if you even know how to perform such a plebeian task."

He chuckled at her gibe before going outside to do as she bid.

When he returned shortly with a bucket of water, they sat on two barrels and ate in relative silence. The quiet of the barn lulled her senses, and when they were finished, Maura suddenly realized that she was exhausted. She also became aware of another problem: The lack of privacy.

She had intended to remove her tight bindings, but now she decided against it. After a quick trip outside to the bushes, she discovered that Beaufort had taken the lantern up to the loft. Maura followed him up the steep wooden stairs and found him in the rear corner, using a pitchfork to make up a bed with fresh straw.

When he had spread out her cloak over the straw and staged a blanket to use as a cover, he gestured at his improvised pallet. "After you, my sweet."

It was then that Maura realized he intended for them to share the bed.

She raised both her eyebrows at him. "Evidently I gave you the wrong impression. It is bad enough that I am traveling alone with you. I am not sleeping with you, too. I do have some notion of propriety."

"You astonish me, vixen," he said, beginning to untie his cravat. "You steal a prize racehorse, but balk at sharing a pile of straw, even though we are both fully clothed. Besides, it is damned chilly in here, so you will have to keep me warm. It is the very least you can do after putting me to so much trouble."

Her eyes narrowed. "I did not force you to come, remember?"

"No, but now that I am here, we can curl up together and share our body warmth." Unwinding his cravat, he tucked it inside his hat. "If it will make you feel safer, you can think of me as your elder brother."

Utterly impossible, Maura thought, shaking her head in exasperation. She did feel safe with Beaufort, up to a point; he wouldn't let any harm come to her, she was certain. At the same time he was so very dangerous to her. He made her feel too much, assaulting her body with erotic sensations and filling her heart with inexplicable yearnings.

And yet, as she suspected, he wouldn't allow her a choice. His tone turned a bit curt when he reprimanded her. "Quit being so missish, love. You have nothing to fear from me. I am too tired to attempt a seduction just now."

Maura hesitated a long moment before reaching up to remove her floppy felt hat.

He waited until she lay down on the cloak before he

snuffed the lantern flame. Then joining her, he spent another minute tugging off his boots. Finally, he drew the blanket up over them both and curled her into the curve of his body, her back to his front, his arm draped lightly over her waist.

Maura lay there rigidly in the darkness, wondering if she could trust him.

It was only a short while before his soft even breathing told her that Beaufort was asleep. She remained fully awake, however, watching as the faint light of dawn filtered through the shuttered loft window, much too aware of the hard, masculine body pressed against hers.

Ash awoke with his lust raging. From the sunlight streaming into the loft, he judged it to be midmorning.

He was painfully aware of Maura asleep in his arms, but he lay there savoring her warmth. This was certainly a first for him, spending a chaste night in bed with a beautiful woman, fully clothed. He could feel Maura's lithe body beneath her many layers of peddler's garb. Sometime during the past hour, she had sunk into a fitful doze, yet even in sleep, she had turned his loins hard and aching.

It felt strangely right to hold her like this, though. Resting his mouth on her pale gold hair, Ash breathed in her scent and marveled at how swiftly his attraction for her had escalated. Maura Collyer was a delectable mix of contrariness, a valiant warrior on one hand, bursting with courage and determination, and a soft, delicate female on the other. He felt a renewed stab of admiration for her daring rescue of her stallion. In her own way, she was every bit as much a rebel as any of the Wildes.

Yet nothing was going as he'd planned. Intent on exploring his sister's legendary lovers theory, he'd considered courting Maura to see where it led, and of course, to help her in her fight with Deering.

Instead, he'd wound up aiding and abetting her theft, sleeping on an uncomfortable bed of straw in a cold barn loft, and facing the very real prospect of a frantic dash to Scotland as a fugitive.

This was not what he'd envisioned when he'd vowed to take his fate into his own hands, Ash mused wryly. Rather than shaping his destiny, he was fast losing control of it.

He'd gotten himself into an even bigger fix when it came to Maura herself. He had her in his arms now, just where he wanted her, but he couldn't do a damn thing about it. He was her protector now, so he couldn't make love to her.

There was, however, no longer any doubt that he would pursue her, Ash thought as he quietly eased back from her delectable body. Something about her called to him, something that aroused the powerful, primal urge to claim her for his own.

Whether or not she was his ideal mate was less certain. He could easily see them becoming lovers. But could he imagine waking up to her every morning? Sharing a marital bed, a home, children? A future together?

And before he could address that intriguing question, he had to resolve her dilemma with Deering. He wouldn't let Maura become an outlaw, even if for the moment he had to go along with her mad scheme.

Right now, she trusted him to devise a better solution to her dilemma. Actually, a plan had begun to take shape in his mind, but he needed time to execute the details.

Meanwhile, he could make use of their forced intimacy to further his courtship, Ash decided. An opportunity he would never have had if they were safely in London.

Maura stirred restlessly just then and rolled onto her back toward him, as if seeking his warmth. His head pillowed on his arm, Ash watched her slumbering face in the morning light, admiring the fine bone structure, the ivory complexion, the sweet, ripe lips. . . . Her sleep was agitated, though, her expression far from relaxed.

He knew the instant she fully woke. She gave a start, as if suddenly remembering where she was, and locked gazes with him. He was so close, he could count the gold flecks in the hazel depths of her eyes.

Looking away, she shifted her position on their cloak bed and promptly winced.

"What is wrong, love?" he murmured.

"Nothing. I am just uncomfortable sleeping this way."

"A few hours ago you were lauding the benefits of a straw bed."

"It is not the straw. It is the pins in my hair and the tight—" She broke off without finishing.

The tight binding around her breasts, he suspected she'd meant to say. When he glanced down at her bosom buried beneath the blanket and her peddler's coat, a flush warmed the fair skin of her cheeks.

"I should have removed my hairpins before trying to sleep," she muttered to distract him.

When she sat up and reached for the pins, he did the same. "Allow me to help," he offered.

Maura remained still as he probed her hair with his fingers. Finding the pins one by one, he handed them to her so that she could put them in her coat pocket. When he was done, he smoothed out her hair, relishing the feel of the luxuriant tresses.

"Now," he said, curling his fingers over the collar of her coat. "Why don't we see to your bindings?"

Chapter Nine

Maura's breath caught at the huskiness in his voice, but she allowed him to draw off her coat. When he raised the hem of her shirt, however, she stopped him by grasping both his wrists. "I can manage on my own," she insisted.

"No doubt, but there is no need for shyness. I have already seen your breasts, remember? In fact, I have tasted them."

Flushing at the brazen reminder, Maura frowned at him. "You are utterly scandalous."

He smiled into her eyes. "I won't deny it. We Wildes are a scandalous lot."

His bewitching charm made her shiver with awareness, and once again she couldn't resist him. When she released her grip on his wrists, Beaufort unwound the strip of linen around her breasts and made a soft, sympathetic sound in his throat. The binding had chafed her skin and left red marks in a dozen places.

His fingers gently traced the deep indentions on her flesh. "You have beautiful breasts . . . too beautiful to suffer such abuse."

As he pressed her back into their makeshift bed, her heart began thudding in her chest. "Lord Beaufort . . ." she protested. "You promised not to seduce me."

"I never promised. I said I was too weary last night to think of seduction. This morning is a different matter altogether."

She watched helplessly as he covered her breasts with his warm hands, aroused by his touch.

"Let me soothe your hurt, sweetheart," he murmured as he bent down to kiss the swells.

Maura's breath fled altogether then. When he took one rosy nipple in his mouth, she let out a soft whimper and shut her eyes at the delectable sensation.

His sensual assault continued, his hot lips suckling, his rasping tongue taunting and teasing. Then he moved to her other breast, filling her with pleasure, making her quiver.

Moaning, she tilted her head back to give him greater access. By now tremors were flooding her body, while between her thighs, desire throbbed.

Yet strangely enough, he suddenly left off. With one, final, soothing kiss to her chafed skin, Beaufort pushed himself up and heaved a sigh. "I regret I cannot do more than merely worship your lovely body."

Her eyes flew open, and she saw hot desire gleaming in his green gaze.

"Why did you stop?" she asked unsteadily.

He pulled her to a sitting position and helped her don her coat again. "Because my conscience won't allow me to go any farther."

Her brows drew together in puzzlement. "I thought you didn't care a whit about propriety."

"Normally I don't. But seducing a virgin under my protection would hardly be honorable, now would it?"

Maura swallowed her sharp disappointment. "No, it wouldn't—but I am astonished *you* realize it."

He smiled. "You should count yourself fortunate, love. It is not like me to be so noble."

She heard the rueful humor in his voice, yet she didn't believe him. His nobility went deeper than his blue blood, she was certain of it.

He proved her point when he planted a light kiss on her hair and then changed the subject. "What do you say that we take to the road now rather than waiting until dark? I know you wanted to hide out during the day and only travel at night, but it might be best to put some distance between ourselves and Deering. And while this barn is pleasant enough, killing time here for an entire afternoon is not high on my list of delights, no matter how stimulating the company."

Collecting her dazed senses, Maura frowned thoughtfully. "I suppose that might be wise. If we keep to the country lanes, we should be able to avoid detection, even if Deering somehow has managed to pick up my trail from London. I have a rough map of the district, which Gandy had his friend draw up."

"That Gandy of yours is highly resourceful," Beaufort observed.

Maura's heart warmed at the mention of the elderly man who had been more like an uncle than steward to her since her father's passing. "He is indeed. I don't know what I would have done without him these past two years after losing my father."

Beaufort rose to his feet and began folding the blanket. "The water bucket is almost full. I'll step outside and give you privacy to wash."

Pushing her hair out of her eyes, Maura nodded gratefully. "Thank you."

"Shall I assist with your bindings?" he asked helpfully, the amused note in his tone indicating that he was provoking her again.

She couldn't stop a fleeting smile. "Not this time, my lord," she replied, "although your generosity is duly noted."

She was thankful that Beaufort's honor had curbed his lustful impulses, and yet strangely regretful as well.

A foolish sentiment, Maura warned herself as she gathered her cloak and other belongings and followed him down from the loft.

While eating a hurried meal of bread and cheese, she showed Beaufort her hand-drawn map and debated the best route for their journey. After saddling the horses and loading Emperor's back with the peddler's gear, Maura left five shillings for the barn owner and latched the door tightly behind them.

Then they got on their way, riding north and west toward Oxford, keeping to country lanes as they'd discussed.

Her spirits rose after the first mile, in part because the sun came out. In the brightness of a lovely spring day, it was easier to believe she might actually succeed in her mission. And yet she knew her optimism was also due to her traveling companion.

She still felt a strong undercurrent of sexual aware-

ness between them, but strangely, there was little awk-
wardness, almost as if they had been together for years.

Eventually, however, Maura broke their comfortable
silence to address what had been preying on her mind
since yesterday. "Katharine confessed that she is attempting to matchmake for you."

"So she is," Beaufort agreed mildly, not nearly as
disturbed as Maura expected.

"I am surprised you sound so calm. To hear Kate tell
it, females have been relentlessly hounding you to
marry for years. You can't be happy that she has joined
their ranks."

"She claims she has only my best interests at heart."

Maura studied him in surprise. "Well, she has gone
daft if she thinks we will play the part of legendary
lovers to prove her ridiculous theory."

Beaufort shook his head. "I've come to believe her
theory is not as farfetched as I first presumed."

"Whatever do you mean?"

"You must realize that our Wilde family history is
rife with famous lovers—both our ancestors and more
recently. My own parents' romance was legendary, as
was Skye and Quinn's parents'. Kate is hoping I will
follow tradition and find a grand passion in marriage
with my soul mate. It's a family legacy."

Maura stared at him. "Are you saying you actually
believe that certain people are fated to be together?"

"I cannot discount it."

This astonishing admission left her momentarily
speechless. It stood to reason that Beaufort took pride
in his family name. Wildes were known for their passionate natures as well as for creating scandals. But
none of that applied to her, Maura reasoned.

"Well, perhaps *your* family is accustomed to imitating legendary lovers in fairy tales, but mine is not. The very notion of my being Cinderella is absurd. I bear little resemblance to the girl in Perrault's tale. My stepmother never made me sit among the ashes or sent me off to a cold garret, and my stepsisters are sweet, lovable girls. And more to the point, I most certainly do not need or want a prince to come to my rescue."

"I well know it," Beaufort murmured, clearly amused. "If I had ever mistaken you for a damsel in distress, you would have obliterated my assumption countless times over these past two days."

Suspecting that he was mocking her, Maura went on as if he hadn't spoken. "I refuse to be the pitiful weakling stepchild who cannot fend for herself and must rely on magic to win a husband." She sent him a narrow-eyed glance. "I am not looking to marry anyone, your lordship. You needn't worry that I will cast my lures at you."

"It never once crossed my mind," he said dryly. "But you have aroused my curiosity. I presume your father's scandal is a prime reason you are still unmarried? And that your unsavory experience with Deering helped foster your dislike of men, or at least of noblemen."

"It is true that Deering gave me a bad taste for noblemen."

"That I can comprehend. Deering is a lecher of the first order."

"What of your own lechery? All you think about is lovemaking."

The slow, wicked smile he flashed her was pure, unadulterated charm. "I beg to differ. I frequently think about many other things. Just now for instance, I am wondering where our next meal will come from, and where we will sleep tonight. But I admit, making love to you does have enormous appeal."

Maura made a dismissive sound. "Let me be clear, Lord Beaufort, I have no intention of becoming your lover—legendary or otherwise."

"Why not?"

The frank question made her falter. The brazen truth was, she wanted to know what Beaufort's lovemaking would be like. She didn't want to remain a chaste, lonely spinster for the rest of her days, never satisfying her feminine yearnings, her curious wonder, her craving for a tender touch.

And yet she had other considerations besides herself.

"I don't wish to incite another family scandal, for one thing," Maura answered honestly.

"Why would you fear a little more scandal?" he asked. "Isn't that like locking the barn door after the horse has been stolen, so to speak?"

She almost smiled at his pointed reference to her.

"No, vixen," Beaufort mused aloud, "you don't strike me as someone who is overly concerned about propriety or what society thinks of her."

"I do not care overly much," Maura admitted rather quietly. "Society's strictures became much less important after I lost my father. Compared to matters of life and death, some things just seem so . . . trivial. But I have to think of my stepsisters. I don't want to hurt their chances to marry well."

"If your theft lands you in prison, it will surely hurt their chances. If you really cared about them, you would return to London immediately."

Maura knew he was right about prison. "I do care

about them, so my best course is to keep my distance. My stepmother will disown me anyway, once she learns what I have done."

"In that case, us becoming lovers shouldn't matter."

"Your motives matter to me," Maura retorted. "As I said, I believe you are amusing yourself at my expense. I have no desire to be the plaything for a bored aristocrat who is only searching for entertainment."

"You are certainly a cure for my boredom," Beaufort agreed. "But I am not merely thinking about myself. It seems a shame, all that fire and passion of yours going to waste."

"What about your professed intention to be noble? You said last night that seducing me would be dishonorable."

"So it would. But if *you* make the choice, the equation would change entirely."

At the distinction, her brows drew together. "I am curious. Would you let your sister take a lover?"

The look on his face answered the question for her.

"I didn't think so," Maura said archly.

"As you mentioned last night, you are not my sister."

"You are trying to protect me as if I were—at least when you are not thinking about seduction." She returned to a familiar theme. "You know you don't need to make this journey with me, Lord Beaufort."

"I thought we settled this issue last night. I am not letting you hie off to Scotland alone."

"I am quite accustomed to being alone."

"A pity. That cannot be enjoyable for you."

Maura had no response for his apt observation. It felt as if she had been alone for a very long time—first because her father had focused his love and attention on his second family, and more recently, with Katharine and Skye in London, living their own lives. Sometimes the loneliness had overwhelmed her. . . .

Maura shook herself out of her reverie. If she hoped to defend herself against Beaufort's wicked charm, she had to keep her emotions in check. She couldn't dwell on how much he eased her loneliness.

Or how fiercely she was attracted to him.

Or how wonderful it had felt lying with him last night, wrapped in his arms, safe and warm and protected.

"I think perhaps the horses need rest and water," Maura announced abruptly.

From Beaufort's knowing look, she realized the discussion was not finished, but she turned off the lane and headed across a meadow in search of a stream.

After dismounting, they allowed the horses to drink and graze while they ate the remainder of her provisions for lunch. The trouble came when they prepared to mount again. Maura had removed her floppy hat, and when she tried to replace it, some locks of her hair tumbled free of their pins.

"Allow me," Beaufort offered.

She stood obediently as he repinned her tresses, but when he tucked a stray wisp beneath her hat brim, his fingers brushed her cheek. At the intimate gesture, the sharp sexual awareness lingering in her body returned with a vengeance; that same, tingling, nervous sensation Maura felt whenever Beaufort was near.

Her eyes locking with his, she saw hot sparks of desire flash there in the green depths. Then slowly he leaned closer, as if he might kiss her, and Maura dropped her gaze to his mouth.

A mistake, she realized, for she couldn't help recalling how that sensual mouth had suckled her breasts with such exquisite tenderness this morning. . . .

The scorching memory made tension race through her, as did his caressing voice.

"Lovely Maura," he murmured in the same husky tone he had used in the loft.

Maura swallowed hard, wondering if she would have the willpower to pull away when her own desire for him was so strong.

Beaufort himself, however, ended the enchanted spell. With a rueful smile, he lowered his hand from her cheek and turned away to see to the horses.

Back on the road again, they passed a small farmhouse and were hailed by the farmer's wife, who mistook Maura for a real peddler. When the plump matron asked to see "his" wares, Maura had no choice but to stop. She wound up selling the housewife a rose-scented sachet and a pair of scissors, but it was Beaufort who turned the misunderstanding to their advantage.

Maura watched in awe as he sweet-talked the woman into supplying them mugs of ale right then, and for their evening supper later, two mutton pies, an apple tart, a loaf of bread, and a quarter rind of cheese.

Just one more example of his irresistible charm, she thought, shaking her head in helpless amusement.

The afternoon grew warmer, however, and depressed her mood once more. Whereas the night had been chilly, the sun was now beating down upon them remorselessly, so Maura was glad when they had to stop to water the horses again.

She gathered that Beaufort was feeling the heat also, for he removed his coat and waistcoat and cravat. Seeing him clad in an open-necked shirt and tight-fitting buckskin breeches, Maura couldn't help admiring his vital maleness. His shadowed jaw made him look slightly disreputable, so that he looked more like a brigand than a nobleman enjoying a ride in the country.

He must have noted her appearance as well.

"You look uncomfortable again, vixen."

"I will survive. But Emperor has begun to sweat, so the sheen is returning to his coat. Will you hold his reins while I apply more mud?"

Beaufort did as she asked, positioning the horse on the swampy bank of the stream.

When she scooped up a handful of wet earth and began working it between her fingers to make a paste, he spoke directly to the stallion. "I trust you appreciate the sacrifices your mistress is making for your sake, big fellow."

Emperor gave no indication that he understood the admonition, and at the first brush of mud on his skin, he tossed his head and sidled away from Maura's touch.

"Easy, Emp," she said soothingly. "I am sorry, but you look too much like a champion racehorse."

The stallion instantly calmed at the sound of her voice and stood docilely while she covered him in mud.

Beaufort watched her quietly. "You have a magical touch with horses."

"I suppose I was born with it. I love horses." She

cast him a provocative glance. "Honestly, I like horses better than most people. Certainly better than most members of your class, my lord."

"You are most assuredly an uncommon young lady."

Maura smiled and wrinkled her nose good-naturedly. "I have been out for five Seasons, and I am hardly young—nor much of a lady, for that matter. I own a breeding stable, so I am no longer considered respectable. You wondered earlier why I am still unmarried; that largely explains it. I am not the kind of wife gentlemen generally seek to wed."

"Your occupation has nothing to do with whether or not you are a lady. I find you refreshing—a woman ahead of your time. Indeed, your very uniqueness gives you more freedom to take a lover."

A heartbeat passed before Maura fully registered his comment. Then she almost laughed at his persistence. "How plainly must I say it, my lord? I am not interested in taking you for my lover."

"A pity. You don't know the immense pleasure you are missing."

She did laugh then. "Your vanity knows no bounds, does it?"

He raised an eyebrow. "Are you accusing me of vanity?"

Maura didn't reply, but she couldn't quell her smile as she finished muddying Emperor's coat and turned away to wash her hands in the stream.

Realizing how lighthearted she felt just then, she shook her head in bemusement. It astonished her, not only how comfortable she was sharing her most intimate confidences with Beaufort, but that the desperation and helplessness she'd endured for weeks had somehow abated.

A dangerous development to let down her guard so completely around him, Maura reminded herself, and yet she just couldn't bring herself to care.

Chapter Ten

Maura's light mood lasted for several more hours—until her luck seemed to turn for the worse. Thus far they had met few people along their journey, but they made the mistake of riding across a field. When they emerged at the rear of a farmhouse, they were instantly greeted by a pack of barking dogs.

Surrounded by teeth-baring animals yipping at their horses' hooves, Maura felt her throat go dry. Next, a rough-looking fellow stormed out from behind the nearby chicken coop, aiming a musket directly at them, and her heart gave a painful leap.

Beaufort swung his mount in front of her to shield her, but thankfully, his protection proved unnecessary. The farmer lowered his weapon and called off the dogs, before tipping his hat in sincere apology.

"Begging yer pardon, guv'nor. We've 'ad a spot of trouble with foxes getting into the coop, so I let the dogs run free in the yard."

Maura swallowed her alarm, yet once again she was grateful to have Beaufort at her side.

She was still musing on her abrupt change of heart

when they came to the small village of Fawley. As they passed a modest inn, Beaufort proposed stopping there for the night, but Maura shook her head, preferring to ride another few miles before dark.

"We have enough food to last another day. And we need to press on if we hope to reach Oxford by tomorrow."

"It would be infinitely more pleasant to sleep in a real bed tonight," he reminded her.

"True, but I don't want to risk Emperor being recognized. We only need to find a meadow with a stream and a few trees. A pile of leaves makes a comfortable bed."

"Behold me in raptures," Beaufort said, his tone dust-dry.

"It will not kill you to sleep under the stars," she replied, smiling.

Beaufort cast a glance at the sky to the west. "I wouldn't count on seeing any stars tonight. Those clouds look as if a storm is brewing."

His words were prophetic, for a while later the wind picked up. Soon the gusts were making the horses nervous. Behind her, Emperor tossed his head and tugged on his lead, and even Maura had difficulty soothing him.

"We ought to return to the inn and wait out the storm," Beaufort suggested.

"Perhaps the next village will have shelter," Maura replied, hoping to ride as far as possible before they were forced to stop.

The rain began some ten minutes later, a dull drizzle that seemed bearable at first. But then the storm intensified, lashing them with icy fingers.

When the torrent had soaked through her cloak and drenched Beaufort entirely, Maura realized how foolish she had been to insist that they try to brave the storm. She was cold and shivering already, so she knew Beaufort had to be even more miserable with no cloak or greatcoat to protect him.

To make matters worse, a mail coach rumbled by, forcing them to the far edge of the road. It was all Maura could do to avoid sliding off the verge into a rain-swollen ditch.

Then disaster struck. Frip tripped in a rut and fell to his knees, almost spilling Maura from her saddle, which caused Emperor to rear behind her and yank the lead out of her hand.

Spinning on his haunches, the stallion plunged down the muddy bank, then stumbled as he scrambled up the other side of the flooded ditch.

Her heart in her throat, Maura guided Frip after him, slithering down the slick embankment and back up again. She could barely see through the sheets of rain, but at least Emperor had halted.

Murmuring a prayer, she flung herself off Frip's back and ran to the stallion. She could tell he was favoring his front left foreleg, and upon inspection, realized that he had thrown a shoe, pulling off part of the hoof wall in the process, perhaps cutting into the quick or bruising the sole of his foot.

When she urged the stallion to take a step forward so she could judge the damage, he visibly limped.

Dismay and guilt welled up inside Maura as Beaufort dismounted behind her.

"That settles it," he declared. "We are returning to the inn. This foolishness has gone on long enough."

"Yes," Maura agreed meekly. "We will need to find a blacksmith to replace his shoe."

While Beaufort took the reins of their riding mounts, she carefully led Emperor back across the ditch. He was still limping, although not as badly, so that Maura doubted he would be permanently lamed by walking all the way back to the inn. Yet she still worried he might be recognized.

"The rain is washing off his disguise," she called to Beaufort.

"In this downpour, no one will note his appearance. But you might be remembered in your peddler's garb. When we arrive, keep your cloak and hood close around you and let me deal with the ostlers and innkeeper."

They trudged slowly back to the inn and led the horses into the stables, where Beaufort arranged for their mounts to be cared for, including a new shoe for the stallion and a poultice for his injured foot.

When they entered the inn, accompanied by a burst of wind and rain, the innkeeper said regretfully that all the rooms were occupied but one.

"My wife and I will take your remaining room," Beaufort told him. "And we require a hot meal and a bath as well."

The innkeeper bowed deeply, evidently recognizing authority when he encountered it. But then Beaufort had the kind of bearing and self-assurance that proclaimed his nobility and commanded respect, Maura knew. He was dressed for the part as well, despite his stubbled jaw and sopping-wet clothing.

She, on the other hand, was hardly attired as his genteel wife. When she hesitated to follow the innkeeper toward the stairs, Beaufort scooped her up in his arms.

Startled, she kept her face buried in his chest but lodged a whispered protest. "I am *not* your wife."

"You are temporarily, if you want to protect your reputation."

"If I hope to protect my reputation, I ought not share a bedchamber with you."

"Don't be an idiot, my love. It will be no more scandalous than sharing a barn loft or a bed of leaves in the woods. And you are shivering so hard, your teeth are clacking."

That much was true, Maura acknowledged as another tremor shook her.

Upstairs, the innkeeper shepherded them into a small bedchamber that overlooked the stableyard. A fire was laid in the hearth but not lit—a situation the innkeeper quickly remedied before bowing himself out with the promise of a tub of hot water and a good dinner to follow.

Alone, Beaufort set Maura on her feet. When he started to remove her cloak, though, she tensed. "I can undress myself, thank you."

"Never fear that I mean to ravish you, vixen," he admonished, his hands still on the garment. "I am hardly in the mood for lovemaking, being cold and hungry myself, and you look like a drowned rat. None of which is conducive to passion."

The gleam of humor in his eyes reassured her enough that she relinquished her cloak and watched as he hung it on a wall peg to dry. Then he surprised her by striding to the door.

"I will leave you to undress and bathe in privacy,"

he informed her. "Once you strip off your wet clothes, wrap yourself in a blanket and go sit by the fire. I'll check on the tub and hot water, and I'll try to scrounge up some dry clothing for us both."

Observing his own drenched state, Maura was suddenly struck by another wave of guilt. "You should be the one to stay. You are soaked to the skin yourself."

"To quote your own words, I will survive. I spied a fire in the taproom where I can warm myself. And I can visit the privy outside and leave the chamberpot here to you. You cannot be seen in public, remember?"

She hesitated to accept his generous offer. "It doesn't seem fair that you should have to make any more sacrifices for my sake."

Beaufort flashed her a grin. "I am willing to act as your prince just this once, Cinderella. Now, buck up. The situation is not as bleak as it seems."

He must have seen her despair, Maura realized, judging by the sudden gentleness in his eyes. Feeling another swell of gratitude, she murmured as he turned again to go, "Lord Beaufort?"

"Yes?"

"Thank you," she said simply.

That irresistibly charming smile appeared again before he let himself from the room.

Alone, Maura shed her wet garments and wrapped a blanket around her body, then went to sit before the now-crackling hearth fire. It was a measure of how much she had come to trust Beaufort that she was calmly waiting for her bath to be delivered.

Amazing, Maura thought, shaking her head in awe and bewilderment. It was even more remarkable that she would permit him to act as her prince, since she rarely leaned on anyone.

No doubt the growing intimacy between them had disastrously weakened her defenses. And now she faced a fresh dilemma. Being trapped in a bedchamber with Beaufort for an entire night would sorely test her willpower.

For a moment her mind returned to the hayloft that morning . . . to the memory of his heart-stirring caresses, the tantalizing feel of his kisses on her bare skin.

She had to fight his beguiling effect on her, Maura knew. Even though he'd said the choice to become lovers was solely hers, she wasn't certain she could resist her desire for him much longer.

Ash had his own reasons for leaving Maura alone just then. The first was to take himself away from temptation. If he wanted to have a prayer of controlling his lust, he couldn't remain in the same room with her while she bathed.

Just the thought of seeing her luscious body naked had the power to arouse him. He'd lied when he'd assured Maura of her unappealing appearance. She seemed to have no idea how exquisitely beautiful she was, and even wet and bedraggled, she could make his body yearn.

At the same time, her forlorn air had only heightened his protective instincts. He wanted nothing more than to make all her troubles magically disappear and then spend the rest of the day and night warming her chilled flesh and showing her just how much he desired her.

He couldn't perform magic, Ash reasoned, but he could help Maura vanquish her troubles if she would only let him.

He wasn't about to tell her his additional reason for wanting privacy for himself, though. Her gratitude would be short-lived if she had even an inkling of the betrayal he was planning.

Upon making his way downstairs, Ash sought out the innkeeper and requested changes of clothing for himself and his "wife," as well as paper, pen, and ink. Then he offered to pay extremely well for a messenger to ride to London immediately with two letters.

When his host readily agreed, Ash used the innkeeper's own rooms to quickly don dry clothes and then sat down before a warm fire to compose a note to Katharine—saying that he was taking good care of her friend and not to worry about them, but including some specific instructions for his coachman and two of his grooms.

It took him three times as long to pen a more complex missive to Bow Street. The Bow Street Runners were a private police force, and Ash intended to hire the elite company of thief-takers for his own purposes. In fact, it wouldn't surprise him if Deering had already engaged the Runners to search for Maura and her stallion.

She would be furious at him, Ash knew, but he needed to force her hand and bring an end to her mad flight as quickly as possible. If she kept on this path, she could very well ruin her life.

Moreover, he was taking destiny back into his own hands.

And finally, Ash admitted, his actions would give

him greater leverage over Maura, which he needed to gain her agreement for an even more ambitious plan he was concocting.

His private feelings for her—which were becoming rather complicated—would have to wait to be sorted out. And so would helping her to regain legal owner-ship of her stallion.

For now, Ash vowed, he simply intended to save Maura from herself.

Chapter Eleven

The storm was still raging when Beaufort returned, sinking Maura's spirits yet again, despite the fact that she was now clean and mostly dry. She had finished bathing and was sitting before the crackling fire, combing out her freshly washed hair. For warmth, she'd draped the blanket around her, over the modest gown the innkeeper's wife had loaned her.

Beaufort wore modest attire also, Maura saw, noting his linen shirt, fustian breeches, and leather slippers.

"Have you eaten?" he asked.

"No. They brought dinner a moment ago, but I waited for you." She gestured at the small table by the window, where a tray of covered dishes lay.

"Come," he suggested.

There was only one chair at the table, since Maura had dragged its twin before the fire. When she rose to relinquish hers, Beaufort carried it back across the small room.

While he inspected the various dishes, she went to the window and restlessly peered out.

"It is frustrating that I must stay in hiding," she muttered.

"You brought it on yourself," he said without much sympathy.

"True."

"Come and sit down. You will feel better after you have eaten a decent meal."

He was holding out her chair for her and clearly wouldn't sit until she did. With a sigh, Maura joined him and let him serve her rabbit stew and bread pudding. But even though the fare was tasty, she did not have much of an appetite.

"You are right," she observed, picking at her stew. "The storm may not let up soon. And even after Emp's shoe is replaced, he could still be too lame to travel."

"Yes. We may have to remain here tomorrow or even longer."

Beaufort seemed too cheerful to her mind. "You are gloating because you managed to get your way after all. If I didn't know better, I would say you arranged the storm somehow."

"I don't have any such magical powers or I would have used them to better purpose. Certainly I would have persuaded you to take shelter here before we were drenched."

When she started to argue, Beaufort startled her by snatching her fork and shoveling a bite of pudding into her mouth.

"Now, be a good girl and chew. You need to stop moping over what cannot be changed."

Maura shook herself, knowing that he was right again. She reclaimed her fork, suspecting that he would forcibly feed her if she wouldn't do it herself.

When they finally finished the meal, she did indeed feel better, not so much because her stomach was full, but because Beaufort had somehow managed to lighten her mood. He would not allow her to despair, she realized, torn between gratitude and unwilling humor.

When two inn servants came to take away the dishes, Beaufort asked for more hot water to be brought for his bath.

Once they were gone, he turned to Maura. "I trust you don't mind if I shave and bathe," he said, rubbing his stubbled jaw with a grimace of distaste.

"Of course I don't mind," she murmured, although she wondered how she would deal with him in such close quarters. The small bedchamber was crowded, what with the table and two chairs, a bed and nightstand, a washstand, and now the round wooden tub at one side of the hearth. The thought of him naked in that tub was most unsettling.

While the servants brought more buckets of hot water, Beaufort went to the washstand and began lathering his face with soap. Maura retreated to the window but found herself watching him in fascination as he used a straight razor to scrape off his growth of whiskers.

"Does that hurt?" she asked curiously.

"Not unless I cut myself."

When he finished, he rinsed the soap from his face and drew his shirt over his head. Maura was unprepared for the shock of heat that flooded her at the sight of his smoothly muscled torso.

Beaufort started to remove his breeches, but when he caught her staring at him, his hands stilled on the waistband.

"I should have warned you I am about to undress," he said with a grin. "You are welcome to watch me bathe, if you like."

Cheeks aflame, Maura quickly turned away.

Behind her, Beaufort finished stripping off his borrowed clothes. When she heard him step into the tub, she couldn't help glancing over her shoulder.

His back was to her, but the golden glow of firelight highlighted his naked beauty. He was starkly masculine, with broad shoulders, narrow hips, taut buttocks, and sinewed thighs and calves.

Her stomach tightening with awareness, Maura averted her gaze and did her best to ignore the ripples of sexual attraction that were coursing through her.

She heard him sink into the water, then splash as he soaped his body with a cloth. It was perhaps five minutes later when he stood and stepped out of the tub. Her gaze was unconsciously drawn to him again as he reached for a linen towel to dry himself.

A small gasp escaped her when she caught sight of his body in profile. She had never seen a nude man before other than sculptures or paintings. Her fascinated gaze followed the line of wet dark hair trailing down his belly and settled on his loins. He was completely aroused, Maura realized, her throat going dry.

He seemed not the least embarrassed by her scrutiny, yet his smile was wry when he spoke. "You do have a certain effect on me, I confess."

He had an unmistakable effect on her as well. His presence was powerfully seductive, even across the room.

She couldn't find her voice to respond, though.

"Why do you seem so startled by my appearance?" he asked as he moved toward the fire and used the towel to rub his hair dry.

"You are not . . . what I expected."

"What did you expect?"

His form was that of a Greek god's, Maura decided, but in one respect, he was built very much like a stallion. His shaft was thick and long—although the nest of dark curling hair that cradled his phallus was somewhat different from a male horse's.

"I thought your male . . . extremities would resemble a statue, not a stallion."

"I shall take that as a compliment," he said, humor lacing his voice.

"My observation was not intended as flattery," she protested. "I was merely comparing facts. You have hair there . . . where a stallion does not."

He laughed softly. "I can see how your knowledge of male anatomy could be warped by all the time spent in your breeding stables."

Maura lowered her eyebrows at him. "You think my naïveté humorous?"

"No, darling, I think your naïveté charming. As a gently reared young lady, you are expected to have limited sexual experience."

He was ribbing her, although gently, she realized. "I am not completely ignorant," she professed. "I know how horses mate. And I must admit, it does not look pleasant."

"How so?"

"A stallion mounts a mare from behind, and there is a great deal of grunting and squealing. While it might be gratifying for *him*, I doubt the mare finds the procedure very enjoyable."

"Procedure?" Amusement danced in his eyes as he turned fully to face her. He had wrapped the now-damp towel around his lean hips, but the sculpted muscles in his chest and shoulders and arms still proved a distraction. "Lovemaking between humans is hardly a 'procedure,'" he said. "And we people usually prefer to face each other when we make love."

"I realize that," she murmured. She might know little about carnal relations, but she'd had enough whispered discussions with her friends to understand the rudimentaries of lovemaking.

"I assure you, a frontal coupling can be exceedingly enjoyable," Beaufort added, "although varying positions can add spice."

Maura gazed back at him mutely, her feelings an odd mix of embarrassment and confusion, intrigue and yearning. Doubtless it was shameful even to be discussing the subject of sexual positions, but she had always been highly curious about lovemaking beyond her pragmatic knowledge of equine breeding.

"My offer still stands," he said, his tone a degree more serious.

The offer to become her lover, he meant.

Maura slowly shook her head, although with a large measure of regret. "I haven't the luxury of expanding my limited sexual experience. Without benefit of marriage, I intend to remain a virgin."

"There are other ways to make love that don't involve penetrating your body or breaching your maidenhead."

She hesitated. "Is that so?"

"Yes. I can give you pleasure without taking your innocence."

When she was silent, his timbre dropped even lower. "Shall I show you, sweetheart?"

A shiver of raw sensation slid down her spine as she stood debating.

Beaufort must have noticed, for he held out his hand to her. "You are cold standing there by the window. Come here and let me warm you."

Did she dare go to him? Maura wondered. She was indeed a little chilled, despite her blanket. And there was a blazing fire a mere few steps away, along with a man who could create a blazing fire within *her*. She knew what could happen if she crossed to him.

She knew what *would* happen between them.

Without conscious thought, Maura found herself moving closer. Then she was standing before the fire, staring up at Beaufort, at his sensuous mouth, the strong planes of his face, the sheer intensity of his eyes. She saw warmth there in his gaze . . . the promise of something thrilling. His expression seemed unbearably intimate, as if he could see into her very heart.

Perhaps he could, she thought when he murmured, "Do you want me, love?"

If she were honest, she had to answer *yes*. He aroused something fierce and passionate inside her. No doubt this wild desire she felt was madness, but just now she wanted to surrender to his spellbinding enchantment.

Even the practical, sensible side of her wasn't protesting. He was right; she could act on her desire with relative impunity. After journeying across England with him and spending their nights together, becoming Beaufort's lover could hardly taint her reputation any more.

Maura closed her eyes, knowing her decision was already made. It seemed the most natural thing in the world to step into his arms and let the heat of his body banish her remaining chill. As she pressed her face into his bare shoulder, she could smell the clean warmth of his skin, feel the silken texture against her cheek.

He held her that way for a short span. Then bending his head, he put his mouth against the side of her neck, where her pulse raced wildly.

"Do you want me, Maura?" he repeated more firmly, although still leaving her the choice.

She took a deep breath and lifted her face to his. "Yes," she whispered.

He hesitated for another heartbeat, searching her face for any sign of reluctance. He must have been reassured by her expression, for he lowered his head and captured her mouth with an urgency that caught her by surprise.

Holding her against his fully aroused body, he kissed her hard, his mouth hot, wet, open against hers, giving her a tantalizing taste of his need, compelling her to respond.

Just as suddenly, he broke off the kiss and caught her arms, then stepped back, as if forcing himself to slow down.

"You will be the death of my willpower," he muttered, his tone softening to rough gravel.

He had already annihilated *her* willpower, Maura

thought dazedly. She could hear the racing thud of her heartbeat as he smiled faintly at her.

"We need to go slowly," he said, more to remind himself than her, she suspected.

His first step was to cross to the bed and fetch a pillow. Returning to her side, he slipped the blanket off her shoulders and spread it on the floor before the hearth, with the pillow at one end.

Then he undressed her, removing her stockings and gown. When she stood naked before him, he unfastened the towel around his waist and let it fall to the floor. Maura's breath faltered at his magnificent male nudity. The hiss and crackle of the fire seemed loud in the hushed silence as he drank her in with his eyes and she did the same with him.

When a shiver danced over her skin, an expression of regret fleetingly swept his features.

"I am neglecting my duty," he murmured, his voice low and vibrant. "I promised I would warm you."

Taking her hand, he drew her down to the blanket and stretched out beside her. With their heads sharing the pillow, her back to the fire, he pulled her close. His skin was hot, sleek, smooth against hers, Maura noted as he ran his hand along the curve of her spine.

Her eyes fluttered shut when he began caressing her body . . . her hip, her thigh, her breast. . . . His warm hand stopped her breath. His palm molded the ripe swells, making glorious sensations clamor through her.

Then he kissed her again, renewing the rush of enchantment. It was like drinking fire.

He spent a long time making love to her mouth, slow

languorous kisses that sent fresh heat welling and spiraling between them. At the same time, he began to stroke her stomach.

Feeling desire pool between her thighs, Maura gave a helpless murmur of pleasure. Her skin seemed to melt under his touch, even before his hand moved lower. Reaching her loins, he probed her downy curls with his seeking fingers until he held the hot center of her in his palm.

When Maura gasped at the sweet shock of it, he drew his mouth back.

"Lie still," he ordered, his voice resonant and sensual. "Let me pleasure you, Maura."

She obeyed him, although restlessly. His fingers resumed caressing her silky curls, slowly rubbing over the swollen lips of her sex. Then his thumb found the slick bud hidden between her folds.

Maura shuddered at the riveting pleasure he gave her. In response, Beaufort only increased the pressure, deliberately circling. The tiny pearl was already hard and aching by the time he slowly slid one finger into her slick heat.

The yearning within her grew as he stroked her inside and out. Maura whimpered again in delight . . . then in disappointment when his enchanting caresses ended and his bewitching mouth broke away from hers.

Dismayed that he had stopped, she opened her eyes, missing the heated wetness of his kiss, but he was only shifting his position.

His handsome face tender, he rose up on his knees and moved over her, positioning himself between her spread thighs with his hands braced on either side of her shoulders. His sensual mouth was still damp from hers when he lowered his head to her breasts. He nuzzled her softly, his lips roughly tender, his tongue tracing burning caresses around her fullness, teasing her nipple, massaging it in shuddering waves with his tongue.

For a time he went on attending each crest, stroking and suckling till both were hard, aching points before moving lower. With slow, exquisite care, Beaufort kissed the bindings marks marring her skin. Then his head dipped even further, his mouth skimming along her body, brushing over the sensitive skin of her abdomen.

As his hot lips worked their spell, Maura shifted fitfully on the blanket.

"Be still," he ordered, the words husky against her skin.

How could she possibly remain still? She was hot and trembling, every muscle in her body quivering.

He seemed to touch every inch of her, setting burning tendrils of arousal ablaze inside her. And that was before he shifted his weight back on his heels and used his fingers to spread her thighs wide. . . .

Her breath caught in a tangled thread as his hands slid beneath her buttocks. When she realized his intent, Maura went rigid, her fingers grasping reflexively at his hair. "Beaufort . . . ?"

Pausing, he glanced up at her, his smile tender. "Call me Ash. I think we have progressed beyond such formalities by now, don't you?"

"Very well . . . Ash. What do you mean to do?"

"To kiss the heart of your sex with my mouth and tongue. Don't tense your body," he commanded, his voice rich and dark. "You'll enjoy this, I promise."

Without waiting for permission, he lowered his wicked mouth to trace a sensuous path over her woman's mound. When he settled on her pulsing cleft, Maura gasped at the bright flare of sensation.

"Oh . . . my . . . heaven . . ."

Her hips jerked as a moan escaped her, which only made his fingers tighten on her buttocks.

"Don't fight it, love. . . ."

Holding her still so he could have his fill of her, he grazed his tongue over her with consummate skill, stroking slowly, the pressure hot and rasping. When he drew the sensitive nub of her sex into his open mouth, sucking gently, Maura began to writhe and twist.

She was trembling violently now, shaking with need more powerful than she had ever known. Her fists clutched in the thick waves of his hair, her moans turning to soft sobs as fire leapt from his mouth to her flesh.

"That's right, give in to it. . . ." he urged.

She could do nothing else. The mounting fire inside her burned hotter and hotter until her entire world was blazing.

At last the exquisite torment was too intense to bear. Her body convulsed, sending starbursts of sparks flying through every part of her.

As she arched her spine, his lips kept on plying her, dredging the final spasms of bliss from her shaking body.

In the hushed aftermath, he placed a final tender kiss on her stomach, then stretched out beside her again and held her while the last tremors subsided.

Her face buried against the fire-warmed skin of his shoulder, Maura lay weak and dazed, panting harshly, listening to her still-pounding heart. She was no longer cold in the least. In truth, she felt gloriously overheated, boneless with sensation.

Beaufort . . . Ash . . . had given her incredible pleasure, the kind she had only dreamed of before. He was a splendid lover, just as he'd claimed. He was everything she'd always fantasized about and more.

"Is it always like this?" she whispered hoarsely.

"Like what?"

She raised her gaze to his. "So . . . intense."

His green eyes were thoughtful and warm. "No. Such intensity is actually rather rare."

Maura hesitated to reply. She had only slowly begun recovering her senses, yet she knew their act of lovemaking was not complete. Ash had felt none of the shattering pleasure he had given her, she realized. He still was full and swollen; she could feel the hard ridge of his manhood against her stomach.

When she tilted her hips tentatively, shifting toward him, he winced as if in pain.

"Don't . . ." he warned.

"Don't what?"

"Arouse me any further."

"Why not?"

"Because I might explode."

Her eyes widening with uncertainty, she brought her hand up to splay against his bare chest. "What if . . . I wanted to arouse you? The way you did me?"

He exhaled a slow breath, but he didn't reject her request outright. Nor did he stop her when she traced a tentative path down his chest to his loins, or when she let her fingers cover the thick pulsing heat of him. The feel of that hard arousal caused her stomach to contract—and his as well, she could tell.

His jaw tense, he kept his gaze locked with hers. His stillness spoke of rigid control when she began to caress him the way he had done her, with slow, rhythmic touches.

She relished touching him, Maura realized, watching his handsome face. His entire body vibrated with strength and life, while his skin was hot enough to scorch.

Evidently he was not happy with her efforts, however, for he soon brushed her fingers away.

"Was I doing it badly?" Maura asked in a small voice.

His short laugh held pain and humor both. "No, not at all, sweetheart. I just can't bear your torment any longer. Give me a moment," he added more harshly as he closed his own fingers around his swollen shaft.

In several sharp strokes, he brought himself to release. He shut his eyes momentarily, grimacing as his body shuddered, then went still.

Realizing he had spilled his seed into his hand, Maura felt a vague stab of disappointment. She had wanted to be the one to pleasure him. But perhaps he preferred to retain control of a seduction and didn't like ceding too much power to her.

It was an intriguing question, Maura thought as he eased his body back from hers.

She lay there feeling uncertain when he rose and went to the tub to wash away the evidence of their passion. Seeing his superb body bronzed by firelight, she felt her breath catch again, but she kept quiet as he returned to the blanket.

When he lay down beside her again and gathered her in his arms, she tensed with shyness, then made herself relax. After the intimacies that had just passed between them, it was foolish to feel bashful around him.

He might have been thinking along similar lines, judging by his next remark:

"This blanket is comfortable enough for now, but when we sleep, I propose we share the bed."

Maura glanced regretfully out the window again, where the rain was still pouring down. "I suppose you are right."

Ash was not as sanguine about sleeping with her as he pretended, however. After tasting Maura's sweetness just now, he wasn't certain he could endure the torture all night long, certainly not in the nude.

"Did you bring a nightgown with you?" he asked.

"No. There wasn't room in my saddlebags, and it would have seemed odd for a peddler lad to be in possession of a nightdress. Why?"

"Because you'll need to put on some clothes when we turn in. I don't dare spend the night in bed with you with no barriers between us."

At her questioning glance, he expounded. "I might act on my lust in my sleep. I don't trust myself not to ravish you."

Her smile held a warm glint of humor. "I am not certain I trust you either."

That enchanting, provocative smile of hers made fresh desire flare inside Ash.

Forcibly holding his hunger in check, he let his head fall back on the pillow. He lay there savoring the feel of her, remembering his body's response when he'd undressed her for the first time. He had made love to innumerable lovely women before Maura, but none of them had ever aroused him so strongly or kindled this sharp swell of possessiveness inside him.

Like Maura, he hadn't expected the intensity, either. It astounded him, the power of his desire for her.

Which only heightened his dilemma.

Bringing her to pleasure had given him a primal satisfaction, as did knowing he was her first lover. Yet he wanted more.

Even now he had to fight the savage urge to drag Maura beneath him and make her fully his. His efficient, dispassionate climax had eased his physical pain for the moment, but he wouldn't be sated till he rested deep and tight inside her.

Yet honorably, to have that right, he would have to wed her.

Ash was understandably leery of taking such a drastic step after so fleeting a courtship, even if there was no denying that Maura had gotten into his blood. He doubted she would accept a proposal of marriage from him, in any case.

Which meant that he would have to resort to coercion to implement his plan. Thus, he was very glad for the storm and even for her stallion's temporary lameness, since he needed a powerful excuse to keep

Maura at the inn with him until his letter to Bow Street bore fruit.

In the meantime, Ash knew, he would have to keep a strict rein on his desire and refrain from claiming her warm, delectable body for his own.

Chapter Twelve

Maura's enchantment lasted through the night as she slept in the bed, wrapped in Ash's arms. Her frustration, however, returned by morning. A chill drizzling rain was still coming down, making the conditions for travel unpleasant if not actually precarious.

After a breakfast of poached eggs and cold beef, Ash visited the stables and reported back that the stallion's shoe had been replaced, but he was still favoring his left fore despite a poultice. Ash also unearthed a two-day-old newspaper and brought Maura a novel that a passing traveler had left behind. Yet she kept vigil at the window, fretting over the dreary weather and watching the occasional activity in the inn yard below.

It was clear that Ash felt none of her urgency.

"Stop pacing, Maura," he exhorted for the second time that morning. "You are wearing a groove in the floorboards."

"I am worried that Deering's minions are on my trail. He doubtless has them searching for me."

"His minions will be looking for a lone Miss Collyer, not the wife of a nobleman."

At least they looked more the part of husband and wife this morning, since Ash had retrieved her traveling dress from her saddlebags and had donned his own dry, superbly tailored garments.

Maura did cease her pacing, but when she wouldn't leave her window post, Ash returned to his familiar refrain. "You know, love, it is still not too late to call off this misadventure."

"I am not letting my horse fall into Deering's clutches ever again."

"Nor will I. In fact, I have a viable solution to your dilemma. I can stable Emperor at my country estate. Neither Deering nor his minions would be able to touch him there. And you and I could return to London with no one the wiser to your theft."

Maura's brow furrowed as she considered his generous offer, but then she shook her head. "I could never be certain Emperor would be safe at Beauvoir, so close to Deering. Scotland is a much better hiding place. Besides, as I've told you before, I don't want to drag you into my battles."

"You have not dragged me. I flung myself in willingly."

Before she could reply, she heard the sound of hoofbeats in the inn yard. When she peered out the window again, a sudden chill ran down her spine.

"What is it?" Ash asked when Maura jumped back from the window to avoid being seen.

"There are two riders down there," she breathed hoarsely. "They could be Deering's men. . . ."

Rising, Ash came to stand beside her. "They are not Deering's men. They are mine."

"Yours?" Bewildered, Maura inched closer to the window. The two sodden riders dismounted and tethered their equally sodden horses to the hitching post in front and made for the entrance door.

"They are Bow Street Runners," Ash explained mildly.

She turned to stare at him in disbelief. "You *kn-knew* they were coming?"

"Yes. I summoned them from London yesterday shortly after we arrived here."

Shock and fear ran through Maura so strongly she could scarcely breathe. "You. Summoned. Them. You summoned the law."

"Yes, but you needn't worry, darling. Here, put this on."

Pulling a gold signet ring off his third finger, Ash slipped it onto hers. "This will aid our pretense."

Since the ring was far too large for her, Maura automatically curled her hand around the warm metal to keep it from sliding off, even as she stared blindly up at Ash. "How could you betray me this way?"

"I promise I will explain later, love. For now just hold your tongue and let me handle the Runners."

How could she hold her tongue when she wanted to cry and rail at him? But what choice did she have?

It was not long before a businesslike rap sounded at their chamber door. Maura stood frozen in her tracks while Ash bid entrance.

Evidently he recognized the taller of the two wiry men who stepped into the room. "Ah, Mr. Linch, welcome. You made good time."

"We set out as soon as your letter arrived, your lordship," Linch replied. "You said the matter was urgent."

"Indeed it is. Shut the door, if you please." Ash slid his arm around Maura's rigid shoulders. "My love, this is Mr. Horace Linch of Bow Street. Linch, this is my betrothed, Miss Collyer."

Maura winced at his blatant falsehood, but kept silent when Ash got straight to business.

"As I said in my letter, until recently the stallion belonged to Miss Collyer before being sold to Viscount Deering. Two nights ago I took Emperor from his stall at Deering's London residence as payment for a gaming debt."

At his second lie, Maura turned to stare up at Ash. So *that* was his plan: Establishing her innocence by claiming *he* had been the one to steal the priceless horse from Deering's stables—and contending that his disagreement with the viscount was merely a civil dispute between two peers.

Maura knew she had guessed correctly when he continued.

"You see, Mr. Linch, I wish to handle this matter privately with Deering while ensuring the stallion's safety. As you can imagine, my betrothed is exceedingly worried for her beloved horse." He smiled fondly down at Maura. "I have hired Bow Street to protect Emperor, my love, so you may calm your fears."

When she remained mute with astonishment, he returned his attention to the agents. "I have sent for my coach and servants. When they arrive later today, you are to escort two of my grooms and the stallion to my estate in Kent and safeguard them, since Deering may take issue with how I chose to confiscate my property. You are well armed, as I requested?"

"Aye, my lord," both Runners replied at once.

"Good. I don't expect any serious trouble, but I want you to be prepared. Naturally you will be well paid for your efforts."

"Thank you, my lord," Linch said, apparently content with the financial arrangements.

"I trust I can count on your total discretion? I don't want Deering to know where we have taken the stallion until I tell him myself."

"Most certainly."

"Excellent. Then you may wait for my servants downstairs, Mr. Linch. Our good landlord will provide you with dry clothing and a hot meal at my expense. As soon as you are safely off to Kent with the stallion, Miss Collyer and I plan to return to London in my carriage."

As he ushered the Runners out the door and shut it behind them, Maura shook her head in bewildered awe. Even when Ash turned back to her, she remained speechless.

He stood there eyeing her warily, as if expecting her to explode at any moment.

"I cannot believe your gall," she finally murmured. "You lied to them about stealing my horse and then bribed them to hold their tongues."

At her calm tone, his guarded expression seemed to relax a measure. "So I did. But my tale was effective. You saw how they reacted to my confession of guilt . . . with complete indifference."

"Oh, I understand your reasoning. They won't be eager to inject themselves into the middle of a feud between two wealthy, spoiled noblemen."

"Precisely."

Maura gave Ash a reproachful look. "Why did you not tell me what you were planning?"

"Because I knew it would alarm you enough to send you haring out of here. I had no desire to continue our ill-advised trek to the wilds of Scotland, especially under such appalling conditions."

"I could still take Emperor and ride for Scotland," she warned, even though they both knew her threat was an empty one.

"You will not get far now that Bow Street knows where to find you."

"You needn't gloat, you devious wretch," she muttered.

Ash allowed himself a small smile. "Why am I a wretch? I collect you should be thanking me."

"Whyever should I thank you for deceiving me so completely?" Maura retorted.

"I had no choice. You wouldn't wait for me to devise a rescue plan, or listen to reason, no matter how often I tried to persuade you to turn back. Consequently, I needed to come up with some means to force your hand."

"You . . . you . . ." She broke off, devoid of appropriate words to express herself. She was profoundly relieved and grateful that he had actually come up with a good plan. It was the underhanded way he had gone about it that vexed her.

"Traitor?" he supplied helpfully as he ambled over

to the table and rested a hip on the surface, as if preparing for a long argument with her.

He wasn't even pretending remorse, Maura thought with renewed exasperation. "Traitor will suffice. You are utterly without shame. I thought Katharine's scheming could rival Machiavelli, but you are far worse."

"I should hope so. I am seven years her senior and a man to boot. Kate must contend with the limits of her gender."

Noting how pleased Ash looked with himself, Maura crossed her arms defensively over her chest. "Some prince you turned out to be, betraying me this way. I never should have trusted you."

"Yes, you should have, love. I have just solved your immediate problems, not only protecting your precious horse but saving you from prison or a miserable career as a fugitive." His voice softened. "I was not about to allow you to be branded a felon and spend the rest of your life hiding from the law, Maura."

His genuine concern mollified her to a large extent, yet she didn't want to appear to capitulate too easily. Ash had too much annoying self-confidence as it was.

"But you just gave those officers of the law enough evidence to prosecute you," Maura countered. "You could be branded a felon yourself."

"That won't happen. If my claim of a gaming debt is challenged, I can say I stole the stallion on a lark. We Wildes do such scandalous things all the time. At worst, the ton will engage in another round of tongue-wagging and head-shaking, and one more blot against my character will hardly matter."

Maura shook her own head at his prediction. No

doubt Ash's rank would shield him from any legal punishment, since a nobleman could literally get away with murder unless convicted by a jury of his peers. "You are awfully sure of yourself, aren't you?"

"I have faith this is the best way—and that you are wise enough to realize it."

She hesitated. "Can you promise me that Emperor will be completely safe at Beauvoir?"

Ash gave a firm nod. "I'll swear to it, Maura. Deering won't dare trespass on my lands."

After the trials her poor horse had been through the past fortnight, she was loath to let Emperor out of her sight. Yet she knew Ash's trusted stablehands could be counted on to take the stallion safely to Kent, certainly if he was escorted by two armed Bow Street Runners.

"Very well, then. . . . Thank you."

Apparently, though, Ash wasn't finished. "We still have a serious problem. Deering will never believe that you had no hand in the theft, which leaves you vulnerable to his retaliation. Unless you have me by your side, that is."

His statement puzzled her. "What do you mean?"

"My plan is simple. You return immediately to London as my betrothed, under my protection."

Maura felt a strange flutter in her heart at Ash's suggestion of a betrothal. "You are not actually proposing marriage, are you?" she asked warily.

His half smile was wry. "No, love. Neither of us is ready for that drastic a step. I am only proposing the *pretense* of a betrothal."

"Even that seems rather drastic. I see no need for us to pretend an engagement."

"There is every need. For one thing, a betrothal will help mitigate the gossip if it gets out that you shared my intimate company for the past two days. But more to the point, if we're betrothed, I can keep you safe. Deering will have to deal with me directly, and he will think twice before taking me on, I assure you."

"Perhaps, but you needn't go to such lengths as a sham betrothal."

"But I wish to, sweetheart. I can handle Deering far better than you can, by mere virtue of my rank and fortune if nothing else. You know I am right."

It was frustrating but true, Maura admitted reluctantly. Being affianced to the Marquis of Beaufort could indeed offer her significant protection.

She glanced down at the signet ring on her finger as she stood debating. The trouble was, a betrothal would expose her to another, more seductive danger. Namely, Ash himself.

When she remained silent, he pushed away from the table and began walking slowly toward her. "I realize you have difficulty swallowing your stubborn pride, vixen, but I am already up to my neck in your affairs. And you should know by now that I won't give up. You might as well concede gracefully."

That was also true, Maura acknowledged as he slid his arms around her waist and drew her close. He was determined to take on her battles for her, despite her objections.

"Your practiced charm will not sway me, Ash," Maura declared, making one last effort to hold her own with him.

"No?" He gazed down at her, giving her the full

effect of his lazy smile. A smile that sent a sweet, treacherous stab of longing straight through her body to her heart. "Shall we put it to the test? I calculate that we have at least two or three hours until my coach arrives. I have until then to convince you."

Chapter Thirteen

Before she could reply, Ash lowered his head for an unhurried kiss, reminding her of the passion they had shared last evening.

He was using his ruthless charm to seduce her into accepting a betrothal, Maura knew. And he was completely succeeding. His mouth was hot and open on hers, compelling her response, and in only a heartbeat she felt herself melting.

She had to be stronger than this, Maura thought dazedly, even as he sent hot shivers through her body. With supreme effort, she pressed her hands against his chest and made him break off his bewitching kiss.

"We need to discuss this further," she said breathlessly. "I cannot possibly think when you are rushing me this way."

"Very well, but if we are to have a long conversation, we should make ourselves comfortable."

Taking her elbow, Ash guided Maura to the bed and drew her down to sit beside him with their backs against the pillows. Then he slid his arms around her.

"I like holding you," he explained when she started to argue. "Now, what do you wish to discuss?"

"To begin with, your notion of needing to protect me from Deering," Maura said. "Surely I will be safe enough on my farm."

"I am not taking that risk. And you won't be returning to your farm just yet. You will travel with me to London today instead."

Her puzzlement resumed. "Why must I travel to London at all? Especially when I should be home helping Gandy with the spring foals."

"Two reasons," Ash said. "First, to dispel any suspicions of your being a horse thief by showing yourself in public. If there are rumors connecting you to Emperor's disappearance, you can refute them and laugh them off."

His suggestion made sense, but dispelling rumors was not a high priority for Maura. "What is the second reason?"

"You will have to face Deering if you want to restore your father's honor."

She went very still. "I don't understand."

"You blame Deering for your father's death, isn't that so? He accused Noah Collyer of cheating and deliberately ruined his reputation."

"Yes."

"Well, I should think you would want to prove your father's innocence."

Maura felt her heart give a painful leap. Her most heartfelt desire—one she never would let herself consciously acknowledge—was to clear her father's name and restore honor to his reputation.

"I would give *anything* to prove his innocence," she said in a shaken voice. "It is my greatest wish. But I don't believe there is any chance of it."

"There is if I help you."

Maura stared at him, her mind awhirl. "You are actually serious."

"Utterly serious. This is your chance to change your father's legacy, Maura."

She was already weak with relief, knowing her stallion would be safe for now, but she hadn't dared let herself hope for more.

"I never dreamed it could actually happen," she murmured almost to herself.

"It is no dream. I intend to make Deering pay for what he did to your father."

"But how?"

"One step at a time, love. Once I make clear to Deering that your horse is safely in my possession and that we are affianced, we can determine what comes next. In any event, our betrothal will provide the perfect excuse for me to confront Deering on your behalf. Don't fret," Ash added when he saw her frown. "Our engagement is only temporary. You can cry off as soon as we declare victory over him."

Maura bit her lower lip in doubt, and yet . . . If there was even the remotest chance of erasing the black stain on her father's reputation, she had to take it.

At her continued silence, Ash prodded her. "If you don't return to London with me, you will be letting Deering win. You don't want him to win, do you?"

"No, of course not."

"Then you need my help."

She did need him, Maura admitted. And in truth, it

would be an enormous relief not to be alone in her fight against Deering any longer.

"Thank you," she murmured gratefully, gazing up into Ash's green eyes.

His expression softened. "You shouldn't thank me just yet. You need only agree to a betrothal."

"Then I agree." She drew the signet ring off her finger. "But I had best return this. It is so loose I fear I will lose it."

He took the ring and slid it onto his finger, then turned her face up to his. "Now give me a kiss to seal our bargain."

Maura complied willingly—and instantly felt her senses start swimming again. When Ash's caressing mouth moved to the side of her neck, trailing light kisses along her skin, she arched to give him better access and threaded her hands in his hair to draw him closer.

When he pressed her down among the pillows, however, she managed a half-hearted protest. "Ash . . . I have already agreed to your plan. I don't need any more persuading."

"I know."

"Then what are you doing?"

"Kissing you. What better way to while away the time until my carriage arrives?"

Agreeing fully, Maura closed her eyes in surrender as he nibbled tenderly at her throat, until his next comment came:

"This could be our last chance for lovemaking for some time. Once we return to London, there may be little opportunity."

Indeed, it might, Maura thought with regret. She wanted this time together with Ash. Perhaps too much.

Recalling her resolve to maintain her defenses, Maura found the strength to untangle herself from his embrace and sit up. "This is extremely unwise, lying in bed with you, kissing you."

Ash followed suit, although more reluctantly. "Come now, sweetheart. You need some pleasure in your life. You've had so little of it recently."

Brushing a disheveled tress back from her face, she raised an eyebrow at him. "Oh, so you are only thinking of me?"

"For the most part. Although easing my own ache is also a consideration."

Seeing the wry glimmer of humor in his eyes, Maura laughed softly. After the stress and turmoil of the past weeks, it was good to be able to share a lighter moment with him.

"I think you are cruel to deny me," Ash added in a plaintive, clearly teasing tone. "As your betrothed I ought to have *some* special privileges."

"Oh, and what privileges might those be?"

"If I could, I would spend the rest of the day exploring your delectable body."

Maura shook her head in reproach. "You are wicked."

"What is so wicked about wanting to make love to you? If we were in Scotland, we would be legally wed by now, since we declared ourselves to be husband and wife before witnesses."

"But we are not in Scotland, nor are we wed. We are not even betrothed for real. And now that I consider it, just pulling off such a sham will be difficult. No one in your elite circle will believe you actually wish to marry me."

"Why not?" Ash asked.

"I am a horsebreeder by profession. That disqualifies me to be your marchioness. And I am most definitely not cut out to be your fairy-tale princess."

"Certainly you are."

Maura disagreed. "No, my Lord Beaufort. You have long been a prize on the Marriage Mart and the bane of every matchmaker's aspirations. No doubt the ton will be shocked to hear that you chose me for your bride."

"It will be no more shocking than anything else I have done. For that matter, no one would be surprised if I eloped with you. My own parents eloped to Scotland many years ago, although there was a little matter of an abduction beforehand." Ash chuckled. "The bride—my mother—was more than willing, but her papa didn't approve of the union, so the groom had to force the issue."

Maura's eyes widened. "I knew about your parents' elopement, but not that it was an abduction."

"It's true. But my parents were actually fairly tame compared to some of my aunts and uncles. Jack's mother—my Aunt Clara—caused a great scandal in her time, falling in love with a foreign prince and bearing a child out of wedlock, then living abroad alone. And Quinn and Skye's parents caused their own scandal. Angelique was a French noblewoman engaged to wed a wealthy count when my Uncle Lionel stole her affections and married her himself. And then there was the Wilde ancestor who had to decamp for America because he killed a rival in a duel.

It started a bitter feud between our families that continues to this day." He smiled a bit. "See, I told you our current generation of Wildes have a legacy to uphold. Our love lives are varied and interesting, to say the least."

"Apparently so," Maura observed wryly.

Ash went on as if she hadn't interrupted. "You may trust me when I say that pretending a betrothal will merely add to the exciting annals of our family history."

Maura hesitated again, wanting to give him one last opportunity to change his mind. "Beaufort . . ."

"I asked you to call me Ash."

"Ash . . . you don't have to fight Deering with me. You can still withdraw your offer."

His own gaze narrowed on her. "Not a chance, love. I am not abandoning you now that I've gone to all this trouble to save you from yourself. Besides, I desperately want the challenge. My life was becoming far too dull."

"Well, then . . . if you are sure. But I won't hold you to a betrothal. We will end our engagement at the earliest opportunity. I won't have it said that I trapped you into marriage."

"There is that prickly pride again," Ash said with a taunting smile.

Maura answered him with much more seriousness. "Perhaps it *is* my pride, but I also don't wish to act the hypocrite. It has always galled me that my stepmother manipulated my father into marriage because she wanted security and wealth. I refuse to be anything like Priscilla, marrying only for material gain. And I don't care to marry you, in any case."

His mouth curved. "I know—I don't need reminding that you are fiercely independent."

Maura pursed her lips thoughtfully. "It is not only independence I want," she said with complete honesty. "Only true love would ever induce me to marry. And from what you have said, you feel the same way. You expect to find a grand passion in marriage, and I gravely doubt that I am your grand passion, any more than I am your ideal princess."

At his contemplative silence, she searched his face. He clearly had his own doubts as well, she could tell.

But she faced the greater danger, Maura realized. After all, what did a rake like Ashton Wilde know about true love, despite his family legacy? She didn't dare let herself succumb to him, for she knew he could break her heart.

Finally he cleared his throat. "Perhaps we are not fated to fall in love, but meanwhile . . . I will settle for passion. I want you, sweet Maura." His hand reached up to stroke her cheek. "You want me, too, admit it."

Of course she wanted him. His merest touch stirred something deep inside her. Yet her yearning for him was more than sheer physical desire.

Maura drew a deep breath, striving for willpower. Then his hand suddenly fell away, making her feel sharp disappointment in addition to relief.

"Perhaps kissing you *is* unwise," Ash murmured, "since it will prove too much temptation. Therefore, I will just hold you."

He drew her close while waging a struggle for willpower similar to Maura's. When she gingerly laid her head on his shoulder, Ash deliberated how to deal with his growing feelings of tenderness for her.

He knew he had to tread carefully. If he wasn't sincere about wooing and wedding Maura, he could cause her grave hurt, for she was far more vulnerable than she liked to pretend.

Alternately, he could be in peril himself if he came to love her and failed to win her love in return.

Frowning, he pressed a light kiss against Maura's temple. How had this fair-haired hellion accomplished something that no other woman had ever done: Make him seriously contemplate matrimony, and even worse, matters of love?

Until now he'd always viewed the question of love with a healthy wariness. Although he bore a fierce love for his closest family members, he'd maintained a deliberate emotional distance from outsiders. Oh, indisputably he was as lusty and passionate as all his Wilde relations, possibly more so. But to this point all his love affairs had been shallow and superficial and had never once come close to touching his heart.

In truth, he'd sometimes wondered if he was even capable of feeling the kind of romantic love that usually afflicted his clan.

It was a profoundly alluring fantasy, though— fulfilling the primal desire to find his perfect mate. Finding the one special woman who was his equal. Who belonged with him and to him. Who completed him and made him half of a contented whole.

Yet for his own self-protection, he'd never subscribed to the principal Wilde doctrine that it was better to have loved and lost than never to have loved at all. After the grief of losing his parents, he had never wanted to risk that terrible pain, not even for the priceless prize of experiencing a grand, lifelong passion.

He would be a sad fool, however, to let his perfect match slip through his fingers for fear that he might suffer an unrequited love.

The simple fact was, whether or not their betrothal ended in marriage and a passionate, timeless love, just now Ash very much wanted to be Maura's hero and prince. And granting her wish to vindicate her father's honor was his best chance to prove himself her prince.

Chapter Fourteen

The Beaufort coach and grooms arrived in good time, so that by early afternoon, Maura was standing in the inn yard saying farewell to her stallion.

She felt anxious for Emperor, even though she knew he would have the best of care from Ash's trusted stablehands and with two armed Bow Street Runners to act as escorts to his new home in Kent.

"And at least you can be properly groomed again, my handsome fellow," Maura murmured as the horse nosed her palm, searching for treats.

She fed Emperor the fat carrot she'd obtained from the inn's kitchen and stroked his face and ears while she waited for Ash to finish speaking to his grooms. When he was done she added her own instructions for Emperor's care.

Finally Ash gestured toward his waiting carriage. "We had best be on our way. It will be late when we arrive in London as it is."

"I hope we are doing the right thing," Maura said, her doubt and worry rising up again.

"We are," Ash assured her.

When he reached up to brush her cheek with his knuckles, Emperor pushed between them and butted his shoulder. Maura softly scolded the horse for his poor manners and apologized to Ash. "He knows better. He is just being protective of me."

"You may tell him that I will take good care of you," Ash promised before handing her into his well-sprung carriage.

They traveled all day, and when night fell, he pulled Maura into his arms and cut off her protests. "This is another advantage of a betrothal—it allows us more freedom when we are together. Now, go to sleep."

She slept soundly in his arms until he murmured in her ear, "Wake up, princess. We are here."

Maura stirred awake, only to realize that she was draped all over him.

"What is the time?" she asked as she untangled herself and sat up.

"Just after ten o'clock."

Self-consciously, she smoothed the straggling wisps of her hair, which she'd pulled back in a tight chignon, and straightened her cloak as she peered out into the dark night.

The coach had drawn to a halt in front of Priscilla's house. There were lights shining from several of the first-floor windows, but none in the upper floors, suggesting that her stepsisters were asleep, but that her stepmother was still up.

With Ash's assistance, Maura alighted from the coach. As he escorted her up the steps to the front door, she took a deep breath, bracing for a confrontation, and no sooner had she let herself into the house than Priscilla came charging into the entry hall.

Maura knew Ash had followed her inside, but Pris must not have seen him, for she immediately launched into an impassioned lecture.

"How *could* you, Maura? I implored you to think of your stepsisters, but you blatantly disregarded all my pleas!"

"What pleas are those, Priscilla?" Maura managed to ask calmly.

She heard Ash shut the front door behind him, but her stepmother was still too upset to notice that they had an audience.

"You know perfectly well what pleas! I begged you not to make an enemy of Lord Deering, but you went and stole his property from under his very nose!"

Striving for patience, Maura forced a grim smile. "And *you* know that Emperor is my property, not Deering's."

"Not since the sale over three weeks ago—and now you have not only gravely offended his lordship, you have aroused his wrath at *me*!"

The hypocrisy of her complaint incensed Maura, since Priscilla had escalated the conflict by selling Emperor in the first place. But apparently *she* considered herself the victim, as evidenced by her next words:

"Deering blames me for failing to control you, you infuriating girl, as if I ever could! And now he intends to punish us all for your transgressions."

Her anger and bitterness were genuine, but so was her distress. She was near tears, Maura realized. It took her aback to see Priscilla distraught enough to shed tears.

To her knowledge, her stepmother rarely cried. The last time was when her husband—Maura's father—had died.

"What do you mean, 'punish us'?" Maura asked skeptically.

"He threatened Hannah and Lucy with complete ruination, and it is all your fault!" That last accusation was issued in a quavering voice that was almost a sob.

Dismay speared through Maura. At least now she understood the reason behind the tears, for Priscilla truly did love her daughters.

"What does Deering plan to do?" she breathed.

"What do you care? You are the most selfish creature alive." Gulping in a steadying breath, Priscilla raised herself up to her full height. "I'll thank you to leave my house at once, Maura. I cannot afford to have Lord Deering for an enemy."

Maura stiffened instinctively. "May I remind you that this has been my home far longer than it has been yours?"

"That cannot matter to me. I have to protect my daughters."

Maura opened her mouth to argue but shut it again, since she deeply sympathized with Priscilla's desire to shield Hannah and Lucy from the viscount's intrigues.

Before she could decide how to respond, Ash stepped forward and spoke for the first time. "You should also give a thought, madam, to protecting your stepdaughter."

Priscilla gave a start upon noticing the tall nobleman. "Lord B-Beaufort . . ." she stammered. "I . . . forgive me, I did not see you there."

"Obviously." He returned a chill smile as he moved to stand beside Maura. "And clearly you are not aware that you are addressing my future wife."

"Your wife!"

"Yes indeed. Miss Collyer has made me the happiest of men by consenting to give me her hand in marriage. We came to tell you the glad tidings ourselves, but I can see you have no interest in wishing us well."

As Priscilla stared, her mouth gaped open for a dozen seconds, and eventually Ash broke the silence. "If you wish to speak to her once you are in a more remorseful frame of mind, Miss Collyer will be staying at my home in Grosvenor Square with my sister and uncle."

Her shock was evident in the way her previous fury dissolved into sputtering confusion. "My lord . . . You cannot mean that you intend to *marry* her? When she has behaved like a common thief?"

Ash's expression became amused. "You are sadly mistaken on both counts, Mrs. Collyer. In the first place, Maura is extremely *uncommon*. . . ." He sent Maura a loving look. "And in the second, I took the horse myself. Emperor is now my property, in my possession."

Leaving his declaration at that, he took Maura's elbow. "Come, my sweet. Your stepmother knows where to find you once she is prepared to offer you an apology."

Turning away, he shepherded Maura out the door and into his waiting coach, where she sank against the leather squabs with a growl of mingled frustration and dismay.

"I should have expected something like this from Deering," she muttered as the vehicle began moving. "It is just like that dastardly man to take his wrath out on two innocent girls."

"I promise you, they will come to no harm," Ash said consolingly.

"He is not one to make idle threats," Maura fretted.

"Nor am I. We will deal with Deering and make him regret that he ever dared tangle with your family."

His solemn reassurance made her feel marginally better, but then she recalled Ash's stated destination. "I should find lodgings somewhere . . . perhaps a hotel."

"There is no need. You don't want to live in a hotel alone, certainly not when my home is open to you." When Maura frowned, Ash added more firmly, "It's perfectly acceptable for you to reside with me, since mine isn't a bachelor establishment. My sister is your close friend, and my Uncle Cornelius is a pattern card of respectability—at least compared to the rest of our family. And if you wish, I will write at once to my aunt, Lady Isabella Wilde, and ask her to come to London to act as your chaperone. Aunt Isabella married into my father's side of the family and is now widowed."

"I could never ask you to go to such lengths—" Maura began.

"Don't be daft. Your staying with us will make the pretense of our betrothal more believable."

"Perhaps, but I have already taken excessive advantage of your generosity."

Ash just smiled that knowing smile of his. "I see your chin locked in that stubborn position of pride again. But there is no need for pride. You know Katharine would go to any lengths for you, and so would the rest of my family. We will all present a united front against Deering."

It was undeniable how comforting his declaration was, Maura realized. For even though she knew her feelings of abandonment were absurd, she felt quite alone since she no longer had a place in London to call home.

"Thank you," she murmured.

At her abrupt surrender, his expression turned dubious, as if he expected more arguments from her. But Maura knew he was right. As an unmarried lady, even one who was almost a spinster, she would only benefit from the connection with his noble family. And if she temporarily went to live with Ash and Katharine, it would indeed support their sham betrothal.

Evidently Ash accepted her capitulation as genuine, for he said, "Come here," and drew her against him.

Held in the light, protective circle of his arms, Maura had the overwhelming sense that she was safe. She cherished that feeling—which was possibly why she felt the need to voice a token protest. "You don't need to cosset me, you know, Ash. I am not entirely a weakling."

He chuckled at that. "No, that you are not. In fact, you are one of the strongest women I know, and that includes my own family. After everything you have endured, you are still fighting and spitting fire."

It was true that she had grown stronger with adversity, Maura agreed silently, but all the same, she was profoundly glad to know that Ash was on her side and that she wasn't alone.

* * *

Katharine, too, was clearly on her side. When they arrived at Grosvenor Square, Katharine had just retired for bed, but came racing downstairs in her dressing gown.

She immediately threw her arms around Maura while scolding her at the same time. "I cannot believe you set out for Scotland all on your own, you darling idiot! You know I would have helped you get your horse back. You gave me such a fright, I could gladly strangle you."

Maura couldn't help but smile when Kate included Ash in her diatribe. "And you, brother dear . . . how *dare* you send me that cryptic note telling me nothing and ordering me to send your coach and grooms—But what the devil have you both been up to? I have been *dying* with curiosity."

When Ash hesitated to answer in the hearing of his servants—his butler and two footmen who were standing by to take their outer garments—Katharine pulled him and Maura away from the vast entry hall, into the nearest parlor for privacy. There they gave her an abbreviated version of events, including the theft of the stallion, their subsequent travels, and the storm that had abruptly ended their journey.

When her brother announced their temporary betrothal, Katharine's beautiful face lit up, and she embraced him with delighted exuberance. "Oh, your legend is coming true, Ash, just as I hoped!"

"Not so quickly," Maura hastened to say. "The engagement isn't real."

"What do you mean? How can it not be real?"

Maura left it to Ash to explain that she would stay with them for a short time while they made plans to take on Deering. He truncated the discussion by saying, "We will tell you all about it in the morning, Kate, but for now I am starving." Ash directed his gaze at Maura. "Are you hungry as well?"

Surprisingly, she was. "Yes."

"Then why don't you go upstairs to freshen up and meet me in the kitchens in a quarter of an hour? I'll raid the pantry and rummage us up something to eat. No need to wake the servants."

"I will show you to your rooms," Katharine volunteered.

Maura expected to be grilled further, but astonishingly, her friend did only as promised, escorting her upstairs to a luxurious bedchamber in the guest wing of the enormous house in order to wash and freshen up.

Kate left for a few minutes and returned with a nightdress and dressing gown, then announced that she was going back to bed. "I want to give you and Ash ample time to be alone together. It's clear that he has become your prince, or your knight in shining armor, or whatever you care to call it. But courtship can be a fragile thing, and it is utterly remarkable in my brother's case. I don't want to jinx it by being underfoot."

Her shameless attempt at matchmaking made Maura roll her eyes in exasperation, and when she threatened to throw her pillow at her friend, Kate left laughing.

Maura's humor had faded a little by the time she went downstairs, no doubt because she was beset by weariness and worry. When she reached the kitchens, she discovered it bustling with activity. Evidently, Lord Beaufort's chef had refused to let him fend for himself and roused several sleepy servants from their beds in order to prepare an impromptu supper.

Upon learning that his lordship was in his study, Maura made her way there and found Ash waiting for her. The hearth fire had been built into a cheery blaze and a side table was covered with enough dishes to make a feast, including half a roasted chicken.

Ash dismissed the two footmen, then heaped her plate high and his own higher. Leading Maura to an overstuffed leather couch, he settled beside her with a contented sigh.

"Damn, but I have missed the comforts of home after you forced me to billet in half the barns and backwoods from here to Oxford. No, I don't want to hear your excuses again," he interjected when Maura would have defended herself. "Hold your tongue for now, love, and eat your supper like a good little thief."

He insisted that she finish most of her meal before letting her speak a word, while he kept making idle observations designed to rile and amuse her. Maura could tell that he was set on teasing her in order to lift her mood, and amazingly enough, she soon felt her spirits doing just that.

When Ash finally announced that he planned to send notice of their betrothal to tomorrow's afternoon papers, she wrinkled her nose. "I still doubt anyone will believe that you chose me."

"On the contrary, no one at all will be surprised that

I fell for you. With your irresistible beauty and valiant spirit, I couldn't fail to be stricken."

How could she resist the laughter in his eyes, that heart-stealing smile? Maura wondered. "There you go again, trying to charm me with your absurd flattery."

"There is nothing absurd about my flattery. You should know by now that I hold you in the highest esteem."

She laughed. "What a whisker."

"I swear, I admire you immensely, vixen. Most ladies wouldn't be willing to fight to their last breath for a mere horse, no matter how beloved."

"I thought you strenuously objected to my attempted rescue."

"I only objected to your methods. I thought there was a smarter way to go about it."

"Which means *your* way."

"Of course."

She shook her head in admiration. "You ended up getting exactly what you wanted, Ash. Is there anyone you cannot bend to your will?"

"I admit, you have proven more difficult than most."

"But I still succumbed in only a few days. You wield charm like a weapon."

He regarded her thoughtfully. "We are not so unalike, sweeting. I have a way with people, you have one with horses. I've seen you work your special brand of charm on your equine companions. You would be downright dangerous if you chose to use that magic on men—not that I want to put any ideas into your pretty head."

She responded to his remark with a serious one.

"Just now my pretty head would like to know what you are planning to do about Lord Deering."

Ash shook his own head. "There will be plenty of time to plot the details of our campaign in the morning after a good night's sleep."

When Maura's expression sobered completely, Ash made a tisking sound. "Have a little faith, darling. Everything will work out. You just need to trust me."

"After you went behind my back and summoned Bow Street to force my hand, you expect me to *trust* you? Your subterfuge is exactly why I tend to prefer horses to humans. Horses are far more trustworthy."

Her declaration earned a chuckle from Ash. Despite her retort, though, Maura did trust him—implicitly. She felt cloaked in warmth and security just now, sitting here like this, before a comfortable fire with Ash, even when she was a target for his ribbing. His warm eyes were amused and beguiling and oh so tempting. . . .

Recognizing the danger, she wasn't sorry when he announced that it was time to retire since it was nearly midnight. She even yawned as he set down their empty plates.

Ash escorted Maura upstairs, then stopped at her bedchamber door and lowered his mouth to hers for a tender good-night kiss. Yearning shot through her blood, along with a sweet, aching awareness. She found herself wishing he could stay with her tonight and make love to her, even knowing how foolish her longing was.

But clearly he had more discipline than she did. After a lingering moment, he raised his head. "Sleep well, princess, for we start our newest adventure in the morning."

When he turned away, Maura entered her room and shut the door behind her, smiling softly. For although she would sleep alone tonight, she wasn't alone at all.

Chapter Fifteen

Maura had barely risen the next morning when Katharine swept into her room carrying a breakfast tray.

"Good, you are awake," Katharine said brightly, setting the tray down on the dressing table. "No doubt you were exhausted after all your travels, Maura, so I hope you slept well, for we have a great deal to do today. Why don't you eat your breakfast while I tell you what has transpired this morning?"

When Maura obeyed, Katharine recounted the events thus far. "First, Ash dispatched a footman to our Aunt Isabella's London residence and learned that she is on her way home from Cornwall and is expected here sometime tonight. She has houses in London and Cornwall and on a Mediterranean island off the coast of Spain, courtesy of her three husbands."

"Three husbands?" Maura remarked curiously.

"Yes, three. She has been widowed since my Uncle Henry Wilde passed away five years ago. She is actually half Spanish—her father was a Spanish count and distinguished diplomat. You will love Bella, I am certain, Maura. She is so lively and such fun, even if she is only a Wilde by marriage. I have no doubt she will be happy to come stay with us to act as your chaperone and lend an air of propriety to your visit."

Without pausing, Kate continued ticking items off her fingers. "Second, Ash wrote a notice of your engagement for the newspapers. Third, I sent to Suffolk for more of your clothing, and in the meantime, you will share mine. And fourth, I have called a family council for ten o'clock this morning to discuss how to give that blackguard Deering his comeuppance. Skye is eager to help, and we shall bring Jack and Quinn and Uncle Cornelius into the deliberations as well."

"You have been busy, I see," Maura murmured, torn between amusement and chagrin that her problems were being forced on all of Katharine's relatives. "But Kate, I dislike putting your entire family to all this trouble—"

"Oh, pah. Ash told me you would resist accepting our assistance, but everyone needs a little support now and then. And you know you cannot defeat Deering alone. You needn't even try, Maura, since we will all relish helping you. No, don't you dare argue with me. I've always been extremely fortunate to have my family to call upon in times of trouble. You have had no one—but that will change right this instant."

Thus it was that during her first day in residence at the Beaufort mansion, Maura found herself swept up in the Wilde family consultations. When she had finished breakfast and dressed, she accompanied Katharine downstairs to the library, where, according to Kate, many of their councils took place.

"Ash is typically in charge of our meetings," she confided. "He holds the reins of our family since as the eldest, he had the most responsibility when our parents died. But we usually listen to him and trust him to lead us."

Ash was already waiting in the library when Maura entered. As he rose to greet her, the warm light in his eyes reminded her vividly of last night's sensual kiss.

His uncle's greeting was more formal, but still genuinely welcoming, as he had known Maura since her first visit to Beauvoir as a schoolgirl. Lord Cornelius Wilde was a classics scholar of some repute and looked the part, with his silvering hair and heavy eyebrows, although his refined bone structure and tall, lean build lent him an unmistakable aristocratic elegance.

Lord Cornelius, Maura knew, possessed a powerful intelligence, but was uncomfortable in most social settings, so she wasn't surprised when he politely asked to be excused from the discussion. Then retreating to a comfortable chair near the hearth, he donned his spectacles and opened a leather-bound tome.

Ash had just seated Maura and Katharine at a large table near the window overlooking the gardens when his handsome half brother, Lord Jack Wilde, strode in. Lord Jack's overlong raven hair and unshaven jaw gave him a rakish air, while his amused, irreverent manner was a frequent source of exasperation for Kate, Maura knew.

Lord Jack clapped Ash on the shoulder before expressing amazement at his engagement. "You shocked the devil out of us, brother, agreeing to be leg-shackled. I never thought you would do it, despite the obvious temptation of so lovely a lady. . . ." So saying, he turned to Maura and bent to kiss her cheek. "Welcome to the notorious Wilde clan, Miss Collyer. I will be delighted to have you as a sister, but I trust you know what you are letting yourself in for, aligning yourself with my libertine of a brother."

Maura found herself blushing at Lord Jack's charming flattery even as she shot Ash a questioning look. "You did tell him that our betrothal is only temporary?"

"Yes, he knows," Ash answered dryly, just as Skye and her elder brother Quinn, the Earl of Traherne, arrived.

Skye embraced Maura joyously and Traherne bowed over her hand.

Like Maura, they were fair-haired, but Skye's tresses were a lighter shade of gold than her brother's. They both had deep blue eyes, unlike Ash and Kate's vivid green color and Lord Jack's dark brown. Additionally, Lord Traherne shared his uncle's aristocratic elegance and keen intelligence, but possessed a dry, biting wit and a zest for adventure that the older gentleman completely lacked.

When they were all settled around the table, Ash explained how he and Maura had been occupied for the past several days, recounting their efforts to spirit the stallion away from London and their subsequent decision to return and confront Deering's malevolent lies about her late father. Maura was quite glad that Ash gave not even a hint about their physical intimacy, yet they couldn't escape questions about their betrothal.

When Lord Jack ribbed her about being his brother's "Cinderella" though, Skye came to her rescue. "Stop teasing Maura, Jack," Skye said sweetly, "or I swear I will make your life miserable."

He gave a mock look of terror before insisting with an amused drawl, "She will have to endure a great deal of ribbing if she means to spend any time with us. But I own I would go easier on her if she would allow me to purchase one of her famous stallion's offspring."

Maura couldn't help smiling at his broad hint, but before she could reply, Lord Traherne commended her influence on his sister. "I recall you play a mean game of cricket, Miss Collyer, but more crucially, you managed to correct Skye's horsemanship when I failed for years."

She had learned to play the rough-and-tumble, very male sport of cricket from Katharine and Skye, who had been taught by their brothers when they were short on team members, and in turn, Maura had improved both young ladies' riding seats.

Skye laughingly objected to his criticism, however, which resulted in an argument about his teaching abilities versus her equestrian talents, but Maura could clearly see their fondness for one another.

As if sharing her reflection, Katharine took the opportunity to lean closer and whisper in Maura's ear. "We may quarrel and bait each other unmercifully, but we would fight to the death if any one of us was threatened. So there are advantages to having a loving family, even if they are forever provoking you and prying into your affairs."

Advantages, indeed, Maura thought wistfully. She

had always wanted a close-knit, loving family, although Priscilla had made that impossible from the very beginning, insisting that Maura be sent off to boarding school alone, away from her beloved father and friends.

Watching the Wilde cousins, she felt that undeniable sense of longing again—a feeling that was suspended when Lord Jack returned the conversation to fairy tales and mythological lovers and ended with, " 'Tis a pity Uncle put such radical literary ideas into Kate's head."

At that, Lord Cornelius looked up from his book with a sheepish expression. "I assure you, I did not encourage Katharine. She devised her hypothesis about legendary lovers all on her own. I merely provided the scholarship."

Ash spoke up then. "I would rather not dwell on her theory when we have more pressing matters to consider, namely how to vindicate Miss Collyer's father."

"I presume you have some ideas about how to proceed?" Traherne asked.

"Yes," Maura seconded. "*Have* you any ideas?"

"A few," Ash said. "The goal is to make Deering retract his accusations and admit that he lied when he claimed your father played with marked cards."

"Is that even possible?"

Ash nodded. "I believe so, but it will require careful forethought and planning. The first step should be to inform him that the stallion is now in my possession, since nothing will inflame Deering more. And I want to put him on notice that you are under my protection. I have no illusions that he will simply ignore the theft. Given his outsized pride, he may even retaliate for the brazen insult to his dignity."

"A personal warning will have more effect," Traherne advised.

"Agreed," Ash said. "I plan to call on him as soon as we conclude our discussions here. It would also help to spread word of my engagement to Miss Collyer, to make Deering's defeat as public as possible. An announcement will appear in *The Star* later today, but I expect there is more we can do."

For a moment the entire family considered Ash with collective bemusement.

Then Skye nodded. "Kate and I will write to our acquaintances and ensure the most vocal gossips know about your betrothal. And Jack and Quinn can go about town today to confirm the story."

Katharine chimed in. "It would benefit Maura to be seen publicly with you, Ash. We have several invitations to choose from this evening. And perhaps we should plan to attend the theater some time when Deering is expected. His box at Drury Lane has a view of ours, and your appearance there with Maura would rub his nose in your victory."

"A good idea. I want him to stew while we determine how to restore Noah Collyer's good name."

"To be truthful," Maura said quietly, "just now I am more worried about my stepsisters than vindicating my father. Protecting them is the most urgent problem. I fear Deering plans to use them as pawns in his battle against me. My stepmother claims he has threatened to ruin them, and I don't doubt he could do it. It would take only a word from him to destroy their chances to ever make a suitable match."

Katharine and Skye both hastened to reassure her.

"We will take your stepsisters under our wing and introduce them to eligible suitors from among our circle," Skye started to say just as the Beaufort butler appeared at the open door of the library and caught Ash's attention.

"Begging your pardon, my lord. Two young ladies have called for Miss Collyer on what they say is a matter of grave importance. A Miss Hannah Collyer and Miss Lucy Collyer."

"Speak of the devil," Lord Jack murmured.

"My stepsisters could be in trouble," Maura said, filled with unease by their unexpected visit, even though they were prone to exaggeration. She didn't like the thought of interrupting the family council, but she worried that Deering had already taken some vindictive action against the girls.

She sent Ash an apologetic look. "I am sorry to leave you, but I should speak to them about their 'grave matter.'"

"Go ahead," he urged. "We are nearly finished here."

"If you see Deering, will you please tell him my stepsisters are under your protection also?" Maura asked Ash earnestly.

"Of course. You needn't doubt it for one second."

"Thank you," she breathed, sending another contrite glance to his whole family.

The gentlemen all stood as she hurried from the room. Maura followed the butler to a small parlor, where she found Hannah and Lucy pacing the floor in agitation.

Both girls flung themselves at her, embracing her with a stranglehold while speaking simultaneously. At first she could understand little from their garbled declarations, but they were clearly upset, and eventually she realized they were apologizing profusely for their mother's cruel actions in evicting her.

Extricating herself from their hugs, Maura tried to reassure them. "I don't care about having to leave, truly. Are *you* all right? Lord Deering hasn't harmed you, has he?"

Her younger stepsister, Lucy, dashed a tear from her eye. "Harmed us? No . . . at least not yet. We are fine, Maura. We just wish to tell you how outraged we are that Mama barred you from your own home!"

"Yes, it was abominable!" Hannah added just as passionately. "Especially since *we* are the ones who will suffer from your banishment. We don't want to lose you as our sister, Maura."

It seemed ironic that she should be the one offering consolation for being expelled from their family home, but Maura smiled comfortingly. "You could never lose me, my dears. But your mother will not be happy that you are here visiting me."

Hannah frowned. "Well, there you are mistaken. Mama gave us permission to call on you this morning. Indeed, she encouraged us to come and even let us have the carriage."

Maura must have looked skeptical for Lucy hurried to explain. "Mama said she regrets sending you away last night."

"Did she now?" Maura replied in surprise.

"Yes, because of your betrothal to Lord Beaufort, you see."

She felt her mouth twist with faint humor. "I suppose I do see." Priscilla must have recalled that a marquess trumped a viscount and that making an enemy of her stepdaughter's future husband was extremely unwise. No doubt she would try to endear herself to Ash, just as she had Noah Collyer.

Hannah took over the explanations then. "Mama believes she acted too hastily and has offered to let you come home. But Lucy and I have discussed it at length, and we think you should make her grovel a bit—but only if you won't hold it against us, Maura." Hannah glanced around the elegant parlor adorned with flocked silk wallpapering, velvet draperies, and expensive chintz and rosewood furnishings. "So long as you are staying in this splendid house, it won't be a hardship for you, will it? In fact, you may be much happier living here. But we don't want you to forget us."

"Surely you know I could never forget you," Maura said. "And it may be best if I keep away from you at present. Your mother is right: My associating with you could bring Deering's wrath down upon your innocent heads."

"We don't care!" Lucy declared loyally.

Hannah was less certain on that score, however. "It *is* rather worrisome. Mama lives in dread that he will destroy our chances to find husbands. Given our family scandal, even a whiff of censure from Viscount Deering would drive away any potential suitors. But that cannot be allowed to matter—and it is not as if we had any suitors beating down our doors to court us anyway."

"Certainly it matters," Maura asserted. "But I promise you, Deering's threat will never come to pass. My friends mean to lend you their patronage. If the entire Wilde family is seen to support you, Deering will find it difficult to bring about your ruination. In fact, Skye and Katharine have offered to take you about society so that you may meet some eligible gentlemen."

"Oh, that would be famous!" Lucy exclaimed, while Hannah professed, "Mama will be vastly relieved."

And so will I, Maura thought, grateful to her friends.

Although, she added to herself, it would mean yet another reason to be indebted to Ash and his family, not just for protecting her stepsisters, but for averting a possible murder. For if Deering dared to harm Hannah or Lucy, she would strangle him with her bare hands or shoot him with her pistol, and then she truly would be thrown in prison and hanged, this time for slaying a nobleman rather than merely stealing back her stallion.

While Maura was consoling her stepsisters, Ash was conferring with Quinn in the library. By then, the Wilde family council had disbanded, with Skye and Kate repairing to the drawing room to attend to their correspondence, Jack to return to his own home, and Uncle Cornelius to prepare for an appointment with a colleague.

Quinn remained behind to discuss possible ways to take down the viscount.

"You would have the most leverage over Deering," Quinn suggested, "if you could reveal him as a cheat as well as a liar. When he played against Collyer, were the cards actually marked, and if so, who marked them? If it was Deering, he might attempt to cheat in the future, given high enough stakes. If you were to play him at cards, you could contrive to expose him."

"An excellent notion," Ash said with a thoughtful nod. "I'm glad you occasionally put that brilliant mind of yours to good use."

Quinn smiled. "Let me know if you need assistance against him. I would relish the opportunity."

"At some point I may require your help, but for now, I hope to let Miss Collyer orchestrate his defeat as much as possible. She has a large score to settle with Deering and needs the satisfaction of routing him herself."

"That I can understand," Quinn said. "What confounds me is how easily you allowed yourself to be caught up in Kate's preposterous theory. Only a few days ago you were bent on making your own destiny."

"I still am," Ash contended.

"Have you determined if she is your true love?"

Ash hesitated. "I don't yet know."

His cousin's amused blue eyes held a hint of mockery—a cynicism that was not unexpected. Of all the Wilde cousins, Quinn was the least likely to believe in such unproven possibilities as lovers who were fated to be together.

But given his closeness with his cousin, Ash felt the need to expound. "I imagine I will know in short order. Although it seems longer, it has only been three days since we embarked on this endeavor together. Our betrothal should prove a good test." He paused another moment. "I do feel *something* for her, I admit. But pray, don't tell Kate or I'll mill you down."

Quinn returned a pained grin. "I wouldn't dream of it, for it would only encourage her matchmaking." Rising from the table, he gave a friendly squeeze to Ash's shoulder. "But pray remember, my own freedom depends upon your success or failure. Kate will hound the rest of us unmercifully if you end up losing your heart to your legendary lover."

His cousin's assertion left Ash pondering his ever more complex feelings for Maura. Admittedly, his carefree bachelor's existence had begun to lose its flavor. He had no wish to wind up like his Uncle Cornelius, alone and unloved but for his relations' children.

Furthermore, Ash was willing to concede that he had never wanted a woman more than the honey-haired vixen who had invaded his life so profoundly this past week. His admiration for her had grown even more. Maura was courageous, smart, resourceful, passionate, and sensual as the devil, yet at the same time comfortable and familiar. She would easily fit into his family, with their bonds of loyalty and affection and repartee.

But that didn't mean he was prepared to take the enormous step of marrying Maura, or ready to risk turning his heart over to her.

On the other hand, his desire for her was increasing by the minute, and having Maura living in his house only a few corridors away would prove a grave challenge to his honor and, even more, to his sorely strained willpower.

Deering was not at home when Ash called, so he continued on to White's Club for Gentlemen where the viscount sometimes lunched. He found his quarry relaxing on a comfortable couch, perusing *The Racing Chronicle*.

"Ah, just the man I was looking for," Ash said easily. Upon settling in an adjacent chair, Ash proceeded to reveal the stallion's current whereabouts.

He had to give the viscount credit: Deering hid his anger tolerably well, responding merely with a cold stare. "I wondered how that she-devil managed to outwit my stablehands," he muttered. "I should have known she had an accomplice."

"Oh, no, the theft was my doing entirely," Ash claimed. "I had no difficulty at all seizing the horse from your stables. You really should have taken better care of your property, my friend."

His thinly veiled taunt had the desired effect, for Deering's countenance darkened.

"I advise you to let the matter rest now," Ash suggested. "It looks better for you if I claim to have acquired the stallion as payment for a gaming debt than if the ton thinks you were bested by a mere young lady who was only reclaiming her rightful property. And did I mention," he added with a pleasant smile, "that the she-devil, as you call her, has promised to be my wife?"

He received enormous satisfaction when the viscount's expression slowly turned livid.

Even so, Deering sat in rigid silence for a long moment before finally gritting out, "It was unwise of you to ally yourself with her in this matter, Beaufort. You do not want to make an enemy of me."

"I could say the same of you," Ash replied lightly. "In fact, allow me to be plain. Any action you take against my future bride I will consider to be a direct strike against me. And that extends to her young stepsisters as well. Do I make my meaning clear?"

Deering's fingers clenched on his newspaper so tightly that the page tore in two places.

Content for now to leave his warning vague, Ash rose and sketched a casual bow before turning and striding away.

He had not made an outright declaration of war, but he had no objection to employing all-out warfare if necessary. For he had every intention of forcing Deering to recant his previous lies in order to give Maura back her late father's reputation.

Chapter Sixteen

Although Maura had formed no precise expectations when she came to live with Ash, she learned in short order what it meant to be embraced by the Wilde family, who never did anything by half-measures. All his relations rallied around her and claimed her as one of their own, beginning that very evening. The cousins appeared en masse at two select ton functions, where the Marquis of Beaufort treated the cream of society to a firsthand display of his startling betrothal and his evident devotion to his lovely, if somewhat disgraced, fiancée.

Naturally, rumors of Miss Collyer's battle with Lord Deering simmered beneath the surface, but for the most part, she was absolved in the court of public opinion of committing any felony regarding her stallion's sudden disappearance from the viscount's stables.

The cousins' aunt by marriage, Lady Isabella Wilde, also joined in the campaign to close ranks around Maura. Late that night, only moments after the family returned to Ash's home and gathered in the drawing room to discuss their next plans, the strikingly handsome raven-haired widow arrived like a fresh breeze and proved just as lively as Katharine had claimed.

Lord Cornelius had fallen asleep again in one corner of the room, but Lady Isabella, upon hearing the rudimentary details about Maura's plight and Ash's objectives, roused her brother-in-law and insisted that he partake in the discussions.

Jointly the Wildes decided to attend several more entertainments the following evening and over the next few days, so as to be seen about town. Isabella even prevailed upon Cornelius to accompany them, since constantly burying his nose in a book was not good for him.

Thus it was that during the succeeding week, the entire clan set out to conquer the ton on Maura's behalf and embarked upon a full-blown charm offensive—an endeavor at which she could only marvel. The delightfully infamous Wildes might be known for their amorous scandals, but it was fascinating to watch them win over their detractors with their bewitching appeal.

Maura's stepsisters also benefited hugely from their attentions. When Skye asked what challenges the girls faced in finding husbands, Maura answered honestly. "Given our tarnished family honor, it will be difficult without the added enticements of significant fortune or beauty. But Hannah has a voice like an angel, and Lucy plays the pianoforte with real artistry."

"Then we shall hold a musical evening," Skye declared, "to showcase their talents and make them appear in the best possible light. Kate and I will invite some potential suitors, and demand that our brothers encourage their unattached friends to attend. And since the girls need to shine, I will have my dressmaker make them new gowns."

When Maura automatically protested, Skye sweetly cut her off. "Trust me, Maura, bringing Hannah and Lucy into favor will be the most effective way to protect them from Lord Deering."

Additionally, Skye arranged a shopping expedition to Bond Street to buy new accessories, with Ash footing the bill. Maura felt uncomfortable accepting such largesse, but her objections were swiftly overridden.

"Nonsense, you can settle finances later," Skye insisted, slipping her arm in Maura's. "By now you should realize that our family sticks together. It has long been the Wildes against the world, and you are now an indispensable member of our clan."

Maura wasn't as certain that she deserved such distinction, at least until the first evening after Isabella's arrival, when the cousins met for dinner at Grosvenor Square before attending a gala event.

They assembled in the drawing room first, and when they went in to dinner, Maura found herself seated on Ash's right. Naturally, she felt a trifle nervous at the formal family gathering, yet she needn't have worried, for she fit right in.

She even managed to win Jack's devotion when she agreed to privately sell him a yearling sired by Emperor, thus bypassing Tattersalls, where the premiere stock in England was bought and sold.

Theatrically, Jack placed his hand over his heart while warning Ash. "I am in love with your betrothed already. If you don't marry her, I will."

Maura had to laugh at his absurdity. But at least his

enthusiastic response helped her decide upon a way to repay Ash.

"I wish to reimburse you for all the expenses you have incurred this past week," she murmured to Ash when his family's attention was diverted by a tale Isabella was relating. "So I thought I might give you one of Emperor's get. If you like, you may have your pick of any horse in my stables. I expect last year's crop of foals will be spectacular."

"There is no need for such a lavish gift, but I will accept since you require it to salvage your outsized pride," Ash said mildly, although his arch smile told her clearly that he was ragging her.

It had indeed become a point of pride for her to prove that she wasn't a penniless Cinderella in need of a prince's charity and that she was determined to meet Ash measure for measure.

Eventually the talk at the table turned to horses, and Isabella mentioned that one of her friends on the Mediterranean island of Cyrene, the Earl of Hawkhurst, possessed superb stables that even Maura might envy. "Hawk visits England occasionally in search of breeding stock. If you wish, I will give him your direction so that you might do business together."

Maura agreed readily. "My stable master would be very happy to speak to him. We are always looking to improve our breeding lines."

Then, when dinner was over, she learned about a unique custom in the Wilde family. Instead of the ladies repairing to the drawing room while the gentlemen enjoyed their port, they all remained at the table and shared fond stories about their parents in order to keep their memories alive. Maura found herself laughing at the tales, until they toasted each parent in turn in what was obviously a solemn ritual.

Unexpectedly, she was taken off guard as an old memory of her own late family rushed up to swamp her, of her father and mother the last time they were together before her mother had taken ill with fever.

Then even more unexpectedly, the Wilde cousins raised a glass to Noah Collyer. Emotion rose up in Maura's chest and tightened her throat. Their consideration touched her deeply, yet it was knowing they had truly made her part of their clan that momentarily overwhelmed her.

When she met Ash's eyes and saw the tender sympathy there, she felt a sense of belonging she hadn't felt since childhood.

Maura managed a grateful smile before forcibly swallowing her threatening tears and rejoining the gaiety. Her wish to end her loneliness had been fulfilled in spades, and the feeling of belonging lingered. She couldn't possibly be lonely when she had the love and acceptance of this extraordinary family surrounding her. It was beyond wonderful that she could claim this new connection, even if she also knew that the bond was fleeting and would remain only as long as her betrothal to Ash lasted.

Reality returned the following day, however. The Wildes had spent another late evening dancing at a ball, so Maura rose rather late that morning. After breakfast, Ash invited her into his study for a private discussion. Clearly he hadn't forgotten the main reason she was even betrothed to him.

"We need to remain on the offensive against Deering," Ash said at once, "so I've begun forming a plan. Pray tell me every detail you can recall leading up to the accusations of cheating against your father. You said Deering lured him to a gaming hell. Do you know the name of the club? And what card games they played?"

Maura could scarcely bear to remember that terrible time, but she disciplined her emotions so that she could answer Ash's questions dispassionately.

"I believe the club was called Sutter's, although I'm not sure of its location. But the game was vingt-un. I will never forget, since Papa and I used to play that when I was young."

"Do you know if the deck was actually marked, or did Deering only claim it to be so?"

Maura frowned as she tried to remember. "At least some of the cards were marked. The ace of hearts was for certain. Papa said there was a small scratch in one corner. That ace had somehow fallen to the floor beside his chair, and he suspected that Deering planted it there. Why do you ask?"

"Because if Deering cheated once, he will likely do so again. I intend to give him the opportunity by challenging him to a friendly game of cards."

The suggestion concerned Maura. "You realize he may accuse *you* of cheating?"

Ash's smile held a calculating relish. "I sincerely hope he tries, for I will be ready for him. If I can catch him in the act and expose his methods, it will go a long way toward proving your father's innocence."

She wasn't convinced Ash's plan would work, though. "Why would Deering even play you?"

"Because he wants the opportunity to win your stallion back."

"Won't he be suspicious if you suddenly offer him his heart's desire?"

"I've come up with a reasonable answer for that," Ash replied. "I'll say that I want Emperor's deed of sale to give you as a wedding gift. I expect he'll believe that pretext readily enough."

Maura's frown deepened as she tried to think through the various possibilities. "What if he doesn't cheat when you play him?"

"Then I might be forced to employ the same ignoble tactics he used against your father. I could fabricate a similar accusation against Deering in front of witnesses and offer to retract my charge if he does the same against your late father. If need be, I'm willing to sink to his level and use underhanded means to gain a confession of guilt from him. However, it's much more likely that he will repeat his previous success."

"You mean, he will cheat you the same way he did with my father?"

"Yes," Ash said. "I suspect Deering either marked the cards himself or relied on someone else at the club to do it for him, so he could deny culpability. Or he might have employed some trick such as mirrors to rig the game. I'll enlist Jack to advise me what deceptions to watch for. Jack has spent a great deal of time in London gaming hells. He might even have played at Sutter's. And unlike your father, I will be on my guard."

Maura nodded slowly in cautious approval. "I should have realized you would consider every angle. But what if Deering refuses your challenge altogether?"

"Trust me, he won't refuse. I'll goad him into it if need be. When I am done, he'll be angry enough to strike back at me, and angry men tend to be reckless."

"I would be delighted to help you goad him," Maura muttered.

"Oh, no, vixen," Ash said quickly. "I don't want to give him any new reason to retaliate against you. I want him directing his wrath at me instead."

Ash's protectiveness still roused Maura's exasperation, but his nonchalance actually worried her. "I don't like the idea of you making yourself his target, either. It could be dangerous."

"I doubt it. Deering usually backs down when facing serious opposition. But given the prior animosity between you two, you need to remain as unthreatening as possible, even charming."

Her eyebrows shot up. "*Charming?* You may have noticed that charm is not my strong suit. And even if it were, I could not possibly be charming to that odious man."

Ash smiled in disagreement. "You have effortlessly charmed my entire family, sweetheart. Just last evening, Jack declared his love for you. You can do the same with Deering."

"But I genuinely like Jack. I detest Deering with every ounce of my being."

"So pretend otherwise for now, just long enough to vindicate your father. It's for a very good cause." When Maura hesitated, Ash prodded her. "If Deering were a horse, you would have him eating out of your hand in two minutes flat. Just think of him as a rogue horse you have to win over."

"He is not a horse," she grumbled. "Even the hind end of a horse would be too flattering for him."

Ash took her hand and made Maura look at him. "Don't make the mistake of letting your hatred get in the way of winning, love. You only have to persuade Deering that you want to mend fences with him and let bygones be bygones."

"Tell me again why I must do so?"

"Because you will lull him into agreeing to play me at cards."

"I suppose you are right," she conceded grudgingly. "Very well, I will try."

"Good. And you must also make a similar effort with your stepmother," he added almost as an after-thought.

"What do you mean?" Maura asked warily.

"I want you to try to turn her against Deering. If she is willing to testify that she stole the deed from you and that he acquired your horse illegally, we will have a good deal more leverage over him."

Maura's first inclination was to scoff at the thought of Priscilla turning against the viscount. "You would do better to charm her yourself. You well know that my relationship with my stepmother is strained at best."

"Do you hate her as much as you hate Deering?"

"No, certainly not."

Maura fell silent as she considered her long relationship with her stepmother. As a child, she'd harbored selfish resentment against Priscilla for taking her father from her. As an adult, however, she'd had to concede that genteel women without independent fortunes were sometimes compelled to marry for security.

She'd also come to realize that even though her father had mourned his first wife deeply, he was lonely after her death, and that while his loneliness had made him vulnerable to a siren like Priscilla, somehow she had filled that emptiness inside him.

"In fact," Maura admitted in a low voice, "until Priscilla betrayed me by selling Emperor, we had arrived at a truce of sorts. But I never could abide how she behaved after Papa's death. She claimed to believe in his innocence, but it was as if she *blamed* him for dying and leaving her mired in scandal."

Ash was unemotional in his reply. "Still, she could be useful to us, Maura. And in this case the end will justify the means."

"Priscilla will suspect some kind of ruse if I suddenly pretend to be gracious and charming to her."

"Even so, you should attempt to make an ally of her. The musical recital Skye is hosting for your stepsisters on Saturday could be the best time for you to speak to her, since she will see firsthand how we are benefiting her daughters."

Maura clasped her hands in her lap and nodded. She wasn't certain she could ever regard Priscilla as an actual ally, but for her late father's sake, she would try.

An hour later, Maura was changing her gown for yet another afternoon outing when Katharine entered her bedchamber. Upon hearing about Ash's plan, Kate fully agreed with her brother's strategy. Yet clearly she was much more interested in his courtship of Maura.

"Have you come any closer to deciding if Ash is your match?" she pressed.

Maura couldn't help but smile. "I am loath to disappoint you, but no."

"Well, just in case . . . I brought you something, although I warn you, it may shock you a little." She handed Maura a red silk pouch that contained several small sponges and a vial of amber liquid. "According to Aunt Bella, a sponge soaked in vinegar or brandy can prevent a woman from getting with child."

Shock, indeed. Maura's eyes widened. "Lady Isabella gave you these?"

"Yes. Skye and I have always been more enlightened than other girls our age because of our brothers, but we don't have a mother to advise us about intimate physical matters. And neither do you. You know a great deal about equine breeding and animal husbandry, Maura, but not about carnal relations between people."

Maura held her tongue, electing not to confide to even her dearest friend that she had learned a great deal about carnal relations from Ash over the past week.

"Aunt Bella has been amazingly frank," Kate explained, "for she is resolute about wanting us to take control of our own fate. She made me promise that I wouldn't wind up *enceinte* unless it was my own decision, as it was for Jack's mother. Our Aunt Clara bore a child out of wedlock, but Skye and I don't mean to follow her example. In fact, we both fully intend to marry someday and so want to remain virgins until our wedding nights. If you don't care about marriage, however, there is no reason you must remain chaste . . . although I truly hope you choose to have a deeper and more permanent relationship with Ash than mere passion."

Maura was eager to change the subject from matchmaking but realized the futility of trying. "Why are you so adamant about seeing your lovers' theory come true, Katharine?"

"Because I care deeply about you and Ash and want you to be happy together. It is not just a silly whim, Maura, or a conceit so that I can prove my skills as a matchmaker. I am pressing you because life is too short not to seize the moment. We Wildes know that better than most, since we were orphaned at such a young age." Katharine paused, as if recalling a sad memory, but then shook herself. "One thing you can say about my family. We may be pleasure-seekers, but in the long run we know that pleasure is empty without love."

"But you cannot force anyone to fall in love," Maura argued. "Your brother does not love me, Kate. He is only pursuing me because you browbeat him into it."

Kate sent her an arch smile. "Can you imagine Ash *ever* allowing himself to be browbeaten? Even by me?" When Maura didn't respond, she added earnestly, "All I am asking is that you give love a chance. You would be insanely happy if you loved Ash and he loved you madly in return."

Indeed, Maura reflected, she would be ecstatic to find that kind of true love with Ash. Not even her deep friendships with Kate and Skye were enough to fill the lonely hole in her heart.

But was it even possible for Ash to fall in love with her?

Granted, he had brought her into his family and wrapped her in a protective cocoon of love, but that was familial love—the deep bond of affection between sisters and brothers. Not a romantic, passionate, soul-stirring sort of love. And even though he pretended to be smitten with her whenever they were in public together, his show of devotion was only part of a charade to convince the ton that their betrothal was real.

Maura let out a wistful sigh. She didn't believe in fairy tales or fated lovers and yet . . . why did she find herself fervently wishing that Ash's pretense of love could be real?

Chapter Seventeen

Her questions about Ash's feelings for her remained unanswered, yet Maura did have the opportunity to meet Lord Deering that very evening—not at Drury Lane Theatre as they'd expected, but at a ridotto given by Lord and Lady Pelham, who were prime leaders in London's political sphere.

Much of the elite company present wore masks and dominoes, but Deering eschewed any disguise, which made him highly recognizable. When Maura spied him across the room, standing near the punch bowl, she slipped away from Ash and brought her cup to be refilled by a servant.

Upon turning back, she made certain to cross paths with Deering and paused to offer him a tentative smile. "My lord, how good it is to see you again."

Deering's expression, which hitherto had been bored, darkened to a scowl as he identified Maura through her mask. Yet she pasted a smile in place, determined to remain calm and, if not charming, then at least pleasant.

"I am pleased to have this opportunity to speak to you, my lord. I wish to apologize for my rude behavior the last time we met," she offered, referring to their physical altercation in Hyde Park when she'd taken his own crop to him.

When Deering eyed her with suspicion, she added sweetly, just as if she wasn't still furious at him for beating her innocent horse. "I was highly upset about losing my stallion then, but now that matters are settled, I am eager to put our past disagreements behind us."

His irritation obvious, Deering muttered an inaudible reply under his breath and turned away.

Maura, however, would not allow him to dismiss her so easily. "Lord Beaufort's cousin, Lady Skye Wilde, is holding a concert tomorrow evening at the home she shares with her brother, Lord Traherne. My stepsisters will be performing, and we would be delighted if you would honor us with your presence."

Deering cast her a sour glance over his shoulder. "Why the devil should I wish to honor you?"

"Because it would show that there are no lingering hard feelings between us. It would also be kind of you to tender your support for my young stepsisters. I know Mrs. Collyer would be thrilled if you would lend us your countenance."

"I think not," he returned stiffly.

Maura kept her tone contrite. "I can see that you are still angry at me, my lord. But I fully intend to return the funds that my stepmother received from you in exchange for Emperor's deed of sale. I want to be completely fair, you know."

His jaundiced look was a mix of distrust and resentment, as if he couldn't determine why Maura was offering him a proverbial olive branch.

"Do please come tomorrow," she begged prettily. "The concert will begin at eight o'clock, with a buffet supper afterward."

With an engaging smile that made her jaws ache, Maura sketched a curtsy and took her leave of the glowering viscount.

Afterward, she went in search of Ash, whom she found occupied with partnering their hostess in a minuet. Then she herself was solicited for the next set of dances. The moment she was free, she spied Ash speaking to the viscount, but it was nearly an hour later before she had the opportunity to speak to him in private, to report on her progress and ask about his.

"I did as you asked," she told him. "I was all charm and politeness to Deering, even though it made my skin crawl."

Ash nodded in approval. "Your sacrifice was worthwhile, since you paved the way for my success. When I told Deering I wanted a chance to win the deed for your wedding gift, he leapt at the chance to play me, and he agreed to meet me evening after next. I allowed him his choice of locations, and not surprisingly, he chose Sutter's. Jack has played there before and says it's a fairly reputable club, so I doubt the proprietor or employees were involved in marking the cards when Deering played against your father."

Distracted by the first part of his announcement, Maura gave a small frown. "That is only two days from now."

"Is that a problem?"

"No, not at all. It is just that . . . matters are coming to a head more quickly than I anticipated."

"The sooner we expose Deering's cheating, the sooner your father can be exonerated."

She would be thrilled to have her father's good name restored, but Maura suddenly realized how short time was growing. If their plan succeeded, in a few more days it could all be over and her betrothal to Ash would end—which meant she would have to decide quickly about the terms of their parting.

She said nothing to Ash just then, for she hadn't fully resolved the conflicting forces warring inside her, a struggle between desire and prudence. But later, after they returned home, she committed to her momentous decision when she managed another private moment with him.

"Will you come to my room tonight?" she murmured.

His gaze was searching as it swept her face. "Why?"

"Because I want to be your lover."

A flicker of fire lit his eyes, yet he didn't instantly leap to accept her invitation as she'd expected.

"You said the choice to become lovers was mine," Maura pressed at his hesitation, "and I have chosen. I don't want to be seen wandering the halls of your house, however, and your apartments are closer to your sister's than is comfortable. So you will have to come to me."

When still Ash didn't reply, Maura eyed him uncertainly. "Isn't your offer to show me passion still open?"

His taut mouth relaxed in a smile. "Yes, if that is what you want."

"I do. I want to make the most of our remaining time together."

"Very well, I will come to you tonight, a half hour after we retire."

His tame response puzzled Maura, for despite his words, Ash seemed reluctant somehow, as if he wasn't as eager to fully consummate their intimacy as she was. Yet time had taken on a new urgency for her, since they had so little of it left to be together.

She had no chance to discuss his reticence further, though, because Lady Isabella claimed his attention by asking him to pour her a glass of sherry.

Maura was left wondering if Ash's latent scruples were coming to the fore. From the very first, he had claimed his honor wouldn't allow him to seduce her, and it would hardly be the act of a gentleman to take her virginity. Or perhaps he just didn't believe that she was truly serious about wanting to be his lover in full.

If so, she would simply have to convince him, Maura concluded, beset by conflicting feelings of nervousness and anticipation about the night to come.

Ash could not have explained his hesitation to Maura, for he wasn't certain he understood it himself. There was no question that he wanted to make love to her; he did, badly. Yet he wasn't pleased with her reasons for deciding to become his lover.

Maura wasn't committing herself to a future with him or planning for their betrothal to result in marriage. In fact, it seemed evident that she meant to bolt as soon as her need for him was over.

When she admitted him to her bedchamber an hour

later, the fleeting smile Maura gave him only confirmed his suspicions. She was tense and on edge, he realized as she quietly closed the door behind him and backed away. Not precisely the reception he wanted.

Ash remained standing by the door as he took stock of her appearance. Maura wore a simple batiste nightgown, and he could see shadows of womanly curves through the delicate fabric. The room was dim, lit only by a low-burning lamp and the hearth fire, but the golden flames lent an ethereal glow to her ivory skin and gilded the fair hair that flowed down her back.

In return, Maura noted his brocade dressing gown, which he wore over his trousers, and clasped her hands together as if to bolster her courage.

"I see this was a mistake," Ash murmured. "You are having second thoughts."

"No, not at all."

"Then why do you look as if you fear my ravishment?"

"I don't fear it. . . . It is just that . . . well, you seemed so reluctant to accept my invitation that I knew I would have to take the initiative and seduce *you*, but I am not experienced at seduction, and I worry that I may botch the whole thing."

At her rushed, breathless explanation, a surge of tender amusement stirred inside Ash, yet her reply still didn't satisfy him. "Your nervousness doesn't explain why you only now decided we should become lovers."

"I told you why. We may only have a few days left together before we go our separate ways, and I want to make the most of them."

Her conviction that they would be going their separate ways did not sit well with Ash, yet he couldn't refute her rationale. Nor could he claim that bedding Maura would make any difference to their current relationship, or to their future. Just because they became lovers did not mean they had to marry. If he took her now, he was not necessarily sealing their fate forever.

"I want to be with you, Ash," she added when he was silent. "Even if it won't last. Please, stay with me tonight."

"Not unless you are certain of your own mind."

"I am certain. I am four and twenty and I am unlikely to ever marry. I don't want to die a barren spinster without ever knowing what it is like to have a lover."

As declarations went, that was unsatisfying also, although he should be pleased that she had finally let down her guard with him enough to give him her body. And even if she wasn't professing her undying devotion to him, he couldn't force himself to turn down her offer. It felt natural and right being with Maura, and he could finally sate his powerful, possessive desire for her.

However, there were other considerations. "You realize that if there is a child, we would have to wed?"

"But there won't be a child. I know how to prevent that from happening."

Crossing to her bedside table, she opened a drawer and drew out a small pouch. He knew exactly what the pouch contained since two of his former mistresses had relied on the same precautions.

"Sponges? Where did you get those?"

Her blush suggested embarrassment. "It doesn't matter."

She was right, he conceded. It didn't matter how she had learned a Cyprian's tricks. And even without sponges, he could withdraw from her body to keep his seed from taking root, if he found the willpower. . . .

His continued silence made Maura frown, though. "I did not expect you to refuse my invitation, Ash. Do you not want to make love to me?"

"Certainly I do. I would have to be dead not to want it."

"Then why are you waiting?" she demanded in a disgruntled, impatient tone. "I should not have to beg and plead with a rake like you."

Ash felt a quiver of tender laughter deep in his chest. "No, you shouldn't. Very well then, you are welcome to seduce me."

She still looked discomfited by his suggestion. "What should I do?"

"You can begin by kissing me."

Dutifully she took a step closer and raised her face to his. Her warm, soft lips were pliant and willing, yet he could feel the tension in her body when he divested Maura of her nightdress and tossed it aside.

Ash began talking to ease her nervousness as he shed his own clothing, starting with his robe. "I confess surprise that you are taking such care to prevent conception. You don't want children of your own?"

The diversion seemed to work, for her expression immediately softened. "Yes, I do want children, although not outside of marriage. I've helped to birth any number of foals and have seen the miracle firsthand. It is the most amazing thing imaginable."

"I will take your word for it."

"Have you never seen a foal being born?"

Her question somehow seemed endearing, as if it was perfectly common for a genteel young lady to know about such things as equine birth.

"I can't say that I have."

"You have missed out on a remarkable experience. When a foal tries to rise on its spindly little legs to take its first steps toward its mother . . . well, there is nothing more precious."

Ash smiled to himself as he projected his thoughts into the future. If Maura was half as good with children as she was with horses, she would make a wonderful mother.

He very much liked the idea of Maura being the mother of his children, Ash thought as he paused for a moment to look his fill of her. She was perfect, from her ripe breasts, to her slender waist, to her gently flaring hips, to her creamy thighs, to her long, shapely calves and feet. He could picture her lovely body swollen with his son or daughter—an image that warmed him to his core.

It crossed his mind that pregnancy would bind Maura to him, but he knew she had to come to him by her own choice, of her own free will. He intended to influence her decision, however, by making her crave him as much as he craved her.

Sitting on the edge of the bed, Ash removed his slippers and stockings and trousers, and when he finished undressing, he beckoned to Maura. "Come here, sweeting."

When she obeyed, he drew her between his spread thighs, bringing his naked loins fully against hers.

The hot shock of contact made her draw in a sharp breath . . . a sound that was repeated when he reached out and fondled one nipple lightly. It stiffened and seemed to thrust out against his fingers.

Her nervousness had dissipated somewhat at his first caress, but not enough, Ash knew. Wanting to distract her further, he lowered his mouth to her tantalizing breasts, suckling her as his hand swept downward to the blond curls between her thighs. When he fingered the damp folds at her apex, her breathless moan told him he had succeeded in making Maura forget any trepidation she'd felt at offering her body to him. And when he found the nub of her sex, her body jolted.

She clutched at his shoulders, uttering his name in a pleading rasp.

"Easy, love," he murmured in soft reassurance, then went on stroking the exquisitely sensitive flesh. In only moments she tilted her head back.

Feeling her helpless trembling, Ash gently thrust a finger into her silken warmth. Maura whimpered in pleasure. He slid a second finger into her, pushing deeper, and she gasped, clamping her thighs around his caressing hand.

Sucking again on her stiffened nipple, he kept up the arousing rhythm with his fingers, probing and withdrawing, until her hips strained restlessly against his hand, instinctively seeking relief from the feverish passion he was building within her. He could feel the heat rising from her flushed skin, hear her rasping pants as she reached the brink of climax. A heartbeat later, he felt her jerk and twist with sweet convulsions until she fell limply against him.

Satisfied for the moment, Ash slid his arms around her and held her until her tremors subsided.

When finally she regained a measure of strength and stirred against him, he drew back to gaze into her gold-flecked eyes. "Do you still want to continue?"

"Yes," Maura whispered. "The sponges . . ."

"Allow me."

Gathering her in his arms, he lifted her onto the bed to lie beside him, then proceeded to wet a sponge with liquid from the vial. Then he made her open for him, parting her moist flesh to slide the sponge within her woman's passage.

She was wet silk between her legs, her body already prepared for his taking. In response, Ash felt his shaft clench with savage need, yet he knew he had to take intense care in satisfying Maura and bringing her to pleasure.

"We need to go slowly," he murmured. "I want to be gentle for your first time."

In answer, she gazed up at him trustingly.

Calling on all his willpower, he began the exquisite task of claiming her. His caresses were slow and erotic, designed to tempt and promise and arouse. First he cupped her breasts, defining their shape, molding her softness. Then he found her molten heat below, enticing her hips into an undulating movement.

Hunger danced in the air between them, while firelight glowed in her eyes.

When Ash slid his thigh between hers, however, he hesitated. He was burning with lust, desire, need, yet having Maura beneath him like this filled him with an immense tenderness. As he gazed down at her beautiful features, the feelings rioting through him were more powerful than any he had ever experienced, his mind and body burning with a fire of enchantment.

Similar feelings were flooding Maura. She wanted Ash, ached for him, yet he was controlling the pace, deliberately wielding his seductive powers again, weaving a spell to make her helpless with desire. A shiver stole through her, while a sweet fever rose and spread through her veins.

His eyes seared her like naked flame, making heat invade every part of her. With deliberate care, he eased over her, spreading her thighs with his own.

The tenderness in his eyes was as devastating as the wildness. When he entered her partway, she drew a sharp breath. For a long moment, Ash remained still, feathering soft kisses over her flushed face, her eyelids, allowing her to grow accustomed to his alien hardness stretching her, filling her. As her tension eased, he pressed in a bit further, progressing in slow increments, until finally he was sheathed in her virginal tightness.

"Am I hurting you?" he asked.

"No," she lied breathlessly, and yet her body was softening, warming around him. Every part of her throbbed at the feel of Ash's hard flesh joined with hers.

After another long moment, he began moving gently inside her, using his consummate skill to coax a sensual response from her. When he thrust even deeper, Maura's thighs parted to accept more of him, and she tentatively lifted her hips to follow his rhythm.

Soon she felt a hot, coiling tension rising and spiraling through her. Soul-scorching heat seared her from the bright center of sensation at her core.

She felt the answering fire in Ash's body, heard the wanting in his husky voice as he grated out her name. He seemed to be having difficultly controlling his own need, just as she was.

When he withdrew and sank into her again, she whimpered, wordlessly pleading, helplessly needing. . . . He thrust harder, and Maura suddenly erupted.

Her senses exploded. She moaned and clung to Ash, her entire body shaking. Claiming her mouth once more, he kissed her, capturing her rasping cries of bliss and wonder as he surrendered to his own climax deep within her. Maura felt his violent shudders, yet she welcomed his urgency.

When at last Ash went still, she lay there beneath him, dazed and trembling. It might have been an eternity before she regained enough awareness to realize that he was still buried within her while she pulsed with incredible pleasure.

Wishing their joining could last forever, Maura pressed her face into the smooth, muscular wall of his chest, savoring the warm glide of her skin against his, the feel of his heart beating.

His tenderness made her ache with longing. It was the tenderness that affected her most, the care he took with her, even though it was his passion that had swept her into a whirlwind of fire.

When he raised his head to gaze down at her, the fire was still there, burning hot and bright in his eyes. She felt a tremendous pleasure that he seemed awed by what had just happened between them. His need called to something feminine and powerful inside her.

Without speaking, he smoothed a tendril back from

her forehead and kissed her again with exquisite gentleness, as if cherishing the taste of her. The soft mating of their breath made her heart melt with tenderness. She let the feeling pour through her and warm the lonely places inside her.

A moment later, Maura nearly protested when Ash eased away and rolled onto his side, but thankfully he only pulled her against his naked body and lay there with her, their arms and legs braided like longtime lovers.

"I will stay with you for a few hours."

Maura nodded, gravely disappointed that they could not spend the entire night together, but knowing that Ash would have to return to his own rooms to avoid being seen.

She wished with all her heart that it could be different. Making love to Ash had made her feel whole, complete, treasured—which was a foolish and dangerous sentiment, Maura reminded herself.

She no longer had any doubt that Ash desired her. But passion was not love, and if they continued such intimacy, the risk of losing her heart to him would only increase exponentially. He was luring her into his web of enchantment, making her dream and wish and yearn for things she ought not even be thinking about.

With a heavy sigh, Maura closed her eyes and buried her face in his warm chest. She was glad their pretend betrothal might soon be over. For as much as she hated returning to being alone, it was better to be alone and lonely than to endure the pain and heartbreak of an unrequited love.

Chapter Eighteen

To Maura's delight and gratitude, the musical evening to showcase her stepsisters' talents proved a smashing success. Skye had converted the grand Traherne ballroom in Berkeley Square into a recital hall and arranged for professional musicians to complement the amateurs, with a poetry reading by a renowned actress to round out the concert program. She had also spared no effort or expense to fill the mansion with guests who could benefit the young Misses Collyer, including a profusion of eligible young men who might be potential suitors.

Skye was playing fairy godmother to her stepsisters, Maura knew, just as Katharine had taken on the role for *her*. Once again she felt the warmth and affection of Ash's family, who were closing ranks around her as if she were one of their own.

The girls did indeed shine. Their modish new gowns helped give them enough confidence to overcome shyness and nerves and deliver a fresh and honest performance. When Hannah sang in a sweet, pure voice and Lucy skillfully accompanied her on the pianoforte,

Maura watched with the same love and pride as Priscilla. Both girls looked so animated, they seemed quite pretty.

Afterward, a bevy of young gentlemen flocked around them, asking to be presented. Skye had given Hannah and Lucy much-needed lessons in conversing and appearing at ease in male company, but their popularity was also enhanced by the persistent, if false, rumors that they both had sizable dowries.

Maura had never seen her stepsisters so happy, although she herself would have deplored being displayed on the Marriage Mart in such a blatant fashion. As Lord Beaufort's future marchioness, however, she had more than her share of people fawning over her.

Ash had remained by her side during the performance, but during the intermission before supper, they separated to pursue their own goals. Maura was charged with charming her stepmother this evening, while Ash was bent on enchanting every female in the company on behalf of her stepsisters, particularly the most socially influential dowagers.

Maura couldn't help following his progress in the crowd, or noting the charisma he exuded. Becoming lovers had given her a heightened awareness of Ash . . . of his touch, his voice, his laughter, his smile. And as their gazes locked across the room, the memory of passion still shimmered between them. Heat flooded Maura as she remembered him moving inside her, the richness of him filling her.

In truth, she had been in a daze the entire day after spending much of the night in his arms. Then shortly before the evening began, he'd taken her aside and stolen a kiss that made her blood sizzle. It was absurd how easily he was able to melt her with his kisses and reduce her to such raw, exposed need.

That thought was foremost in Maura's mind when Ash flashed her a slow, intimate smile that pierced her heart.

Averting her gaze, she deliberately shied away from analyzing his dazzling impact too closely and instead tried to discipline her rioting thoughts to focus on the task at hand. She had promised to do her utmost to recruit Priscilla as an ally.

As expected, Viscount Deering had not attended the musical, but Priscilla had. Pris's greeting at the start of the evening had seemed remarkably chastened. Evidently she regretted acting so hastily in cutting ties with the future Marchioness of Beaufort, no doubt because she wanted to remain in the marquis's good graces, since his patronage could benefit her daughters more than a mere viscount's could.

Maura was about to go in search of her stepmother when Priscilla sought her out first.

"I wish to thank you, Maura," Priscilla said in a tone that was amazingly contrite. "Not only did you devise this splendid opportunity for my daughters to consort with high society, you persuaded Lord Beaufort to fund their dowries."

Maura barely managed to hide her surprise. She had thought the whispers about the Collyer sisters being heiresses were completely fabricated. "You give me too much credit for his generosity, Priscilla."

"Oh, no. I am certain he would never have offered if not for you. He promised to add five thousand pounds apiece to the portions your father left them."

The large sums partly explained the eagerness of the

gentlemen who currently surrounded Hannah and Lucy, Maura realized. She was supremely grateful to Ash for his kindness to her stepsisters, although wondered how she would ever repay such a gift, and exasperated that once again he'd acted behind her back to avoid her objections. No doubt he wanted to bribe Priscilla into supporting their case against Deering, but even so, he should have discussed the matter with her first.

She would vocalize her opinions to him later, however. Meanwhile, she had a job to do with her stepmother.

"I expect you are relieved," Maura observed. "Their having independent fortunes should bode well for their marriage prospects, as well as help to protect them against Deering's threats."

"I truly hope that is the case." Pris hesitated before adding unexpectedly, "I owe you an apology, Maura. I never wanted to take your precious horse from you. I only believed I had no choice."

Maura eyed her with skepticism. "Of course you had a choice."

Strangely, Priscilla suddenly looked distressed. "Perhaps so, but I thought I was doing the right thing for my daughters. And now that odious man—" She broke off and bit her lip.

"What odious man?"

Glancing around the crowded ballroom, Priscilla lowered her voice. "Never mind. This is not the place to discuss it."

"No," Maura agreed, "but there are numerous rooms nearby where we may be private. I need to speak to you about an urgent matter in any case."

When Pris nodded with great reluctance, Maura led her from the ballroom and down a corridor to a quiet parlor.

"By odious man, did you mean Deering?" she asked then. At her stepmother's troubled silence, Maura tried another tack. "If you truly wish to apologize to me, I know how you could make amends."

"How?" Pris asked cautiously.

"If Deering continues to claim ownership of Emperor, you could confirm my version of events—that you sold my horse without my knowledge or consent."

"I don't know if I can do that, Maura. It is more . . . complicated than you realize."

"Then why don't you explain it to me?"

Maura was startled to see Pris twist her gloved hands together, since the beautiful widow was never one to wring her hands. Then even more surprising, Priscilla looked away. "I am ashamed to admit what I did."

"You are speaking in riddles," Maura pressed, trying to quell her impatience.

"You must understand, I was under great duress. I thought Viscount Deering and I had . . . an understanding."

"What sort of understanding?"

"You see . . . in exchange for purchasing your horse, he promised to pave the way for my daughters' debut in society. I knew his patronage would significantly minimize the taint of scandal against their stepfather—"

"You have told me all this before, Priscilla."

"Yes . . . well . . ." Pris took a deep breath and met her gaze again. "I have not told you what happened last week after you stole— After you took back your horse. Deering gave me an ultimatum. He would only lend his support if I . . . if I shared his bed."

Maura stared at her stepmother. "You slept with Deering to curry his favor?"

"Not willingly." Her lower jaw trembled. "That cursed man made me do it."

Maura had no idea what to say. Priscilla was so alluring, it wasn't surprising that Deering had coveted her as an object to add to his collection of prize possessions. But for her to have paid so exorbitant a price? She must have been desperate.

At Maura's speechlessness, Priscilla sent her a pleading look. "I was an utter fool, I know. I thought we had a bargain, and instead Deering reneged on his promise and blackmailed me. He said that unless I complied with his new terms, he would make it known that I had shared my favors just like any whore."

Maura shook her head in disbelief. She had always suspected Priscilla capable of using her body to gain her ends, but her seductive wiles had backfired this time when she'd tangled with a man far more ruthless and dishonorable than she.

"Maura, you must realize . . . I only was thinking of my daughters. After your father died, their matrimonial prospects were nonexistent. There was no one to protect us or stand up for us. We were entirely on our own, with no one to advance our entrée into the ton and no way to finance the vast expense of a Season."

That last complaint struck a discordant chord in Maura. "Papa left you the London house and a significant income, enough to keep you in comfort if you had been in the least frugal."

"But you know I am not frugal. I sold your horse to

fund my daughters' debuts. Then when Emperor disappeared, Deering blamed me. I was afraid he would destroy our lives entirely, Maura, so I did as he demanded." Bowing her head, Priscilla covered her face with her hands. "I am so ashamed. . . . I felt so . . . soiled afterward."

She was weeping by now. Those disconsolate tears were very real, Maura realized.

Unexpectedly, she felt a strong measure of sympathy for the woman who had been almost her adversary for more than a decade. Priscilla was Deering's victim, too. And she seemed genuinely remorseful now.

Moving away, Maura sank down in a nearby chair. She hadn't thought Deering could be any more repulsive, but this latest revelation was utterly appalling. First he had brought about the disgrace and death of an innocent man, then forced the man's widow to steal and whore for him.

Maura's hands curled into fists as a wealth of dark emotion rose inside her along with the echo of old grief. The memory of her father dying in shame made her sick and furious all over again, as did her own guilt for being unable to save him.

"I do understand, Priscilla," she whispered, her voice holding anguish. Clearing her throat then, Maura vowed to keep a tight rein on her emotions and began again. "Blackmail is Deering's weapon of choice. He did the same thing with Papa. He said he would withdraw his accusations of cheating if Papa would agree to sell Emperor to him."

"I know," Priscilla sniffled.

Her response made Maura's heart twist. "Deering actually admitted that Papa was innocent?"

Priscilla raised her head, showing eyes that were red and swollen. "Not in so many words, but he implied it."

"But you sometimes act as if you believed his lies. As if Papa were guilty."

Arresting her sobs, Pris swallowed. "Of course I know Deering lied. Noah was innocent all along."

Maura returned her stepmother's gaze steadily. The acknowledgment coming after all this time was welcome. Yet it was still hard for her to believe in Pris's complete conversion. "How can I believe your change of heart, Priscilla? You wed my father for his fortune."

"I don't deny that," she said quietly. "I was poor, and yes, I married Noah for monetary reasons. But I came to love him, Maura. He was kind and generous and he did not deserve the end he received." She took a shuddering breath. "I wronged him, and I wronged you too, Maura, from the very first. I was jealous of the bond you had with him . . . of the advantages you had over my daughters. You were so beautiful and poised and stood to inherit your father's estate. That is no excuse for the cold way I treated you, I know. And truly, I regret being in league with Deering against you, Maura. If you could bring yourself to forgive me . . . I should like to try and begin anew."

Maura wasn't certain she could be entirely so forgiving, but she did want to be on better terms with Priscilla. "Very well, we can try."

"I sincerely want to make it up to you, Maura."

She hesitated before making her suggestion. "If so, then you will help me clear Papa's name."

Wiping away her tears, Priscilla grimaced. "I don't

know if that is even possible. You've made a mortal enemy of Deering."

Maura's gaze hardened. "On the contrary, he made a mortal enemy of *me* two years ago when he destroyed my father."

"He is still a devious force to be reckoned with . . . and I still fear what he could do to my daughters." She shuddered. "I can't bear to think of him anywhere near them."

"I think you needn't worry about Hannah and Lucy any longer. Lord Beaufort and his family will see that they are safe from Deering and that their futures are secure."

After a long moment, Priscilla released a shaky sigh. "What would you have me do?"

"If you would be willing to make his dastardly scheming public, we could sue him in a court of law."

She look dismayed. "Who would believe me? No one would take my word over his. And my shame would come out. It could ruin me, Maura. I haven't your noble connections to champion me. There must be another way."

Although reluctant, Maura had to agree. Priscilla's testimony against a nobleman of Deering's stature would not carry substantial weight. They would have to find another way to bring him down—which meant that Ash's plan to expose the viscount's perfidious machinations *had* to succeed.

Just then, a rap sounded on the parlor's open door. When Ash entered, Priscilla looked flustered at his presence, no doubt realizing that her tawdry tale would come out. After a pleading look at Maura, she curtsied awkwardly to the marquis and hurried from the room.

"Well?" Ash asked.

Maura shook her head as she rose to her feet. "It is even worse than we feared. Deering is a villain of the first order." Her hands fisted again as she quickly explained how her stepmother had been blackmailed.

"This is no longer about only restoring my father's honor," Maura said urgently. "We have to render Deering powerless to hurt anyone else."

Ash's eyes reflected sympathy, but there was real anger in the set of his jaw and in his tone. "Have no fear, love. Deering's predilection for preying on the weak will end tomorrow night."

He gave her a swift kiss and took her arm. "Come, we need to return to the drawing room. Supper has been served."

He made it sound so simple, Maura thought as she accompanied Ash from the parlor. But she was willing to trust him when he declared that they would prevail.

The buffet table was laden with tempting fare, and much of the company was already gorging on rich lobster patties and delicate meringues. Maura and Ash filled their plates and carried them to an empty table, where he seated her. While Ash was occupied with having a footman pour glasses of wine, Maura's stepsisters passed by her chair and halted long enough to speak to her.

"This is so famous, Maura," Lucy exclaimed, her eyes shining. "We cannot thank you enough—"

"Yes," Hannah interrupted reverently. "We have you to thank for our good fortune, dearest Maura. No fewer than five gentlemen have asked to call on us tomorrow."

"And several of them have been fighting over the privilege of taking supper with us now," Lucy added. "Mama is to chaperone us, of course. Look, she is waving to us now. We had best hurry, Hannah."

Maura followed Lucy's gaze to see Priscilla beckoning them.

Before Hannah complied, however, she leaned down and whispered to Maura. "I keep pinching myself to see if I am dreaming. We have already thanked Lady Skye and Lady Katharine profusely. But please, will you convey our thanks to Lord Beaufort, Maura? I can see why he won your hand and heart."

Both girls quickly kissed her cheek, then hastened to join their mother and their new beaux.

Maura sat frozen in place, though, the echo of Hannah's innocent observation reverberating in her ears.

Surely it wasn't possible.

Her gaze lifted to seek out Ash's tall, powerful form. The roaring in her ears grew louder as the truth sank in. Ash had indeed won her heart. Against her will, against all her better judgment, she had fallen in love with him.

Jolted by the realization, Maura shook her head weakly. Ash had seduced her heart without even trying, luring her into his web of enchantment over the past week, surmounting all her defenses when she had been especially vulnerable.

Her most powerful dream was that she would find love and family and an end to loneliness, and he had shown her explicitly what it meant to be part of a passionate, loving family. She couldn't help loving the Wilde cousins, Ash most of all.

Yet she had no earthly idea what she would do

about her shocking acknowledgment. Ash didn't love her. He was merely playing at the *game* of love, exploring the theory that they could be legendary lovers. As for winning her hand, their betrothal was only a charade, merely a means of defeating a common enemy.

Maura shook her head again, but when Ash returned with their wine and took his place beside her, she realized that any attempt at denial was futile.

It was far too late to protect her heart, for she had foolishly gone and fallen in love with her prince, just as Cinderella had done in the timeless fairy tale.

Chapter Nineteen

Somehow Maura managed to hide her newly-realized feelings of love from Ash for the rest of the evening and during the next day. Too much was at stake for either of them to be distracted by the uncertainty of their future together—although she promised herself that as soon as the issue of her father's vindication was settled, she would squarely face the matter of her feckless heart.

The following night, Lord Jack escorted her to Sutter's gaming establishment. Maura had refused to be left behind, and Ash permitted her participation, saying that she needed the satisfaction of seeing her longtime nemesis exposed. For propriety's sake, however, she went incognito, wearing a hooded domino and mask as genteel ladies often did when they wished to conceal their identities.

Sutter's, Maura realized from the moment they were admitted, was a prosperous club, the decor sumptuous but surprisingly tasteful. There were several large rooms crowded with elegantly dressed gamesters and patrons of both sexes being served refreshments by attentive waiters. She noted a roulette wheel, as well as various card games in progress—some, such as faro, overseen by professional dealers.

Ash was already there, since he had arrived early in order to put his plan in motion. Maura's heart leapt when she spied him sitting at the green baize card table across from Viscount Deering.

It seemed that the game had already begun.

When she took a step closer, Jack firmly grasped her arm and guided her toward the far wall.

"You agreed to observe from a distance, remember?" he reminded Maura. "We don't want Deering to know you were complicit in his downfall, and if I allowed him to see you, Ash would have my head."

Nodding reluctantly, she let Jack seat her so that she could watch the game from well back in the crowd. Shortly, he placed a glass of Madeira in her hand, yet Maura couldn't drink with the knot of anxiety tightening her stomach. Even from a distance she could see that Deering's expression was one of smug, supercilious arrogance. He clearly expected to win—and the next few hours would prove whether or not his confidence was justified.

Ash completely understood Maura's compulsion to be present at the gaming club. He would have felt the same urgency defending his own parents, or any other member of his family, for that matter.

He also understood the imperative for him to succeed. In playing the viscount, not only was he risking the loss of Maura's prize stallion, he was responsible for exonerating her beloved father. A heavy onus indeed.

Vingt-un was partly a game of skill and partly of luck. After being dealt two cards each, the players attempted to reach a combination closest to twenty-one points without going over that number, with court cards counting as ten points, face cards as their numerical value, and aces as either one or eleven points. The deal changed between players, depending on who won the last hand, and the dealer had the advantage of odds.

Upon arriving, Ash had met with the club owner, George Sutter, to insure the game wouldn't be rigged ahead of time by any other parties. Jack had vouched for Sutter's honesty, but Ash wanted the two new decks of playing cards examined by a reliable witness and noted to be free of disfigurements of any kind. He hoped to catch Deering at marking cards during the evening, since a repetition of the viscount's game with Noah Collyer two years earlier would be highly suspect. There was also the possibility that Deering would find a way to accuse Ash himself of cheating, just as he'd done with Collyer.

Ash knew he would have to keep his wits sharp if he hoped to expose Deering for what he was: An unscrupulous bastard who preyed on the vulnerable. But for Maura's sake, he was prepared to do whatever it took. One way or the other, he intended to flush the viscount out.

The game began innocently enough. The cards remained clean at first, Ash was convinced. But as the night wore on, faint scratches started appearing in the lower left corners of certain cards, which led him to conclude that using a sleight of hand, Deering was scoring the backs of the court cards with his signet ring.

It was the final straw for Ash. He had no qualms about employing similar unprincipled means, not necessarily to win the game, but to rile and unsettle Deering as much as possible.

The next time Ash had the deal, he marked several face cards with the same scratch, so that eventually Deering exceeded his point limit when he'd obviously expected a much different result.

When Deering eyed him suspiciously, Ash asked in an innocent tone, "Is something amiss?"

"No, nothing," the nobleman replied, scowling faintly, although he must have known he'd been tricked into playing the wrong card.

Ash flashed a slow, taunting smile to drive home his victory, which earned him a more perceptible scowl.

It was perhaps a quarter hour later when Ash managed to identify the ace of hearts—the same card that Deering had once used to accuse Collyer—and conceal it beneath his coat sleeve before giving over the deal. Then, with his own sleight of hand, Ash flicked the ace beneath the table to land at his opponent's feet.

By then, several curious players had gathered around the noblemen to watch their contest, including one of the club's paid dealers. Thus, Ash had an impartial audience when a moment later, he made a deliberate show of spotting the fallen card beside Deering's evening shoe. After leaning to one side of the table and peering down, Ash froze as if unable to believe what he was seeing.

Frowning, he pointed to the stray card to draw the attention of everyone around them. "You seem to have misplaced part of the deck, Deering," he commented as he bent down to retrieve the card.

Upon turning it faceup on the baize surface, Ash let his jaw harden. "How very convenient that you should have a spare ace lying around," he drawled.

Deering stared at the card as if he'd seen a ghost.

"How did that just happen to fall there within your reach?" Ash pressed.

"I have no earthly idea how it came to be there on the floor," the viscount declared, his expression indignant.

"No? Do you deny that you dropped it there so you could play it later when you most needed it?"

Deering lifted his gaze to skewer Ash with an icy look. "Of course I deny I dropped it."

Ash raised a skeptical eyebrow. "Forgive me if I fail to believe you. You have made a habit of employing the ace of hearts to your own ends before this. I recall this same card was used to accuse Mr. Noah Collyer of fixing your game two years ago."

The viscount's cold glare intensified. "What are you saying, Beaufort?"

"That you have been cheating outright since the beginning of our game tonight."

There were numerous gasps from the spectators standing around the table.

"How *dare* you," the viscount ground out, his defensiveness turning to anger.

"How dare *I*?" Ash countered in a cool voice. "I could ask the same of you, Deering. I have observed you closely all evening. You have been scoring the backs of particular cards this entire time."

He turned over the ace of hearts to display the back, where the plain red surface was visibly marred by a scratch in the lower left corner. "Our proprietor will vouch that both decks were free of defects before the game began, so this identifying mark had to have been made during our play. There are identical scratches on other court cards as well."

At first Deering made no reply, but his livid complexion suggested that he was seething. "You could just as easily have been the one to score the cards," he finally retorted. "Indeed, I suspect *you* are the guilty party, since you are the one who pointed out the marks."

A valid argument, Ash agreed silently before attempting to direct the blame back where it belonged. "That doesn't explain the ace lying at your feet. Did you actually think to get away again with the same fraudulent scheme you used against Collyer?"

His face contorted with fury, Deering uttered a curse that was audible throughout the entire room. A hush had fallen, as if a blanket had been lowered over the crowd to snuff out all frivolity and good spirits. The tension in the club was now palpable.

Ash smiled without humor. "Perhaps I am mistaken. I would be willing to retract my charge now if you admit that you were inaccurate when you accused Collyer two years ago."

"Collyer? What the devil do you care about him?"

"A good man's reputation suffered mightily that night. You could easily clear up matters by explaining the truth of what happened. Even if it comes posthumously for Collyer, his family will be relieved to have his name exonerated."

"What of my reputation? You are impugning my good name, sir!"

By now Deering was almost choleric, yet apparently the allegation of cheating was not enough to compel him to change his account of the game with Maura's father.

Frustrated by his failure, Ash continued pressing. "The similarities between the games are too obvious to believe anything other than duplicity."

His charge had the desired effect, for Deering practically spat out his reply. "You leave me no choice but to defend my honor. You will give me satisfaction, Beaufort."

Ash nodded, gratified that he had goaded Deering into issuing the challenge, since it gave him greater leverage over the viscount. "I am happy to oblige," he responded.

Out of the corner of his eye, Ash saw Maura surge to her feet and take a step toward their table, only to be prevented from approaching by his brother, Jack.

Shifting his gaze from her, Ash glanced around at the crowd. "Pray, give us privacy," he ordered with a sharpness that sent the observers backing away.

"Shall we settle the matter with pistols or swords?" he asked Deering then.

"Pistols," Deering snapped. "You should name your seconds so they may arrange the particulars."

"I prefer to decide all the particulars tonight," Ash countered. "Of course we will have our seconds present to watch the duel to insure that honor is satisfied, but I see no reason to delay our meeting. After first light tomorrow should suffice, say half past six . . . unless you dislike rising at such an early hour. As for place, the field below Granger Hill is a prime location."

He could see Deering internally debating a reply. Dueling was illegal, so the fewer people involved the better. The gentlemen's code required that each primary appoint a second to act as emissary and arrange the details of time and place. Normally at least a full day was allowed to pass to give a cooling-off period in case common sense prevailed over charges made in the heat of anger. But Ash wanted to pressure Deering as much as possible, since the threat of a duel was likely the only way to get him to confess his role against Collyer.

Not surprisingly, Deering faltered, as if suddenly regretting that he'd issued his challenge so hastily. He well knew that Ash was accounted an excellent shot. Yet Deering was highly skilled as well, so the match would not be totally uneven. And he could not back down now without losing face.

As if coming to the same conclusion, the viscount gritted his teeth and gave a brusque nod. "I will rely on Pelham as my second."

His choice of such a reputable gentleman was unexpected, but Ash had no right to question it. "I plan to ask my cousin, Traherne."

"Very well, I will see you early tomorrow morning."

Standing, Deering turned on his heel and strode off, sending unwary bystanders scurrying from his path.

A moment later Maura appeared beside Ash, with Jack trailing close behind her. She still wore her mask, but her distress was audible in the tone of her voice when she launched into a protest. "Merciful heaven, you were not supposed to challenge him to a duel, Ash!"

"He challenged me," he corrected.

Her scoffing sound held a measure of disgust. "You are arguing semantics. I know very well that you purposely maneuvered him into dueling with you."

Realizing Maura was growing wise to his methods, Ash almost smiled. "Just as a last resort. Accepting his challenge was the only way to force his confession. If I had been able to catch Deering dead to rights and prove unequivocally that he'd marked the cards tonight, his cheating would have been publicly exposed. But I only managed to cast doubt on his honesty."

"Even so, you cannot duel. You have to withdraw."

"Whyever should I?"

Maura's lovely jaw dropped in disbelief for a moment. "Because he could very well shoot you. He might even kill you! I never meant for this to go so far. Vindicating my father is not worth risking your life."

"It is to me, love. But it may not come to a duel. Deering is a coward at heart. I suspect he will back down before it comes to actual shooting."

"But what if he does not? You could *die*."

"And so could Deering."

Maura glared at Ash with mingled dismay and frustration. "If you kill him, you will have to flee the country, have you considered that?"

"I wish you had more faith in my skills, darling. I will only aim to wound him."

"That does not reassure me in the least!" Maura retorted fiercely.

Rising from the card table, Ash pressed a finger to her lips to hush her. "Calm yourself, sweetheart. Deering could not retreat just now in front of so many onlookers, but by tomorrow morning he may change his mind. If he wishes to call off the duel, though, he will have to meet my terms and offer a public retraction of the charges against your father."

Without giving Maura a chance to argue further, he shifted his gaze to his brother. "Jack, you will take her home? I need to visit Quinn and arrange for him to second me."

At Jack's nod, Ash turned away. Yet feeling Maura's troubled gaze following him, he knew he hadn't heard the last of her objections.

Chapter Twenty

Maura could scarcely believe the turn her ongoing battle with Deering had taken. It was one thing to try and expose his treacherous connivances by challenging him at the gaming table. It was quite another to shift the challenge to the dueling field, where it could result in Ash's death.

She found no ally in his brother, however, for Lord Jack supported Ash's decision to meet Deering over pistols early the next morning.

"I wish you would speak to Ash and make him see reason," Maura implored as Jack escorted her home.

"I think you are worrying needlessly," he responded in an easy tone. "Ash can take care of himself."

"It is no surprise that you would take his side," she muttered. "Dueling is something only a reckless, hard-headed Wilde would do."

"Did you expect anything else? Our family is known for living up to our name."

Jack's careless grin rubbed Maura the wrong way, even knowing that the fiery, passionate Wilde cousins were proud of their legacy.

"This is no joking matter," she retorted irritably.

Jack seemed unfazed by her fuming. "True, but Ash has never been one to retreat because of a little danger. Besides, he has vowed to defeat Deering, and he won't go back on his word." Jack cast her a speculative glance. "You must admit it is rather princely of Ash—even heroic, some might say—to fight to restore your father's honor."

His not-so-subtle reminder of the legendary lover role Ash was playing did nothing to allay Maura's frustration, nor did his casual dismissal of the risk. Thus, Jack left her at Grosvenor Square without settling the argument.

Katharine was out for the evening with Lady Isabella, and Lord Cornelius had already retired. Maura went directly upstairs to her bedchamber, where she paced the floor and debated what to do. She was still highly upset and worried for Ash. She couldn't live with herself if harm came to him. If she hadn't realized her love for him before this, her gut-tightening fear now would have enlightened her.

She would have to think of some way of convincing Ash to withdraw, Maura decided. Yes, she wanted her father's name cleared, but she wanted much more to keep Ash safe.

A half hour later, she had changed out of her evening gown, yet she still had not calmed down enough to try to sleep. Resolving to make one last attempt to speak to Ash, Maura pulled on a robe over her nightdress and took up a candle, then made her way along the silent corridors to his bedchamber.

She didn't care about being seen by the servants just now. Her reputation wouldn't be worth a farthing to her if she allowed Ash to be killed.

Letting herself inside, she glanced around the masculine chamber, which was done in burgundy and golds. The night was warm enough that a fire wasn't necessary, but even so she shivered as she settled in a wing chair to wait.

It was a long while later before she heard the tread of footsteps out in the corridor. Shortly, the door opened to admit Ash, but he checked on the threshold as soon as he spied her. As if making a decision then, he entered and shut the door softly behind him.

"I suppose you have a good reason for coming to my rooms and risking scandal," he said calmly.

"You know why I am here," Maura replied. "To convince you to abandon this mad duel."

Ash remained silent as he began removing his coat and waistcoat. Supremely frustrated that he intended to ignore her, Maura rose and went to stand before him. Reaching up, she framed his face in her hands and pressed her lips against his.

"Please, Ash, won't you reconsider?" she pleaded.

"I'm sorry, love. We have come too far to turn back now. I will stop when Deering professes your father's innocence and not before."

Maura exhaled a fretful sigh. "Then I will have to try to persuade Deering to withdraw." At Ash's skeptical look, she expounded. "He might, if I give him what he wants . . . my stallion. Your life is more important to me than any horse, even Emperor."

His expression softened as he untied his cravat. "I

am honored, sweetheart. I didn't realize you cared that much."

"Of course I care." She cared *deeply,* Maura added to herself.

"Thank you, but your sacrifice isn't necessary." Ash paused in his undressing to hold her gaze. "You need to trust me, Maura. My plan will work, you will see."

There was nothing brash or cocky about his pronouncement; he was simply convinced he was on the right course. But his self-confidence made her irritation return.

"I do trust you, Ash," she claimed in exasperation. "It is Deering I don't trust."

"I share your feelings. That is another reason to go through with the meeting tomorrow. It will force Deering to fight out in the open. I wouldn't put it past him to employ underhanded means in order to win against me." Ash pulled off his shirt. "I was actually reassured when he chose Lord Pelham as his second. If Deering doesn't back down—which I still contend is a strong possibility—Pelham will be there to act as a reputable witness. In fact, I just spent the past hour hunting down Quinn to act as my second. He will make certain that Pelham is there tomorrow."

"That is hardly reassuring to *me.*"

"Stop fretting, love."

"How can I when you could be going to your death tomorrow?"

"I promise it won't come to that."

He continued shedding his clothing—his evening shoes and stockings, then breeches and drawers. Soon he was sublimely naked. In the soft glow of lamplight,

Maura couldn't help but notice his loins; he was already heavy and aroused, the shaft pulsing and erect between his sinewed thighs.

Contrarily, desire began to shimmer inside her, even before he took her hand and said tenderly, "Come lie with me, Maura."

"Ash . . ." she murmured, a final effort at protest.

"Hush, sweeting."

He was done arguing, Maura realized as he led her toward the bed. He intended to make love to her instead—his way of silencing her. He knew she was helpless in his arms.

He undressed her swiftly, divesting her of her robe and nightshift, then drew her down to lie beside him on the bed and began a sensual assault designed to shred the last remnants of her resistance.

For a while he only caressed her bare breasts. Then his mouth dipped to her swollen nipples. Maura shivered as it closed hot and moist over a sensitive bud. Wet heat pulled her taut inside as Ash suckled her, his tongue laving while his palm slid along the satin of her inner thighs to find the heart of her womanhood.

He aroused her until she was moaning for him, until a desperate fire had built in her yielding, throbbing center. At her urgent pleas for release, he finally mounted her. His hard thighs pressing into her softness, he thrust inside her slick passage with exquisite care, then withdrew in a slow, sensual motion, only to sink slowly into her again.

Settling into a possessive rhythm, he captured her mouth in a searing kiss that compelled her complete surrender. As Maura clung to him, the scent of him filled her senses, the taste of him stole her reason. And as she felt him move inside her, she experienced his spellbinding power again—that special magic only Ash could command. He made her feel whole, complete, as if they had been lovers forever and always would be.

Their whispers and murmurs and moans gave way to cries of passion from their explosive joining. When it was over, they both lay spent and shuddering and flushed with heat.

At last Ash raised himself up on one elbow. Gazing deeply into Maura's eyes, he cradled her cheek. "Don't worry for me, love. I want to do this for you."

His touch was so tender. It warmed her and comforted her and made her heart ache, just as the soft light in his eyes did.

Admitting her resistance totally vanquished, Maura buried her face in his shoulder, yet her emotions were still in turmoil. She couldn't bear to lose Ash, she thought with dismay. Not now, when she had just come to love him so very much.

Ash woke well before dawn, cherishing the feel of Maura's warm, silken body curled against him. Judging by her soft breathing, she was still asleep—a state he hoped to maintain.

He didn't want her waking until after he was gone, for he knew she would try to plead with him again. Yet he intended to follow through with the duel this morning. It was in his power to give Maura what she wanted most in the world, and he wasn't about to give up now. He wanted—needed—to defeat her nemesis for her. If that entailed mortal risk, then so be it. He would die for her, defend her to the death, just as he would for any member of his family.

He considered Maura his family now.

So what did that say about his feelings for her? More crucially, what were her feelings for him?

Maura was concerned for his safety, he knew that without a doubt. It touched him deeply that she was willing to sacrifice her precious stallion for his sake. The trouble was, he wanted more from her. Much more.

Lying here with her now in the dim, predawn light, Ash could acknowledge that he'd crossed a final line last night. He had claimed Maura for his own, with no regrets for any potential consequences. Their joining had felt like a true mating, at least on his part. As far as he was concerned, they were irrevocably bound together.

He was loath to leave her now. He relished waking by Maura's side, reveled in her sweet passion and the incredible pleasure she gave him.

Putting duty before pleasure, however, Ash silently untangled himself from her warm body and eased from the bed. For a moment as he stood gazing, gazing down at her beautiful face in the faint light, that powerful, familiar sense of possessiveness and protectiveness welled up inside him.

Quelling the urge to caress her soft cheek, Ash picked up his clothing from the previous evening and carried the bundle to his dressing room, where he quietly lit a lamp. He checked his pocket watch and noted the time was just after five A.M. More than an hour before he was to meet Deering for their duel.

He dressed and shaved. Then, needing sustenance, Ash went downstairs to the kitchens to raid the pantry for breakfast. He surprised a sleepy scullery maid who was stoking the fire in the hearth. After eating a cold but hearty meal of beef and bread, Ash spent the next half hour in his study, putting some final affairs in order and penning instructions for his family in the event of his hopefully unlikely demise.

When the time drew near, Ash moved to the entrance hall to await the carriage he had ordered for six o'clock. Quinn was to meet him at Granger Hill, so Ash intended to drive directly there. Frankly, he was surprised that his carriage was not already standing at the curb. The footman on duty in the hall had no idea what was taking so long, either.

When five more minutes had passed, Ash felt himself growing impatient, especially since he worried that Maura would wake and come downstairs before he could make his escape. Deciding he would be wiser to depart now, he proceeded to the rear of the house and let himself out.

By then the morning had grown light enough that he didn't need a lantern as he strode down the path to the mews beyond the gardens. Oddly, though, the carriage house was dark, and while the wide doors were open, Ash could detect no sounds of activity from within. Stranger still, he could see that his team of chestnuts was harnessed to his coach, but when he entered the carriage house, there was no sign of his coachman or grooms or stable lads.

"Tom?" Ash called out, but received only silence to his query. His servants were superbly trained and rarely slack in their duties, so their disappearance was not only puzzling but disquieting.

He repeated his coachman's name more loudly, and this time heard a soft groan in reply. His instincts for danger now on full alert, Ash took another step, just as a dark shape came barreling at him across the passageway.

Chapter Twenty-one

The attack caught Ash off guard, and it took him more than a second to react. He felt himself being shoved to the cobblestone pavement, the breath knocked from his lungs. Rolling, he struggled to his feet just in time to ward off a savage blow from a night watchman's baton.

His assailant must have been lying in wait, Ash realized as he tried again to defend himself from the swinging club. When he regained his balance, he lunged forward in a surprise offensive. A lucky blow from his fist managed to knock the lout down, but then another one immediately took his place and was quickly joined by a third.

There were at least three attackers—all armed with batons or cudgels. Big, brawny fellows who looked determined to beat him to a bloody pulp, if not worse.

Raising his fists protectively, Ash danced back out of range, but the two upright thugs came after him at the same time. For what seemed like endless moments he fought off both brutes, while out of the corner of his eye, he saw their even taller comrade lurch to his feet.

Not certain if he could take all three at once, Ash redoubled his efforts, yet he knew he was losing the fight as his shoulders and ribs took the painful brunt of the attack. At the increased ruckus in the carriage house, the nervous horses began snorting and stamping as if preparing to bolt, which shook his coach in its traces, despite the brake being set.

An instant later, Maura's cry of alarm chilled Ash's blood. He didn't want her caught in the melee, yet the moment she ran into the carriage house, she threw herself into the thick of the battle, charging one of his attackers with her bare fists.

When the miscreant whirled toward her threateningly, Ash felt a surge of fear-driven rage more powerful than anything he'd ever experienced.

In reaction, he let fly a punishing blow that sent his second opponent sprawling. Responding just as swiftly, Maura scrambled after the fallen thug's baton and swung it with all her might at the first tough. With a yelp, her target went down hard, like a felled oak. Ash was left with only a final assailant to dispense with.

By the time he succeeded in knocking the lout unconscious, Maura was standing over the other two prone thugs, pointing a cocked pistol down at their heads.

"Don't even think about getting up," she warned in a deadly tone. Ash could hear the fear trembling in her voice, but her eyes were fierce and bright.

She was angry and shaken, but he had never been more proud of her—or more grateful. The fight had concluded almost as swiftly as it had begun. Yet he knew he could not have survived without her intervention. He was still more concerned about Maura just now, however.

"Are you all right?" Ash demanded as they stood staring at each other, breathing heavily.

"Yes," she said unsteadily. "Are you?" Distraught, she scanned his face, noting the scrape on his jaw where it had grated against the cobblestones, and a bruise on his left cheekbone from a beefy fist.

When she raised her free hand to gently touch his injured jaw, Ash reassured her. "I'm fine—but I am worried about my grooms. I need to find them."

Maura nodded in answer. Then, continuing to aim her pistol at her prisoners, she backed away just far enough to calm the frightened horses. Ash almost smiled. He should have known that the animals would be her chief priority, even above her own welfare.

She spoke soothingly to the beasts, bestowing a soft stroke here, a tender pat there. Then her eyes lifted to meet Ash's, suddenly fierce as fire again. "They tried to kill you."

"I wonder," Ash replied thoughtfully.

He nudged the unconscious thug with his boot. Her attention directed downward, Maura inhaled a sharp breath at the man's attire. "He is dressed in Deering's colors! These are *his* servants!"

One was indeed wearing familiar livery, Ash realized. "I don't doubt they are. Keep your pistol trained on these fellows, will you?"

"Gladly."

"Don't move if you value your life," Ash advised the defeated bruisers who were still conscious.

While Maura stood guard over them, Ash made a quick check of the carriage house and found one of his grooms on the floor behind his coach, clutching his head and groaning. Three other servants were tied and gagged in the tack room, including his coachman, Thomas.

After freeing his chagrined staff and devising a compress for his injured groom's head, Ash returned to Maura's side. Deering's minions had remained perfectly still where they lay, but he could see they were quaking in fear at the punishment they would likely receive.

"Let's tie them up and see what they have to say for themselves."

In short order his own servants had accommodated his wishes, although none too gently, in payment for the harsh treatment they themselves had received earlier. Maura could then safely uncock her pistol and return it to her cloak pocket, and Ash was able to confirm what he'd suspected: The thugs were indeed employed by Viscount Deering. They had come on foot to infiltrate the Beaufort stables—their orders to disable the marquis's servants and commandeer his coach, then incapacitate him for a time so he would be forced to forfeit the duel.

"See?" Ash said quietly to Maura. "Killing me was not their aim. They merely hoped to keep me from reaching our meeting."

"For once I am in complete agreement with Deering," Maura muttered. "I should have tried that method of forestalling you myself."

Ignoring her gibe, Ash sent a stable lad for reinforcements from the house, then turned to his coachmen and quietly issued a new set of orders. Once Thomas had climbed into the driver's seat, Ash shepherded Maura into his coach.

"Just where are we going?" she asked, clearly none too happy.

"To the dueling field, of course."

Her eyes glittered dangerously. "I am not letting you face Deering over pistols!"

"I daresay there will be no duel now. We have enough leverage over him to render him powerless."

That gave her pause. "What do you mean?"

"Deering has violated our gentleman's code of honor with a vengeance, and we have incontrovertible proof from his own servants. He won't be able to cover up his machinations now."

When she looked skeptical and unmollified, Ash adopted a conciliatory tone. "Thank you for coming to my rescue, love. I gather you followed me to the stables to prevent me from leaving—"

"I did indeed," she agreed. "I saw you heading there from my bedchamber window, so I threw my cloak on over my clothes and brought my pistol in case you had already left and I had to trail you to the duel."

"Well, I am very glad you came along when you did, since I'm not certain I could have managed to defeat Deering's lackeys on my own." Ash let his mouth curve into a grin. "I would say that you and I make a good team."

Maura was having none of his pacifying, however. "How can you be so nonchalant? You could have died!"

"In truth, I am far from nonchalant. You were remarkably brave, but seeing that brute come after you took ten years off my life."

"How do you think *I* felt, seeing them attacking you so viciously?" Maura demanded.

"I don't know. How did you feel, love?"

"I wanted to hit you myself. I was right to be worried about you, Ash—and I was right not to trust you. You snuck out without even a farewell. I told you I do not want you risking your life for me!"

She looked incredibly beautiful and fierce just then, and Ash couldn't help but feel gratified by her anger on his behalf. Not even his physical discomfort could subdue his high spirits. Although his jaw and ribs ached from the blows he'd taken, and his knuckles were raw from the blows he'd given, not to mention nearly having his head bashed in, Ash only felt elation.

And Maura's fierce protectiveness was the cause.

She had the same reckless attitude as he, putting his safety above her own. Her pluckiness, her courage to overcome great odds all on her own, had always impressed him, as did her determination to fight for what she believed in. She was passionate and opinionated and tart-tongued and sometimes even violent . . . and she was so very, very dear to him.

She had proven herself his match in every way, and Ash knew only one manner to express his feelings for her: Take Maura in his arms and soothe her anger with his lips.

Maura's fear subsided as Ash's strong arms closed around her. She'd been deathly afraid, seeing him set upon by a pack of savage brutes. Now her overwhelming relief that he'd escaped serious injury was buoyed by the fervent hope that he would not have to duel.

And admittedly, she felt awed by how masterfully he

had dispatched his assailants. In all likelihood, Ash hadn't even needed her intervention, despite his avowals to the contrary. When his kiss ended, Maura sighed and laid her head on his shoulder, signaling her surrender.

As Ash gently stroked her hair—which she'd had no time to pin up—she listened as he speculated on what had driven the assault. "Deering is a coward at heart, so it makes sense that he would try to engineer my forfeit. But he would gain in another way if I failed to meet him. I would be as much as admitting that I cheated during our card game. At least I now understand something that has puzzled me—why he would name Pelham as his second. He wanted a peer with an impeccable reputation to bear witness when I didn't appear this morning. But having Pelham there should work to *our* advantage now."

Shifting her head, Maura glanced up at Ash. "How so?"

His mouth curved faintly. "I don't know if I should tell you, love. You won't like my plan."

"Tell me anyway."

"When we arrive, I will act as though I mean to go through with the duel."

When she started to object, Ash pressed a finger to her lips. "I am asking you to trust me once more, Maura."

She searched his face, finding no sign of prevarication or smugness, merely tenderness and unshakable resolve. "Very well," she agreed, reluctantly swallowing her reservations.

Some quarter hour later the coach slowed and turned

off the road onto a green field that was damp with mist.

The other primary participants were already present. In addition to Viscount Deering, Maura spied Ash's cousin, the Earl of Traherne, standing next to a distinguished elderly gentleman whom she recognized as Lord Pelham from the incident in the park last week, when Deering had cruelly beaten her stallion.

Ash's coach halted near the other carriages. Upon handing Maura down, he called her attention to the small crowd of spectators on the hillside overlooking the field.

"We have an audience," Ash said dryly. "No doubt they are taking bets on the outcome of our duel."

Maura shuddered at such morbid curiosity, but responded tartly to his observation. "What did you expect when duels attract such notoriety? You brazenly announced your intentions to the entire gaming club last night. By now most of London knows about your affair of honor being settled over pistols."

Not denying the accusation, Ash shepherded her toward the edge of the field where Deering awaited. The viscount's features were grim, possibly because his hopes had been dashed when his opponent had kept their appointment after all.

Deering scowled further as his gaze shifted from Ash to Maura. "What the devil is she doing here, Beaufort? Her presence here is completely unacceptable."

"Granted, Miss Collyer's attendance is irregular," Ash replied with his blandest smile. "But I want her to have the pleasure of seeing me shoot you. Unless of course you have decided to recant your spurious accusations against her late father?"

Maura held her breath until Deering responded with a sneer.

"I have no intention of recanting."

Disappointment flooded her, but Ash seemed to have expected that answer.

"As you like." He nodded both to his cousin, Lord Traherne, and to Lord Pelham. "If you gentlemen will indulge me by waiting a few more minutes, I expect some guests to join us shortly."

Deering immediately narrowed his brows. "What scheme is this, Beaufort? Why are you delaying?"

"Are you so anxious to die, Deering?" Ash countered silkily. Receiving no answer, he turned toward their seconds. "Meanwhile, I should like to examine the weapons if I may."

Maura watched Lord Pelham step forward and offer a satinwood box, which contained an elegant matched set of long-barreled dueling pistols.

Traherne nodded his approval. She could tell that his sharp eyes hadn't missed the bruises on his cousin's face, but his casual tone belied his concern. "I have already checked the balance and sights, Ash, but you will want to do so for yourself."

Ash complied, then asked about the specific rules for the duel—number of paces, order of firing, et cetera. The discussion made Maura extremely nervous, but Deering was unnerved also, judging from his tight expression, and that consoled her a small measure.

After final agreement was reached on the rules, little else was said between the duelists. By the time another handful of minutes passed, Deering was looking visibly irritated, and Maura felt her tension rising even further. Even the crowd on the hillside was growing restless at the unexpected delay.

Then at last she heard the distant sounds of a horse-drawn vehicle approaching. Maura turned to watch a wagon roll onto the field and lumber across the grass toward them. She counted half a dozen occupants—three whom she recognized as Ash's servants, plus the three liveried thugs whose hands and feet were bound.

Deering blanched at the sight of his incapacitated minions, much to Maura's satisfaction and Ash's obvious enjoyment.

"I see you understand how drastically our respective circumstances have changed," Ash commented as the wagon came to a stop near the carriages.

"I haven't a clue what you are talking about," Deering snapped, trying to bluster his way out of the net that was closing around him.

"Oh, come now. You may as well give up your pretense of innocence. Your lackeys have turned against you and confessed."

"What did they confess?" Traherne asked curiously.

Ash continued staring at the viscount. "Why don't you explain, Deering?"

"I have nothing to say. This is a complete fabrication. You manufactured their lies—"

"Pray, spare us your sham claims of victimhood," Ash interrupted. Evidently losing patience, he summarized what had happened in his stables that morning, concluding with his speculation as to why Deering had ordered the attack. Traherne's momentary surprise was followed by a soft chuckle, while Pelham seemed repulsed.

"Is this true?" Pelham demanded of the viscount. "You sought to make Beaufort forfeit the duel?"

Deering glanced behind him at his barouche, as if contemplating making his escape. Knowing he'd been caught red-handed, he was clearly desperate to be anywhere else at the moment.

Ash continued to press his case. "As you see, you failed in your aim to disable me. However, under certain conditions, I might be willing to overlook your assault on me and keep quiet about the entire affair."

"What conditions?" Deering asked warily.

"First, you will admit your guilt to Miss Collyer—unequivocally, right now—by confessing the role you played in her father's downfall and why. You were the one who cheated two years ago, not Noah Collyer, because you coveted his prize stallion. Is that correct?"

When Deering hesitated, Ash prodded. "We are waiting, Rupert . . . and do speak up. I want Lord Pelham to hear your admission for himself so you cannot rescind it later."

Under clear duress, the viscount ground out his words. "I admit I am guilty of cheating Collyer in order to gain possession of his stallion."

Maura couldn't help curling her fists as she took a step toward Deering. "You treacherous coward," she said in a trembling voice. "You knew my father was innocent all along, but your despicable accusations led to his death."

"Yes," he said through gritted teeth.

"See, that was not so difficult, was it?" Ash taunted.

Deering glared daggers at him. "Is my admission adequate?"

"Not quite. I want two signed copies of your confession to keep as insurance—one for myself and one for Lord Pelham," Ash said before addressing Pelham. "I would ask that you keep his account confidential for the time being, my lord."

Pelham frowned. "You will let his contemptible deeds go unpunished?"

"I did not say that precisely. I am not quite so noble. No, I want three more things from Deering in exchange for our silence." He turned back to the viscount. "Next, you will sign over the stallion's deed of sale to Miss Collyer. Then you will make a public apology to her— today, in writing—withdrawing the charges you made two years ago against her father and absolving him of all suspicion of cheating. I want to see a retraction in this evening's newspapers."

"Very well," Deering said grimly.

"And lastly, by week's end, you will take an extended trip to the continent and not show your face in England for the next decade."

When his final condition sank in, Deering erupted, practically sputtering in outrage. "You cannot expect me to leave my home!"

Ash smiled at his vehemence. "It is entirely your decision, but if you remain, your dishonor will become universally known. I daresay you will be hounded out of England, and even your closest friends will disavow you."

"Damn you, Beaufort!"

"Protest all you like, but you should be grateful that I am not pressing to have you arrested. Your employees will shortly be on their way to jail, where they will be charged with assault on a peer."

Traherne interjected with a trace of humor, "You should take his advice and go abroad for an indefinite stay, Deering."

When the viscount snarled like a cornered animal, Ash's smile broadened to bare his own teeth. "Buck up, Rupert. I am offering you a chance to avoid total disgrace. But if you should attempt anything like this ever again . . . if you dare act in any manner whatsoever against Miss Collyer, I promise I will hunt you down and kill you, do I make myself clear?"

His tone was amiable, but there was a deadly glint in his eyes. Pelham looked a trifle shocked at such plain speaking, but Deering apparently understood that Ash's threat was serious. He also knew that he had no choice and that he'd been soundly beaten.

"Perfectly clear," he growled, nearly vibrating with rage.

He cast a scathing glance at Maura then, his fury barely contained. She could feel his desire to punish her for his defeat and almost recoiled at the hatred in his eyes.

"This is all *your* doing," he complained bitterly.

Ash took a protective step toward her, but Maura raised a hand to forestall him.

"You brought your banishment on yourself, Lord Deering," she replied defiantly. "You have only yourself to blame."

Wheeling, the viscount marched over to his waiting carriage and flung himself inside. As the vehicle drove away, Ash thanked Lord Pelham for his participation and his discretion. Then Pelham took his leave also, all the while shaking his head in incredulous disgust.

Traherne's reaction was more positive. His eyes gleaming with appreciation, he clapped Ash on the shoulder. "Well done, cousin. And congratulations, Miss Collyer, on the imminent restoration of your father's reputation. This is cause for celebration. I say that when we return home, we gather the family to raise a toast to your success."

Ash answered for her. "Unfortunately, any celebration will have to wait until later, since I must lay charges against those fine fellows." With his head, he indicated the bound thugs. "The wagon is full, however, so if you'll give me a ride to Old Bailey, Quinn, I'll send Miss Collyer home in my coach. There is no need to expose her to the criminal elements she would find there."

"I would be happy to," Traherne agreed.

"My thanks . . . and will you also allow me a moment of privacy with her?"

"Certainly." Ash's cousin glanced up at the crowd on the hillside. "I shall inform the spectators that the duel has been canceled. They will be sorely disappointed to be deprived of their entertainment."

Traherne strode away then, leaving Ash alone with Maura. She stood there speechless, unable to move as she realized the import of what had just happened. She felt stunned by Deering's confession, almost numb with euphoria.

"I cannot believe it," she whispered before her voice cracked.

When she lowered her head and covered her face with her hands, Ash caught her wrists and made her look at him. She could scarcely see him through her blur of tears, but she could tell his expression showed concern as he peered down at her.

"Why the devil are you weeping? I expected you to be happy."

"I *am* happy. I am ecstatic. After all this time . . . I never thought this day would ever come. I only wish that Papa were still alive to see it."

When she sent Ash a tremulous smile of sadness and regret, he looked relieved. Despite their audience on the hillside, he stepped closer and wrapped his arms around her, pulling her to his chest. His strength was palpable, surrounding her, comforting her.

However, Ash being Ash, he couldn't resist provoking her. "I never thought you of all people would turn into a watering pot, vixen."

Maura gave a shaky laugh against his coat front.

Tender amusement sounded in his voice. "I told you that you could trust me, did I not?"

"Yes, I believe you did." He hadn't given up, even when she had begged him to. She owed him a debt she could never repay, Maura knew.

"I am so very grateful to you, Ash," she murmured. "I don't know how I could possibly thank you."

He pressed a kiss to the crown of her head. "You needn't thank me, love. It is satisfaction enough, seeing Deering get his just reward."

His declaration reminded her just how they had come to be in this situation in the first place. The realization served to jolt Maura out of her daze and bring her sharply back to reality.

She had resolved that once her father's name was cleared, she would settle her uncertain future with Ash . . . and now that time was at hand. To be fair, she couldn't hold him to their temporary betrothal. He had only proposed in the first place because he'd wanted to defeat Deering. Now that goal was met, there was no more reason for them to continue the pretense of an engagement.

"Come, Thomas will drive you home," Ash said, interrupting her thoughts. Releasing her from his embrace, he turned her toward his coach. "Quinn is right—we need to celebrate tonight."

Maura, however, doubted she would feel much like celebrating. Not when she had to give Ash his freedom.

Suddenly her throat was clogged with tears for reasons that had little to do with her father's vindication. She should be enraptured just now, since this was a profoundly joyous occasion. Yet as she accompanied Ash to his carriage, all Maura could think about was how badly she wished their betrothal could be real, and how unlikely it was that her wish would ever be granted.

Chapter Twenty-two

During the entire drive home, Maura argued with herself about when and how to resolve her future with Ash. As a gentleman, he could not honorably end their betrothal. Thus, she would have to be the one to do it, or at least give him the chance to withdraw his formal offer of marriage. But the pressing question was, should she broach the subject as soon as Ash returned home?

Her stomach churned with anxiety as she considered his possible responses. In order to protect her, he might decide to continue their deception a while longer, until the conflict with Deering was unequivocally settled and he actually left the country. Or, since Ash had claimed her virginity, he might even offer to marry her for real in an attempt to be noble.

Maura knew she had to make the same effort at nobility. She didn't want to trap Ash into matrimony or force him to be shackled unwillingly to her for the rest of his life.

He would likely leap at the offer of his freedom, Maura feared. He didn't love her. He had won her heart so effortlessly—in scarcely more than a week, in fact—but she hadn't won his.

Admittedly, a tiny piece of her foolish heart held out hope that perhaps in time, with a great deal of luck, Ash might one day change his mind about her and come to see her differently, as something more than an intriguing experiment or a pleasurable game or his chosen lover of the moment. But the sensible part of her knew she was only indulging in fanciful dreams.

Idiotic, pointless dreams.

Ash wasn't the kind of man to fall in love. He frequently called her "love," but that was the same casual endearment he used with his sister and his cousin Skye, and no doubt with numerous other women in a manifestation of his rakish charm. Such endearments were meaningless in revealing the true state of a man's heart.

She would be wise to crush her foolish hopes, Maura chided herself. She didn't dare let herself believe in happy fairy-tale endings when doing so would likely result in devastating disappointment.

Yet despite her vow to be pragmatic, she couldn't keep knots of dread from tightening her stomach at the necessity of parting from Ash now that there was no justification for remaining with him.

When Maura arrived home, she inquired after Katharine's whereabouts and discovered her breakfasting with the rest of the Wilde clan—Skye, Lord Cornelius, Lady Isabella, and Lord Jack—in a family gathering.

They all rose from the table at Maura's entrance, but Katharine was the first to ask with a trace of apprehension, "What news have you, Maura? We have been anxiously waiting to hear the outcome of the duel."

"It has been called off," she announced, which elicited varying expressions of relief from the company. The elders exhaled audibly while Skye murmured, "Thank heaven."

Katharine also blew out her breath, but then said rather cheerfully, "I confess, I was not overly afraid for Ash. This is not the first duel in our family, and my hair would be gray if I worried every time my reckless brothers or cousins"—she directed a pointed look at Jack—"did something dangerous or rash."

"I was not in the least worried," Jack commented with a provoking grin. "As I told Miss Collyer last evening, Ash can take care of himself."

"You were concerned for him, too, dear brother," Kate retorted in a ribbing tone. "Why else would you have joined us at this early hour, long before you usually rise?"

"Perhaps because your chef sets a fine breakfast table?"

Their good-natured squabbling brought a faint smile to Maura's lips, but Skye quickly intervened. "Hush, you two! I want Maura to tell us what happened this morning. We heard from our servants about Deering's treacherous ambush, but nothing since then. Why was the duel canceled?"

Maura told them in detail, recounting how Ash had skillfully compelled Deering's admission of guilt and the conditions under which his dishonor would remain concealed from the *Beau Monde*. At her conclusion, Katharine and Skye both hugged her happily, after which Jack demanded an embrace also.

With reluctant amusement, Maura complied, then thanked all the Wildes profusely for helping to remove the ugly stain on her father's memory. When she asked about the groom with the head wound, Katharine said the lad was resting quietly after being tended and bandaged by their physician and was expected to make a full recovery.

Maura didn't doubt that after the carriage house battle, Katharine had taken charge as mistress of the manor to bring order out of chaos and see to the injured. Kate now assumed her frequent mother-hen role with Maura.

"Do sit down and eat with us, dearest. I'll wager you skipped breakfast and are famished."

Maura's appetite was entirely nonexistent, however, even though she hadn't eaten a thing since yesterday's dinner. "Thank you, but I would rather go upstairs to my bedchamber and repair my dishevelment." Not only did she need to wash and change her clothes and tame her unpinned hair, but she knew she would be terrible company in her present dismal mood.

"Then I will send up a tray for you," Katharine said, linking their arms in a sisterly fashion. She accompanied Maura out into the corridor, where she made use of their relative privacy to resume her favorite theme of late.

"So now that your father's reputation will be restored, Maura, you will surely proceed with wedding Ash, won't you?"

Loath to be drawn into a discussion about her dubious matrimonial prospects, Maura responded with a pained smile and parried the question. "The matter is still unsettled," she murmured, before kissing her friend's cheek and excusing herself.

Yet as she trudged up to her bedchamber, her agitated thoughts remained fixed on that very quandary, like a tongue probing a sore tooth. She badly wanted to delay facing Ash, but perhaps she had best get it over with at once, to learn her fate and end this torturous uncertainty.

When she spoke to Ash, she would dispassionately release him from any further obligation toward her and state her plans to return home to Suffolk, then judge his reaction. If he put up no resistance, she would *not* break down in tears, Maura vowed. She couldn't let her pitiful emotions override her resolve. Nor could she make Ash feel guilty about ending their association. She had to be strong and do the honorable thing.

She would force herself to smile and accept whatever decision he made regarding their future together.

Even so, Maura wondered how she would endure it if he decided their affair was over, for the loneliness and hurt would be unbearable.

She did not have long to wait, since Ash returned by late morning. Maura had planted herself in the front parlor to watch for Lord Traherne's carriage, and as soon as she heard Ash being admitted to the entrance hall, she went to greet him.

She was keenly aware of the dread squeezing her chest, but one look at the worsening cuts and bruises on his face and knuckles drove all thoughts of a confrontation from her mind.

"You should let me tend those scrapes," she said urgently.

Ash seemed surprised by her offer. "You are a woman of many talents, love, but I didn't realize you were skilled as a medic."

"I have cared for plenty of wounded horses in my time."

A gleam of amusement lit his eyes. "Should I be flattered that you are comparing me to a horse?"

Maura ignored his levity. "Where are your medical supplies?"

"Our housekeeper has a store of salves and bandages in her office."

Maura asked the footman on duty in the hall to fetch a basin of warm water from the kitchens. Then she accompanied Ash to the housekeeper's office, where she proceeded to gather the supplies she would need to patch up his injuries.

Once the basin was delivered and the footman dismissed, she ordered Ash to sit down in a wooden chair while she worked. She cleaned his wounds with soap and water and applied basilicum ointment, ministrations which he bore without protest. When she dabbed a damp cloth at the deep cut above his eyebrow, however, he winced reflexively.

"I'm sorry to hurt you," she apologized sincerely.

"It is no matter. My chest pains me more, to be truthful."

"From the blows you took to your torso? Let me see."

After a slight hesitation, Ash opened his coat and waistcoat, then gingerly raised his shirt to bare his chest.

Seeing that his ribs were covered with brown and purple splotches, Maura bit her lower lip in sympathy.

"I will survive," Ash claimed, watching her. "I've suffered much worse brawling with Jack and Quinn during our salad days."

"Is that how you knew to defend yourself from those brutes' vicious blows? Your childhood bouts of fisticuffs?"

"That and various sparring matches at Gentleman Jackson's." He meant the boxing salon run by a former national champion, Maura knew.

She used a gentle touch to probe Ash's ribs. "I don't believe anything is broken. I could make up a warm poultice and wrap your chest, or I could just apply some liniment to ease the pain and bruising."

"The liniment will do. I am not an invalid."

Maura complied, carefully smoothing a pungent yellow ointment over the discolorations and rubbing it into his skin.

"Thank you, love," Ash said, easing his shirt down again. "That does indeed feel better."

Knowing there was nothing more to be done for him, Maura washed and dried her hands, then busied herself returning the supplies to the closet shelf, drawing out the moment as she tried to gather her courage.

Realizing she was purposely delaying, she cleared her throat and began in a small voice. "Ash, I have been thinking."

"Yes?"

"I believe it is time for me to return home to Suffolk."

At his lack of response, she glanced over her shoulder with trepidation. He had raised an eyebrow, as if waiting for further explanation.

"You see . . . Gandy has his hands full with the spring foaling and badly needs my help. And I ought to bring Emperor home as well."

"Of course," Ash said in an even tone.

"I don't wish to seem ungrateful," Maura added in a rush, "by disappearing the instant my problems are settled, but there is no reason for me to remain here." She took a deep breath to brace herself. "There is no reason to continue our charade, either."

Ash's gaze stayed fixed on her. "No reason?" he repeated slowly. "You mean you want to end our betrothal?"

What she wanted was entirely beside the point, Maura thought despairingly. "Yes." There, she had said it. She had provided him the excuse to back out if he wished to.

"You seem to be in a hurry," Ash remarked at last. "Why such haste?"

"I am in no hurry," she lied. "I just no longer need the protection of your name, now that you have dealt with Deering."

His gaze was unusually penetrating, yet Maura couldn't read his enigmatic expression.

"You never wanted to wed me in the first place," she reminded him. "You only proposed a temporary arrangement as a means to protect me."

"True."

At his brusque reply, the pain that stabbed her was sharp and piercing. Maura suddenly felt as if she couldn't breathe.

Ash's next comment was not any more comforting, either. "If there should be a child . . . you know that will change things. You will have to wed me then."

She nodded, although the ache in her throat wouldn't let her speak. Ash was saying he would be willing to marry her if she was with child, but he was offering her no professions of love or even affection. His expression was starkly solemn, devoid of all emotion.

She wanted him to say something—anything—to prevent her from leaving, but his grave silence drew out.

"Very well," he said finally. "When do you plan to leave?"

She had her answer, Maura realized, feeling the pain intensify. If he loved her, he would not let her go so readily.

Blindly she turned back to the supplies and finished arranging them neatly on the shelf. She was crying inside, but she wouldn't let him see it. "Today. This afternoon," she whispered past the ache in her throat.

"You are welcome to stay here longer if you wish."

"I know." Clamping her teeth together to hold back a sob, Maura pasted a smile on her lips as she faced him again.

Ash had risen from his chair and was frowning now. In fact his expression was almost a scowl as he said in that same gruff tone, "You will use my traveling chaise to convey you home."

"There is no need to trouble yourself," Maura managed. "I have my gig here in London."

"I am not letting you travel all that way on your own. Not until I'm certain Deering is gone from England and there is no further risk of his retaliating."

In answer, Maura nodded mutely and headed for the door.

As she passed him, Ash stepped closer. "Maura . . ."

When he reached out a hand, though, she flinched and quickly moved around him. If he touched her now, she would be lost.

She made it out to the corridor by putting one foot in front of the other, but her eyes were so blurred she could barely see.

She would leave for home immediately, Maura vowed. It might be cowardly to flee from Ash so abruptly, but staying would make it even harder for her to tear herself away in a week or two weeks or a month from now, when she fell even more desperately in love with him.

She felt too deeply for him already, that was the agonizing truth.

She would not tell Katharine about her departure this time either, for Kate would only argue and try to convince her to reconsider, and then Maura would break down and sob out her pathetic feelings of unrequited love.

Yes, she could remain here in London for a time, gathering memories of Ash and his family to solace her in the interminable years ahead, when she would be all alone. But living here under the same roof with him would be impossible. Seeing him each and every day but unable to be with him, to touch him, to love him, would be excruciating.

She would have no right to do any of those things. Nor would she be his lover any longer. If she wanted to claim a few moments of illicit passion with Ash, she would have to resort to slinking about his house, stealing into his chamber at night to avoid his servants, deceiving his family and her friends. It was far preferable to remove herself from temptation.

When she made it to her bedchamber, it was all

Maura could do to control her tears. Dashing at her streaming eyes, she retrieved her valise from under the bed, then began searching her drawers and wardrobe for the barest necessities required for the drive home, haphazardly tossing garments into the case.

She had learned long ago that it was useless to long for things she could never have, Maura reprimanded herself. She had to accept that tormenting fact now, even though her heart was breaking.

Two hours later, Ash was in his study, sprawled indecorously on his leather sofa, when Katharine came storming in. "I cannot believe you let Maura go!" she declared.

He pried one eye open to shoot her a baleful glare. "What would you have me do? Lock her in the cellar so she could not escape?"

"Yes! If that was the only way to keep her here."

"Go away and leave me in peace, Kate," Ash muttered.

He had already downed the better part of a liberal brandy, and when he raised the glass to his lips again, Kate took notice. "What are you doing, imbibing such potent spirits in the middle of the day? Is it because Maura left you?"

"Your powers of perception are unparalleled."

Disregarding his testy sarcasm, Kate furrowed her brow. "I don't understand. I thought things were going swimmingly between the two of you. You vanquished her hateful foe and restored her father's honor. That should have made Maura welcome your suit." Her gaze narrowed on Ash. "What did you do to make her flee, Ash?"

"Nothing that I'm aware of."

"Did you cry off from your engagement?"

"No. Maura was the one to cry off."

Katharine looked bewildered. "Why? Did she give you a reason?"

"She only said that there was no point in continuing the charade of our betrothal and that she had to return home to Suffolk to see to the spring foals."

"And you just let her walk out? What did you say to her in return?"

Ash didn't reply at once. He had no intention of revealing his warning to Maura—that if there was a child, she would have to marry him. Instead, he admitted to his second edict. "I insisted that for her protection, she take my chaise home rather than her gig."

Katharine lifted her gaze to the ceiling, muttering "Men!" in a disgusted tone. Then more calmly: "I see I gave you far more credit than you deserve, Ash. Don't you have the remotest inkling about romance? You know how to seduce any woman who catches your eye, but you make a mull of genuine courtship. I'll wager my life that Maura wanted you to propose for real. She loves you, I know she does."

His gaze narrowing on his sister, Ash slowly levered himself to a sitting position. "Did she tell you so?"

"No, not in so many words. Maura is not one to share her feelings, even with me. But I know it in my bones."

"Your bones are hardly the best judge of her feelings."

"And *you* are?" Kate put her hands on her hips. "Speaking of feelings, how do you feel about *her*, Ash? Do you love her?"

He no longer had difficulty answering that question. He loved Maura deeply. The fear he'd felt this morning at seeing her life threatened had relentlessly driven that truth home to him. "Yes, I love her."

His sister exhaled in relief. "Then why the devil did you let her go? She is your ideal match. Surely you see that by now."

He'd come to the same conclusion this morning when Maura had fought by his side, defending him with her bare hands regardless of the peril she faced. Or perhaps his revelation had come last night, when he'd held her in his arms and joined their bodies, moving inside her in perfect rhythm.

If Maura wasn't his consummate match, then he didn't have one on this earth. She fit him as no other woman had or could.

Ash stared down at the last of the golden brandy in his glass as he pondered his inexorable transformation. He hadn't truly believed he would ever know true love—or more accurately, that he would ever *allow* himself to feel love. He'd never wanted to risk that kind of pain. After losing his parents, he'd held himself emotionally distant from outsiders, never letting any woman close enough to touch his heart. He had never expected to live up to his family's celebrated legacy and find his one true mate. Yet he couldn't be a dispassionate, uninvolved bystander any longer. Not with Maura.

Loving her felt profoundly right, and he yearned for her love in return.

Absently Ash gulped a mouthful of brandy. He felt the burn all down his tight chest into his rioting stomach, yet he was more keenly aware of the hot fear that had gnawed at him since Maura had broken off their engagement and declared her intention of returning home. In that moment, he had frozen solid with fear. His mind and heart and body had simply shut down, Ash remembered.

The only response he could think of just then was to clutch at straws. His pronouncement about Maura possibly carrying his child was a desperate way to bind her to him—and the very least romantic declaration he could have made. It was no wonder she had taken his reaction as evidence that he cared nothing for her.

On the other hand . . . despite Kate's avowals, he had difficulty believing that Maura loved him. Oh, she was grateful to him, Ash knew. She had told him so on more than one occasion. The irony was that he'd done his level best to earn her gratitude over the past sennight, but he feared gratitude was all he had.

He looked up to find Kate watching him closely, waiting for his answer.

"Whatever my feelings for her," he finally said, "I doubt Maura believes herself to be my match. She feels indebted to me, nothing more. That isn't love. I don't want her accepting my hand in marriage because of a misplaced sense of obligation. I want more than that."

"Then why didn't you tell her so? In fact, why don't you tell her so now? What are you waiting for?"

What indeed? Ash wondered. Was it fear keeping him here, planted on his sofa, trying to drown his desolate thoughts with expensive liquor?

"You must go after her, Ash," Katharine prodded when he was silent.

"I will. Just not for a while yet."

"How long is a while?"

"A day or two. A week at most."

Exhaling in relief, Kate smiled in approval. "Excellent." Moving closer, she bent down to kiss his cheek. "If there is anything I can do to help you—"

"You've done more than enough as it is," Ash said dryly.

"I know." Her smile turned self-satisfied. "Thanks to me, you had the opportunity to test if Maura was your legendary lover. But it is up to *you* to make her love you."

Ash didn't dispute his sister's observation and in fact scarcely noticed when she left the room. He did know one thing, though. He couldn't force Maura's love. He had to *earn* it. He might have gained her respect this past week, but winning her heart was a much more immense challenge. . . .

His gaze narrowed as he focused on the dilemma he faced. Maura had to come to him of her own free will, but that didn't mean he wouldn't do his damnedest to influence her feelings. She belonged to him—he would just have to make her see it.

However, he would give her a little time to adjust to the significant changes in her life, chiefly to gain some distance from her anguish over her late father. Ash wanted to make a fresh start with Maura. He also had to make certain that her nemesis was out of her life for good. Deering might have poisoned her feelings for any man. . . .

Ash shook off that dismal reflection and came to a new resolve. Even a few days of waiting would doubtless be interminable, but he wasn't ever giving up. He would allow Maura a sufficient interval to reflect and sort out her feelings for him. But if she didn't love him now, he would hound her until she did.

Ash felt a determined smile curve his mouth. Maura was his life's mate, he knew that now without a doubt. He'd felt that remarkable bond between them last night when he'd made love to her, and again this morning when she'd come to his rescue.

He simply had to make her recognize it as well.

He would shape his destiny by sheer force of will if need be, but in the end he would make Maura love him.

Chapter Twenty-three

Situated between Newmarket Heath and the village of Cavendish, the Collyer Stud had the advantage of being close to the racing downs and annual bloodstock sales of Newmarket, yet boasted rich grass pastureland that was ideal for horsebreeding.

Charming streams and roads dotted with poplars and beeches laced the undulating, green countryside, where timber-framed thatched cottages mingled with the grand estates of the Suffolk nobility, occasionally interspersed with cupolas and turrets of various studs and stables.

The Collyer Stud had a quiet beauty all its own, Maura had always thought. Normally she relished the peace and tranquility of her home, but on this particular occasion, six long days after her retreat from London, she gave little thought to the loveliness. She and Gandy had both been up since well before dawn, encouraging a fractious mare through a difficult birth.

They had just stepped outside the stall and were now observing over the half door. Twenty minutes ago, the tiny black foal they'd named Noble Prince after his sire's champion line had stood on its long spindly legs and had successfully begun nursing.

Despite her relief, however, despite the fact that the miracle of birth never failed to awe her and watching precious young foals always raised her spirits, Maura felt drained to the bone. Even so, she welcomed the weariness. Upon arriving home, she'd thrown herself into her work, hoping to make herself so exhausted that she would cease mourning her loss of Ash.

Gandy appeared to be growing more and more concerned for her, though. Tall and wiry, his hair peppered with gray, her longtime stable master still had a spring in his step that belied his nearly sixty years of age. He was the closest thing Maura had to a father since her own father's passing. Actually she thought of Gandy more like a dear uncle, despite the differences in their fortune and stations.

His rugged, weathered face was frowning now as he shifted his attention from the weak mare to her. "Ye should seek yer own bed now, Miss. I can deal with the young 'un and her mama from here."

Maura glanced out the window of the foaling barn. The angle of the sun suggested that it was early afternoon. "It is broad daylight, Gandy. I won't be able to sleep until dark."

He made a face. "If ye won't turn in and lie yerself down for a nap, then take yerself back to the manor. Ye should eat something. Ye missed yer breakfast and dinner."

"So did you."

"But my old bones can get by on scant victuals. Please, Miss Maura."

"Very well, I will go." She had been resting her arms on the door and now pushed away. Before she turned, however, Gandy spoke again.

" 'Tisn't my place to say, but p'raps ye should return to London. Ye aren't happy here. Anyone with eyes can see that."

She was indeed fiendishly unhappy. Three days of heavy rain had darkened her mood even further. Yet she forced a smile. "I will be fine."

"Well, for my sake I wish ye would heed me. Yer papa would have me head to see ye now. He's surely looking down from heaven and cursing me."

"Papa never cursed, Gandy."

"Not in yer hearing, no, but he could swear a wicked streak if he had a ken to."

His observation won a more genuine smile from her, a smile that stayed with her as she made her way down the aisle to the pump.

Her amusement faded as she scrubbed her hands and arms and removed the thick apron that had protected her gown. But at least the dreary weather had let up, Maura thought as she left the barn and trudged toward the manor. The afternoon was growing warm with bright spring sunshine, a welcome change from the recent downpours.

When she grew closer, she noticed a carriage in the stableyard. Her spirits sank when she recognized Priscilla's barouche. Wondering what had brought her stepmother calling, Maura let herself in by the back door, where she traded her half boots for shoes. She still was not at all presentable for company, though, certainly not by Pris's standards, and so she considered going up to her bedchamber to change her gown.

She was rather surprised when Priscilla intercepted her at the back stairs—and taken aback at the thoroughly amiable tone of her greeting.

"There you are, my dear," Pris said, smiling broadly. "I should have known you would be out in the barns. I trust the new foal is healthy?"

"Yes, although the mare had a difficult time dropping. What brings you here, Priscilla?" Maura asked warily.

"Why, I wanted to report the glad tidings to you myself. Lord Deering has left the country! And before that, he made a public apology to your late father in the papers!"

Maura exhaled slowly. Katharine had sent her a copy of Deering's retraction, but she hadn't yet heard of his departure and had been almost afraid that it wouldn't happen.

"That was Beaufort's doing, was it not? And you are the reason Beaufort intervened. I cannot thank you enough, dearest Maura."

"You needn't thank me, Priscilla. I acted for Papa's sake."

"Well, I am beside myself with joy. I confess"— Pris lowered her voice to a conspiratorial whisper— "I found Deering's public humiliation immensely satisfying."

"As did I," Maura said in heartfelt agreement.

"And my daughters are flourishing, now that the Wildes have taken such a particular interest in them. I know you are the sole reason." Pris hesitated, her expression growing solemn as she took Maura's hands in her own. "I must apologize for how I treated you all these years. As I told you last week, I very much hope we can start anew, if that is even possible."

Maura felt her usual guard crumble at her stepmother's genuine contrition. "I hope so too, Priscilla," she replied quite honestly.

"Then why don't we share a nice cup of tea and I can tell you everything that has happened in London during your recent absence?" She took Maura's arm and turned her toward the front of the manor. "You and I never have had a real coze, like mother and daughter, but I should like to try."

Amazingly enough, Maura realized she would like that also. After detouring to the kitchens to ask the housekeeper to bring them tea, Maura went up to her bedchamber to quickly wash and change, then settled in the rose parlor with Priscilla, where they eyed each other hesitantly.

Their conversation began tentatively, even stiffly, but Priscilla appeared determined to persevere and move beyond establishing a mere truce in favor of a comfortable relationship. And after a while Maura found herself relaxing and even smiling. It was her first time being the target of the beautiful widow's charm and a pointed reminder of how her father had been seduced so easily.

When the subject turned to Maura's betrothal to Lord Beaufort, however, she balked at discussing any of the details, merely saying there would be no wedding.

"What do you mean, there will be no wedding?" Priscilla's tone quickly changed from persuasion to exasperation, and even held a shrill note. "What happened, Maura? Did you offend his lordship in some fashion? You never could behave suitably toward an eligible gentleman, with decorum and charm and sweetness . . . honey not vinegar. No doubt you gave Beaufort a disgust of you with your tart tongue and indelicate manners."

Maura's lips twisted in an ironic smile. "For once you misjudge me, Priscilla. The truth is, our betrothal *never* was real. It was only a pretense so Beaufort could challenge Viscount Deering on my behalf."

Her stepmother's mouth dropped open. "Not real? Well then, you simply must make it real, Maura. You must marry the marquis!"

"I'm afraid I cannot oblige you, Priscilla."

"But this is a golden opportunity for you," she chided. "And your family as well. How can you pass it up, marrying a nobleman of his fortune and rank? Surely you want your stepsisters to have such a splendid connection—"

Suddenly Priscilla bit off her last words and stopped the harangue herself. For a moment, she looked as if she had swallowed a sour lemon, but then amazingly, she managed a rueful smile. "Please forgive me, my dear. I promised I would turn over a new leaf. You don't need me to scold you. Truly, Maura, I did not mean to imply that my only thought was for my daughters or that you were deficient in some manner. I sincerely want for you to be happy. Beaufort seemed quite taken with you and you with him. Is there no hope for a marriage?"

"No, I am sorry, there is not." The thought brought a sharp pain to Maura's breast, but she was determined to conceal it.

Priscilla sighed. "Very well, then, I will cease reproaching you. My lips are sealed, I swear. So why do you not tell me about this year's foals? How many of them are Emperor's?"

Since Priscilla had never once been interested in the workings of the stud, Maura was convinced her stepmother was making an enormous effort to reconcile. When she extended an invitation to stay for the night, however, Priscilla claimed the need to return directly to London in order to chaperone Hannah and Lucy at an important engagement the following morning. But she had considered it necessary to come in person and express her thanks to Maura for vanquishing Lord Deering.

They parted on remarkably good terms and actually embraced for the first time in years. Maura saw her stepmother's barouche off, but in the quiet that followed the departing carriage, she had to face her own problems once more. Her heart was so heavy, it felt like a lump of lead had lodged in her chest.

Rather than return to the house, Maura crossed the stableyard and passed the barns, then walked out to the stud paddocks to check on Emperor—something she had done frequently since his return to Suffolk.

A swell of affection filled her when she saw the stallion cavorting in the meadow like a young colt. The enclosed pasture was surrounded by high rail fencing and tall yew hedges and separated from the broodmares and foals by the width of the farm, but he didn't appear to mind the segregation since he had Frip for companionship. The elderly chestnut gelding was contentedly grazing while Emperor raced freely across the grass.

He was very happy to be home, Maura knew. Moreover, the bond they shared had only been strengthened by his ordeal. When she let herself in by way of a sturdy gate, Emperor suddenly plunged to a halt and whipped his head around, as if sensing her. Upon spying her, he let out a piercing whinny and galloped over to Maura, only slowing at the last instant.

For a time he pranced in a circle around her, snorting and tossing his head, hooves dancing, tail raised high as he showed off his regal carriage and noble bloodlines. Sweat shone on his glossy black coat in the sunlight, accentuating the power in his rippling muscles.

However, the stallion finally halted quietly before her, tame as any lamb. Eager for the attention, he offered his face to be fondled. Maura obliged, stroking his ears and the poll between.

"I am glad that one of us is happy, Emp," she murmured. "You at least have good reason to be cheerful since your amorous affairs are far more successful than mine. You are back with your harem, while I am alone once more."

It was a measure of how lonely she was that she was talking to her horse, Maura knew. But even her beloved Emp couldn't cure her heartbreak. The hurt inside her was like an aching wound.

She had brought her misery on herself, though. By letting herself love Ash, she had made her pain and loss infinitely greater. If only she had heeded her own self-warnings and kept her heart closed to Ash. . . . Except that would have been impossible. She couldn't help loving him, any more than she could will herself to stop breathing.

Adding disappointment to her crushing despondency was the fact that her monthly courses had come and gone. She had wanted Ash's child to love, even though becoming *enceinte* out of wedlock would have resulted in a monstrous scandal.

"I believe the poets are wrong," she told Emperor sadly. "It is *not* better to have loved and lost. Losing at love is far too excruciating."

The stallion shook his head at her musings, which drew a faint smile from Maura. "What, you disagree? Priscilla shares your opinion. She thinks I should pursue Ash for his fortune and connections." Maura hesitated, then dared to voice the subversive thought that had been intensifying for days.

"Perhaps I made a mistake returning home, Emp. At least if I had remained in London, I could have been with him."

The prospect of being with Ash again was so appealing it was frightening. Was she seriously considering, Maura wondered, taking her stepmother's advice to join all the other pitiful husband-hunters who stalked wealthy noblemen?

She was disgusted at herself for the very idea. How could she have sunk so low, behaving just like Priscilla, manipulating and conniving to ensnare a wealthy husband?

Except that she would not be pursuing Ash for security or material possessions, Maura declared silently. It would be purely for love.

The inescapable truth was, she desperately wanted to be with him, even if he didn't love her . . . although she yearned for much more. She wanted to share his life, his home, to bear his children, to own his heart as he did hers. She wanted the entire wonderful fairy-tale dream.

But if you truly want such things, an insistent voice inside her prodded, *you will have to fight for them. You have never been a coward, but you are acting like one now. This is no way to prove yourself Ash's match, languishing in the country in this pathetic manner, hiding yourself away, such a vast distance from him.*

"What do you think, my fine fellow?" Maura finally asked the stallion. "Should I return to London and pursue Ash? I would have an ally in Katharine. No doubt I could ask her for advice on winning his heart."

Emperor gave her no answer, of course. Instead, he abruptly pulled away from her and spun around, then with a flash of his heels, took off running again.

Maura's thoughts remained on her dilemma as she watched his exuberant play. Perhaps it was deplorable, but the overwhelming yearning inside her was growing stronger with each passing hour. She needed to return to London and tell Ash that she had changed her mind. She did *not* want to be honorable and release him from their betrothal. And if he had no desire to wed her, then she would settle for whatever he would give her. She was willing to humble herself and beg him to take her back, if need be—

"That stallion of yours is one magnificent animal," Ash said in an admiring tone behind her. "I can see why Deering coveted him."

At the sound of his dear voice, Maura's heart lifted with joy, then promptly plunged back down again when she remembered she had no grounds to feel joy at

Ash's presence. Turning slowly, she saw him standing on the other side of the gate, looking impossibly handsome in a blue coat and buff pantaloons.

Maura raised a hand to her breastbone to calm her clamoring heartbeat. She ought to be embarrassed that he had likely heard her plotting a campaign to capture him—and yet she was too glad simply to see him.

She drank in the sight of him, and realized he was watching her just as intently.

"Ash . . . what are you doing here?" she managed a breathless query.

"I could say I came to claim the yearling you promised me, but I would be lying."

"Then why?"

"I brought you something."

When Ash let himself in through the gate, she noticed he was carrying a gold brocade bag roughly the size of his hand. As soon as he reached her, he proffered the bag to her. "Here, open it."

Maura loosened the drawstrings and peeked inside, only to find a horseshoe that was bent and twisted and beginning to rust.

She sent him a puzzled look. "You brought me an old horseshoe? Whatever for?"

He hesitated, seemingly oddly wary. "That is not just any old horseshoe, I'll have you know. It is the one Emperor lost during the storm a fortnight ago. I returned to Fawley and spent a full day searching for the damned thing."

"I don't understand," she said, still bewildered.

The look in Ash's green eyes was compounded of wry amusement and something more unfathomable and disturbing. "I wanted to remain in keeping with the tale of Cinderella, but I thought you would prefer a shoe for your horse more than a glass slipper for yourself."

When his meaning finally dawned on her, Maura drew a sharp breath and was barely able to find her voice. "You are here . . . in the role of prince?"

"Yes, and I wish to make you a proper proposal of marriage."

She stared at Ash, not daring to believe what she was hearing, since it was doubtless too good to be true. "You must be roasting me."

This time the tender laughter and affection in his eyes was unmistakable. "Surely you know by now that I never jest about matrimony."

Maura's shock gave way to sudden hope, yet her tone held skepticism in addition to breathlessness. "You actually . . . *want* to marry me?"

"That is what I said, isn't it?"

"No, it is not. You said you intend to *propose*. There is an immense difference."

"Very well, vixen . . . I very much want to marry you. The thought of spending the rest of my days without you is unbearable. I love you, Maura," Ash added simply, gazing levelly at her.

"You *love* me?" she breathed, her astonishment not abating.

His eyes were stunningly bright as he took her in his arms and drew her close. "Of course I do. Why else would I have trekked halfway across England for you, hiding out in barns and braving storms and enduring an utter lack of creature comforts?"

She peered up at him. "At the time you said it was to ensure my safety."

"That was only a small part of my motivation. The greater reason was that even then I was falling in love with you. Regrettably, I was very late recognizing my feelings, since I have never been in love until now."

"You *love* me," she repeated in wonder.

Ash smiled at her amazement. "I do, sweet Maura, quite madly. I couldn't help myself. I was drawn in first by your courage and determination when you stole your horse back from under Deering's nose. Then, that morning when you went up against his brutes and bashed one with his own cudgel in order to protect me, I was certain I loved you. How many other genteel young ladies would risk such danger to save my skin?"

Maura shook her head in awe.

"I can see you don't believe me," Ash observed with a rueful sigh. "But I will prove my love for you, I promise you. I know you don't feel the same for me yet, but—"

"You know nothing of the kind, Ash," Maura said swiftly. "Of *course* I love you. How could I not, after everything you did for me? After what you did for my father?"

Ash grimaced. "I don't want your damned gratitude."

"Well, you have it, for eternity. But gratitude is only a small part of why I love you so dearly. There are countless reasons, not the least of which is your vexing protectiveness of me." Reaching up, Maura wrapped her arms tightly around his neck. "But I want to make it clear, none of my reasons have to do with material things. I am not a fortune hunter like my stepmother. I love you solely for yourself, not your title and wealth or even your handsome appearance."

His slow smile was pure magic, reflecting her own joy. Maura's heart suddenly felt hugely full, brimming over with happiness.

Ash pressed a swift kiss to her lips, then drew back abruptly. "If you felt that way about me, why did you dissolve our betrothal?"

"To set you free. I was trying to be noble and not trap you in marriage."

"I suppose your attempt to be selfless is admirable, but I want to be trapped, my lovely Maura. You are my perfect match, and I am never letting you go."

Her brows narrowed. "You could have said something when I cried off instead of letting me think you didn't want me at all."

"You caught me off guard. And in fact, I was trying to be noble myself, letting you choose your own future. I didn't want to impose my will on you."

"That would be the *first* time you ever declined to impose your will on me," she replied archly, although with a hint of humor. "I wish you had told me how you felt and saved me all these days of acute misery."

"I should have done so," Ash conceded. "Kate accused me of not knowing an inkling about romance—which is the prime reason I went in search of that blasted horseshoe. I thought the symbolism would be meaningful to you."

"It is indeed," Maura said softly. "But if you came here to propose marriage, you are exceedingly dilatory, my dear prince. What are you waiting for?"

Ash smiled again. "An excellent question." His expression, although still warm, turned serious. "So my beloved Miss Collyer . . . For the second time in a fortnight, will you do me the immense honor of accepting my hand in marriage?"

"*Gladly*, Ash. With all my heart."

"The perfect answer," he said with that same tender solemnity. "We should seal our bargain with a kiss."

Eagerly Maura complied, raising her mouth to his. However, what began as a tender consummation of their renewed engagement quickly blossomed into something much more heated. Desire flared and smoldered between them. Maura felt a fierce, aching need for Ash rise within her.

When she sank into his kiss, he pulled her even closer, his mouth taking hers with hard, quick urgency. That wonderfully sensual mouth could drive a woman wild, and this time was no exception for Maura.

At her responsive moan of pleasure, Ash's breath turned to a growl in his throat. His hands swept down her back to caress her buttocks, bringing their hips together so that she could feel his rigid hardness through their clothing. Clearly they both yearned to satisfy the relentless hunger shimmering between them. His touch felt rough and almost desperate, which only increased the ache inside her.

She had missed Ash so fiercely. Missed his protectiveness, his charm, his wry humor, his blunt honesty, his tender enchantment, his passionate lovemaking . . .

Their embrace might have progressed to an even more flammable pitch if not for the sound of galloping hoofbeats behind her. Startled from her daze, Maura broke off and glanced back in time see Emperor skid to a stop.

To her astonishment, the stallion tossed his head, snorting and pawing the earth as if in challenge to Ash.

Ash recognized the horse's stance as well. "Easy there, fellow," he said swiftly. "I will take good care of your mistress, I swear to you."

"He isn't dangerous," Maura assured Ash.

"Not to *you*, certainly. I, on the other hand . . . Perhaps we should take this embrace elsewhere, away from his territory. He clearly is jealous of your affections."

Slipping a possessive arm around her shoulders, Ash escorted her safely outside the gate.

"I am sorry," Maura murmured. "Emp has never behaved so possessively before."

Surprisingly, Ash chuckled. "Oh, I fully understand his feelings for you. And I might be angry at his interruption, except that I owe him a monumental debt of gratitude. He is the reason I found you."

Guiding her a short distance away, behind a concealing hedge, Ash resumed his tender hold of Maura. "I suppose it's just as well that he prevented us from going any further. I might have ravished you right there on the grass."

Maura's mouth curved as she gazed up at him. "I think ravishment implies lack of consent. I would have been entirely willing."

"I am flattered, love. But now that we are officially betrothed, I should wait to have my wicked way with you until our wedding night, so as to avoid any further risk of scandal."

Maura eyed Ash with real amusement. "What? I can scarcely believe what I am hearing. A scandalous Wilde determined to avoid scandal? Will wonders never cease?"

"You have a tart tongue, did you know that?"

"I may have heard that sort of spurious accusation once or twice before."

When Ash chuckled again, Maura recalled what he'd said earlier, before their passionate kiss that had kindled Emperor's protective streak. "Do you truly think I am your perfect match?"

"Yes, indeed. You are every bit a rebel in your own way, just as fiery and passionate as all the other females in my clan. You are unquestionably worthy of becoming a Wilde."

His teasing tone made her smile, and yet it meant a great deal to Maura, knowing she would be marrying into his enchanting, delightfully dear family.

"In fact," Ash pointed out, "I tried to show you how I felt that last night before the duel. When I made love to you, I was laying claim to you."

Her eyebrows lifted. "Were you now?"

"Yes. I didn't tell you, because I know how excessively proud you are."

"I was willing to swallow my pride, Ash. In truth, not ten minutes ago I was contemplating how soon I could return to London. I even considered begging you to take me back."

"I should have welcomed *that* remarkable event."

"It is too late now," Maura replied firmly. "I have already accepted your proposal. You will have to be content with my professions of love."

"I imagine I could settle for professions, as long as they are ardent enough. Let me hear them again, Maura."

"I love you dearly, Ash. Do you really love me?" she repeated, wanting the reassurance.

"Fiercely, vixen. My actions should have given me away from the very beginning of our adventure together. I was willing to become a notorious fugitive for your sake. But I would much rather stay here in England and marry you and sire your children."

"I infinitely prefer that, Ash." Maura's heart warmed at the mention of children. "You saved me from a lonely life as a criminal. I realize that it entailed great sacrifice on your part, having to endure those dreadfully primitive conditions."

"Well, if I were forced to, I would do it again. Pray let me know if you have any other crimes you want my help perpetrating, or any other stallions that need stealing. We could schedule our larceny for Tuesday or Wednesday next, between calling the banns for our wedding."

Her eyes brightened. "Our wedding? When will that be?"

"Within the month, unless you prefer sooner. We could be wed by special license if you wish."

"I would absolutely prefer sooner." Her laughter faded a measure, since she wanted to accord this special moment the seriousness it deserved. "I want to marry you as soon as possible, Ash. To be your wife and your lover, to face life at your side."

"I have wanted to be your lover since the moment I first kissed you," Ash responded lightly, but then he, too, sobered as his arms tightened around her. "I love you, dearest Maura. I want you, I need you. I can think of no greater pleasure than holding you in my arms and loving you for the rest of our lives."

Entirely reassured, Maura smiled and raised her mouth to his for another intoxicating kiss. She loved Ash desperately, irrevocably, and she knew now in every part of her heart that he felt the same deep love for her.

Epilogue

London, May 1816

Out of habit, Ash leaned idly against a column in the Traherne ballroom, his pose reflecting the ennui of a jaded nobleman. Yet boredom was the farthest thing from his mind as he watched his bride of nine hours. This was his wedding day. He and Maura had been married that afternoon by special license, and afterward Skye and Quinn had hosted a lavish wedding feast and ball at their magnificent London mansion.

The celebrations were an immense success, judging by the laughter and gaiety of the company. Ash had spent all evening at Maura's side, accepting continuous felicitations from friends and acquaintances, but just now she stood a short distance from him, conversing with her stepsisters while he marveled at his good fortune.

He had never thought he needed anyone, but he'd severely deluded himself. He needed Maura profoundly. He knew without doubt that she was his soul mate, his heartbeat, his love.

Just then Uncle Cornelius rambled past Ash and paused upon spying him. Despite a distaste for grand society, Cornelius had put himself out to mingle with the glittering throng. Even more surprising, he had managed to stay awake long past his usual retirement hour since he wished to welcome into the family the first new Wilde bride in decades.

"I confess," Cornelius observed thoughtfully to Ash, "I initially questioned Katharine's postulation regarding legendary lovers, yet she was surprisingly sapient. You did well to wed Maura, my boy. Exceedingly well."

"So I did, Uncle," he agreed.

"Your parents would have been quite pleased and proud to see this day."

Ash felt a momentary stab of loss at the mention of his late parents, even though his grief was tempered by the intervening years. Yet he knew Cornelius was right. Stephen and Melicent Wilde would have ardently approved of his choice, as would Quinn and Skye's parents, Lionel and Angelique Wilde.

As his Uncle Cornelius wandered off again, Ash returned his attention to his new wife. Maura glowed with life and happiness. She was all woman—vibrant, dynamic, eternally intriguing. He would never tire of watching her.

Her stepsisters, too, seemed animated and almost pretty in their enjoyment of the ball. When their mother joined them, Maura's glow only faltered a slight measure, evidence of her newly forged relationship with her stepmother. A moment later Maura turned to glance around her, as if searching for him.

When she locked gazes with him, the glorious smile she gave him filled Ash with a deep, piercing joy. He wanted nothing more than to make Maura smile like that always, to protect her and make her happy.

As the conversation with her stepfamily continued, he felt a sharp impatience that they were keeping Maura from him. Finally, though, she broke away and returned to his side.

"What kept you so long?" he demanded as he straightened from his causal pose.

"Hannah and Lucy wished to express their appreciation to us once again. They are both being courted by eligible young gentlemen now, and apparently their beaux are impressed that I own a famous racehorse. But happily, the girls seem to be admired for their own sweet sakes, not solely for their connections and the generous dowries you bestowed upon them." Maura's hazel eyes were dancing with amusement as she gazed up at Ash. "Priscilla has high hopes of turning their new suitors into husbands before long, and she gives me partial credit. Is it not ironic that *I* am playing matchmaker?" Maura added with a disbelieving laugh.

"Ironic indeed," Ash said dryly. Having no desire to dwell further on her young stepsisters' amorous affairs, however, he took Maura's elbow and guided her behind a decorative bank of potted palms.

"What are you about, Ash?" she asked with more curiosity than wariness.

"I am hiding you away from prying eyes so I can

steal a kiss from you. To be truthful, I should like to leave the ball altogether and take you home at once."

Her resultant smile was as warm as a midsummer breeze. "I desperately crave a kiss, but it would be rude to leave the festivities so early when Skye and Quinn have gone to such trouble for us."

"It is nearly midnight," Ash pointed out. "And my cousins will understand that I want you all to myself tonight. As for the ball guests, I don't give a farthing for their opinions."

"You *will* have me all to yourself tonight, since Kate means to remain here to afford us privacy on our wedding night. We ought not leave for a while longer."

"You are asking a great deal," he grumbled.

"I know, but sadly, you must curb your lust a few hours more."

In response, Ash slid a hand down the back of Maura's elegant gown and drew her hips against his. Her eyes widened in a pretense of shock. "Ash, behave yourself! We cannot embrace in public, for pity's sake."

"Behave myself?" He raised a dubious eyebrow. "I can see you are already set on turning me into a henpecked husband, giving me orders about proper comportment."

He saw the laughter building in her eyes. "You are hardly in danger of being henpecked," Maura retorted. "It is all I can do to hold my own with you."

"Actually, you do quite well at holding your own, my darling." When her quelling look didn't slacken, though, Ash gave a theatrical sigh. "Very well, but the least you could do is give me a kiss to sustain me until we can finally take our leave."

When he lowered his head, Maura complied eagerly as expected, her luscious lips softening and opening under his. Merely kissing her created sparks of passion between them, and Ash felt the heat start to smolder in his lower body. . . .

They were still kissing passionately when Skye found them behind the row of palms. "Why am I not surprised that you are already living up to the family legend, Ash?"

He might have ignored the cheerful question if Maura hadn't broken off guiltily. Disappointed, Ash turned a baleful eye on his youngest cousin. "Can you not see we are occupied?"

Skye smiled sweetly. "I only wished to tell Maura how delighted we all are to have her join our family. I would have done so sooner, but I haven't had a single moment alone with her since the ceremony." Stepping closer, she took Maura's hands. "I am overjoyed to have you as a sister in addition to a dear friend, Maura. And ecstatic for you as well. No one deserves happiness more than you."

"Thank you," she murmured with a heartfelt smile.

"I foresee a long and glorious union between you and Ash," Skye predicted, "since we Wildes fall in love for life. Granted, we had begun to despair that Ash would never marry and fulfill our parents' legacy, but now there is real hope for the rest of our generation."

Katharine appeared just in time to overhear Skye's last remark. "Yes, Ash," Kate agreed in a provocative tone. "It seems my legendary lovers theory is not so preposterous after all. I expect a suitable acknowledgment from you. I was right about Maura being your destiny, you must admit."

His mouth curved. "Very well, I admit it."

His sister's response was a self-satisfied smile. "Allow me to say I told you so."

"Smugness does not become you, sweet shrew."

Kate laughed. "I think I should be permitted to crow a little. You fought me tooth and nail at first, but you have now proved the possibility that a legendary lover could exist for each of us cousins."

Ash slid a friendly arm around Katharine's shoulders. "I trust your time comes quickly, sister dear."

"I sincerely hope so also."

"You mistake my meaning, Kate," he replied with an affectionate squeeze of her shoulders. "I want you to find your match soon, because now that Maura and I are married, I prefer to have the house to ourselves."

Katharine feigned a wounded look. "Are you actually saying my presence is *unwanted*?"

"No, only that you need to increase the pace of your hunt."

"I am trying, I assure. I promised I would search for my own true love next. But unfortunately, my romantic prospects seem dim at the moment, despite my best efforts."

Ash wasn't surprised, since he knew of few men who could handle a lively spitfire like Kate.

"Kate," Skye interrupted. "I gather you have discovered no prospective match for me yet?"

"I am sorry, Skye, but not yet. To be frank, I think it will be easier to find mates for the men in our family."

When Kate glanced behind her at the ballroom floor, Ash knew she was eyeing Jack and Quinn. Not only had they attended the ball and remained the entire time, they were dutifully conversing with dowagers and dancing with wallflowers in a show of family loyalty.

"She has a Greek myth in mind for Quinn," Skye said mischievously.

"Oh, which one?" Maura asked Kate.

"I imagine his tale will be Pygmalion. But Jack should come next, since his time is growing short."

When Maura looked intrigued, Kate explained. "I have found a possible Juliet to Jack's Romeo, but there are serious impediments to the union—namely, the long-standing feud between our two families and even worse, the young lady's imminent engagement to a duke. No doubt her parents will vociferously object to Jack's courtship, although in his case, having royal blood could be his saving grace."

"Royal blood?" Maura repeated. "Oh, yes, I remember Ash telling me that Jack's father was a European prince."

"Yes. Jack is a love child, but he could claim the throne if he really wished to—which he says he does not. Either way, he must act soon or he will miss his chance entirely. Skye, you are closest to Jack. You will have to persuade him to at least meet his Juliet."

"Certainly I will do my utmost," Skye replied earnestly. "However, you may have an even more difficult challenge than his, since Aunt Bella asked you to find someone for her good friend, Lord Hawkhurst. You remember, Maura, he is the earl who breeds horses on the Isle of Cyrene? Hawkhurst is a widower," she explained, "who lost his wife and young child here in England years ago. Aunt Bella believes he needs a new wife in order to be happy."

Kate's green eyes grew serious. "Hawkhurst is most assuredly on my list. I might even turn my hand to Uncle Cornelius."

Maura appeared skeptical. "I thought Lord Cornelius was a scholarly bachelor who rarely leaves his library."

"True. He is not a typical Wilde with a bent for passion and scandal, but he does have a romantic past of his own. Like Jack's mother, Uncle Cornelius never married because he was thwarted in love. But he is a dear soul, and I want a happy ending for him."

Kate's expression remained thoughtful as she eyed Maura. "Now that you have benefited from my theory, Maura, I think you should assist me in my future matchmaking endeavors."

Hesitating to reply, Maura cast an entreating glance at Ash, who came to her rescue by gently prodding his sister and cousin. "Kate, I expect you to suspend your scheming for this one evening at least. Why don't you and Skye return to our ball guests so I can be alone with my new wife?"

His blunt hint jolted Katharine out of her ruminations. "Oh, of course." With a rueful smile, she kissed Maura's cheek and stepped back while Skye did the same. Then linking arms, the two cousins disappeared behind the row of palms.

When they were gone, Maura shook her head in amusement. "I cannot believe she wants me to aid her. The role of matchmaker is as alien to me as that of Cinderella . . . although at the moment, I do feel like a fairy-tale princess. This gown is worthy of royalty." She glanced down at her short-sleeved gown of creamy, gold-embroidered lace. "But even though my metamorphosis into princess is progressing, I may never become accustomed to being addressed as Lady Beaufort."

Maura surprised Ash then by reaching down to grasp both his hands in her own. "I never expected to become your marchioness, Ash, but there is nothing I want more." Her gaze growing tender, she brought their entwined hands inward to frame her face while gazing up at him.

Love. Her eyes were full of it. Ash stilled, transfixed by that magical look. Her next words enchanted him even further.

"I cannot imagine living without you, Ash," Maura declared solemnly. "I would never want to. You make me feel treasured, cherished, loved."

"That is exactly how you should feel," he said simply, "since I treasure, cherish, and love you."

At his heartfelt affirmation, a hint of a smile returned to her lips. "How soon can we leave the ball and go home, dear husband?"

"You want to go home now? I thought you were concerned about appearing rude."

"I changed my mind. I don't want to waste another

moment before fulfilling the Wilde family legacy. We should probably wait until the stroke of midnight to honor the spirit of our lovers' tale, but after that . . ."

Having similar thoughts, Ash smiled in approval and captured Maura's lovely mouth again.

Chapter One

"*Miss Fortin is* not the grasping husband-hunter you seem to think her, Jack. And she certainly is no spineless ninny either—which you will discover for yourself if you ever deign to meet her. You will like her prodigiously, I swear it."

Recalling his cousin's ardent prediction, Lord Jack Wilde studied the young lady in question from across the dimly lit garden.

He had yet to contrive an introduction to Sophie Fortin tonight, or even approach her. Indeed, because of the long-standing feud between their families, he'd had to employ subterfuge simply to attend the masquerade ball hosted by her great-aunt.

Sneaking behind enemy lines in disguise seemed a craven way of investigating a prospective courtship, Jack reflected with dark humor. Yet here he stood, garbed as a swashbuckling pirate, observing Miss Fortin with a healthy dose of skepticism.

The gardens of her aunt's London residence had

been converted to an open-air ballroom, gently illuminated by colored lanterns. Undeniably, Miss Fortin stood out among the crowd of costumed dancers like a diamond among lumps of coal.

Jack couldn't keep his eyes off her, in no small part because she seemed a profusion of contradictions.

For her costume, she wore a glittering tiara and the gossamer, flowing gown of a royal princess, yet her grace and loveliness had little to do with her attire. A demi-mask concealed her eyes but not the delicacy of her face or the sensuality of her mouth. Her hair was an ordinary shade of dark brown, but the lustrous, curling tendrils piled high on her head had a life all their own.

A thoughtful frown drew down the corners of Jack's mouth. As much as he loathed admitting it, he was intrigued. Judged on outward appearances, Sophie Fortin was a beauty, just as advertised, but with none of the cold remoteness he'd expected. Instead, she had life, vitality, warmth.

That, and a generous, kind smile.

He hadn't expected the liveliness, much less the kindness or warmth. From what he knew about her, he'd imagined either a submissive young miss or a calculating social climber. Why else would she allow herself to be sold to a widower twice her age for the price of a dukedom?

Watching her, Jack felt a primal tug of desire, despite himself. Granted, his bias against her had softened over the past half hour. However, the notion that she might make him an ideal mate was still impossible to swallow.

He had no intention of courting her, of course. Most definitely he was not in the market for a wife. But he'd had no choice other than to arrange a meeting with her.

For that he could only blame the tenacious matchmaking of his sister Katharine and his cousin Skye. Kate's schemes would put Napoleon Bonaparte to shame, Jack suspected. Her campaign to marry him off had begun in earnest last week, the morning after their brother Ashton's wedding.

When Kate was younger, the family had generally indulged her romantic machinations with good humor. But her latest flight of fancy was patently absurd. Kate theorized that the five Wilde cousins—Ashton, Quinn, Jack, Skye, and Kate herself—could find true love by emulating legendary lovers throughout history.

Beyond all expectations, Ash had recently succeeded in falling in love with his "Cinderella," Miss Maura Collyer of Suffolk. Jack's supposed legend was not a fairy tale but one of the Bard's most famous tragedies, *Romeo and Juliet,* with him cast in the leading role of Romeo and Miss Fortin as his Juliet.

"Have you utterly lost your wits, Kate?" was his first reaction. I'm not about to play the pathetic hero who dies."

He put little credence in his sister's outlandish belief in romantic destiny. And even though he was usually ripe for a challenge, he had adamantly refused even to meet Miss Fortin.

In response, Kate and Skye had endlessly sung her praises in an effort to rouse his interest.

"Sophie Fortin has beauty in abundance," Kate professed.

"She is clever and kind," Skye added.

"It is not *her* fault that her parents are determined to land a high-ranking title for her," his sister repeated for the umpteenth time.

Jack's scoffing amusement remained the same. The Fortin chit had to be a timid dormouse, allowing herself to be married off to an older nobleman who had already buried one wife.

"There is no official betrothal yet," Skye countered. "You must act now, Jack, and rescue Miss Fortin from a loveless union before it is too late. Once she is engaged, she cannot honorably fall in love with *you*."

"Her honor or lack of it is hardly my concern," Jack replied, unswayed.

"Just promise you will meet her," Kate begged.

He'd held out until two days ago when Skye cornered him as he left his house. He was late for a curricle race, his head aching from an overindulgence of brandy the previous night. He'd practically tripped over his youngest cousin, who was camped on his front doorstep.

Completely ignoring his professed desire to be rid of her, Skye had climbed into his waiting curricle and refused to get down until she had wrung a promise from him to meet Miss Fortin.

"You know I won't give up, Jack," she said sweetly, "so you might as well concede."

For his own peace and self-preservation, he'd surrendered, knowing his female relatives would hound him relentlessly otherwise.

The masquerade had seemed the ideal opportunity to conduct his surveillance, since disguised as a pirate, he could attend without an invitation and reconnoiter freely in enemy territory. And he could rely on anonymity to contrive an encounter with Miss Fortin and judge her for himself. The unmasking was not until midnight, and by then he would be long gone.

He'd come tonight intending to prove Kate's ludicrous theory wrong. Regrettably, however, he'd been thrown off course by the beauty herself—or rather, by her lovely smile. Jack was drawn to that captivating smile against his wishes. At least he understood why a widowed duke could be smitten enough to consider offering matrimony to a much younger commoner with no fortune.

The dance ended just then, and Miss Fortin's partner of the moment bowed and took his leave of her. Alone, she glanced over her shoulder and caught Jack watching her from a corner of the gardens.

Instead of turning away out of shyness or embarrassment, however, she surprised him once again by suddenly moving his way.

Upon reaching him, she peered up into his mask, trying to see his eyes. "Do I know you, sir? I penned the invitations for my aunt, and I don't recall anyone of your description on the guest list."

Although his pirate costume couldn't disguise his height or athletic build, Jack suspected his identity was safe, since his mask covered the better part of his face and his headscarf concealed his black hair.

"No, we have not met before, Miss Fortin," he answered, amused by her directness. Confronting a stranger was something the females in his family would do.

"Then would you care to explain why you have been watching me these past twenty minutes or more?"

Her boldness impressed him, but he parried her question with his habitual facile charm. "Is it unreasonable for a man to enjoy watching a beautiful young lady?"

Responding to his flattery, she gave a light, skeptical laugh and glanced down at the cutlass he wore sashed at his waist. "Am I in any danger? Pirates are known to take hostages for ransom and carry away maidens for their own wicked purposes."

"If memory serves, I haven't ravished any fair maidens since Tuesday last."

Her enchanting smile reappeared, although whatever reply she would have made was interrupted by her unlikely suitor, the Duke of Dunmore.

"There you are, my dear," Dunmore said in a fond tone. "You promised me your hand for the next set of dances, remember?"

Her purported suitor, Jack noted, had even, rather handsome features but thinning hair that was graying at the temples. In his mid-forties, the duke was also taller than average, but his aristocratic bearing was marred by his slight paunch.

After a brief hesitation, Miss Fortin answered with a gracious smile. "Yes, of course I remember, your grace."

Seeing that entrancing smile bestowed on the nobleman, Jack felt an inexplicable pang of jealousy. Absurd, since he had no claim to Miss Fortin's affections whatsoever.

The duke might have felt a touch of jealousy as well, for he cast Jack a sharp look before offering the lady his arm.

"Who was that pirate fellow?" Dunmore asked as he led her away.

"I am not certain," Jack heard her say as they took their positions on the grass dance floor.

When the music began for a waltz, Jack watched their progress with bemusement, wondering what Miss Fortin saw in the Duke of Dunmore other than his illustrious title and fortune.

They did not appear to be well-matched as dance partners, for Dunmore was remarkably uncoordinated and kept treading upon her toes. Her expression remained serene until the third time he ground down on her foot, and then she couldn't conceal a grimace.

Dunmore seemed to realize he had hurt her, for he halted in his tracks and began apologizing profusely. "My dear, pray forgive my clumsiness."

Miss Fortin forced a smile. "It is no matter, your grace. There are all manner of people who find the waltz difficult to negotiate, since it is so new. But perhaps we should not attempt it any longer?"

When Dunmore readily agreed, they moved back to the sidelines and stood conversing until the dance ended. A short while later, she excused herself.

When she turned toward the house, Jack could see her struggling to hide her limp. She was putting on a game face but was clearly in real pain.

With some thought of helping her, he followed her inside in time to see her hobble down a corridor and slip through a doorway. Curious as to what she was about, he pursued her.

She had taken refuge in the library, of all places, Jack realized upon pausing at the threshold. A table lamp had been lit, no doubt for the convenience of the ball guests, and Jack watched as Miss Fortin sank gratefully onto the sofa nearest the lamp.

Bending down, she raised her skirts to her knees, then removed her left dancing slipper and stocking. She muttered something inaudible before taking off her mask, perhaps the better to see as she examined her toes.

When she grimaced again, Jack stepped forward. "May I be of assistance, Miss Fortin?"

She gave a start of surprise and eyed him warily as he crossed the room to her. Without waiting for her agreement, Jack knelt before her and took her bare foot in his hands.

"Allow me," he said, ignoring her sharply indrawn breath at his boldness.

Her smallest toe was bleeding, he could see. "Does it hurt to bend it?" he asked, gently prodding.

"Yes, but not excruciatingly so."

"Then it is only bruised, not broken," he pronounced. "It should heal in a week or so. Trust me, I speak from experience, having been injured by many an iron-shod hoof in my youth."

Finding the end of his waist sash, he tore off a strip of fabric and used the makeshift handkerchief to blot the blood on her toe.

"You can wrap a piece of cloth around your wound until you can fashion a proper bandage."

"Thank you," she murmured.

At her genuine expression of appreciation, Jack made the mistake of looking up. Her face was so very close that he froze.

She had stunning eyes, he realized. Luminous and thickly lashed. That dark shade of blue was almost violet.

Who had violet eyes? Jack thought irritably, struggling to resist her allure. This near, she was even more of an enchantress than he first realized, and his body reacted accordingly. The stab of desire that shot through him was as powerful as any he could remember.

In self-defense, he summoned a gruff voice. "Why did you allow Dunmore to trample your feet and half cripple you?" he demanded.

She had frozen at his nearness as well, but she looked taken aback by his inquiry. "I was being courteous, if you must know. It would have been unkind to point out his shortcomings. Dunmore cannot help it if he is a terrible dancer. Some people are cursed with two left feet."

"I suppose his rank and fortune can excuse myriad deficiencies," Jack said sardonically. "Isn't that the chief reason for your compassion? And why you wish to marry him?"

She stared at him. "Not at all. The duke is actually a very kind man. I didn't wish to hurt his feelings."

At Jack's skeptical silence, her gaze narrowed. "Why is it any of your concern?" When he didn't answer, she made a demand of her own. "Who *are* you?"

Jack reached up to remove his own mask.

"*You,*" she exclaimed, obviously recognizing him. Oddly enough, she seemed relieved to learn his identity rather than apprehensive as he'd expected, for she settled back on the sofa and regarded him thoughtfully.

"I gather you know me?" he asked.

"Everyone knows of the scandalous Lord Jack Wilde."

"But we have never met? I think I would remember you, Miss Fortin."

"No, we have never met directly. I saw you at the Perry's ball last season, but you never noticed me."

"I cannot imagine why," he said honestly.

"Perhaps because I was dressed in white. You avoid debutantes like the plague."

He grinned at that. "Ordinarily, yes."

"I avoided you that particular night as well, since I had been warned about you." When his eyebrow lifted, she expounded. "Our families have been locked in a blood feud for two generations, remember?"

"Ah, yes, the feud," Jack said. His great-uncle had killed her great-grandfather in a duel over a woman, and then fled to the American Colonies with the prize.

"I always regretted that prohibition," Miss Fortin said wistfully. "I would have enjoyed knowing Lady Katharine and Lady Skye, but I was forbidden to associate with them."

His mouth curved. "Do you always do as you are bid?"

She sidestepped the question. "Do you *never* do as you are bid? No, you needn't answer. From all reports, you live to break rules."

"What reports have you been heeding?"

"Oh, the gossip about you is universal. You are said to be an outrageously irreverent rake who can charm the birds from the trees—at least female birds. If only half the stories are true, I should fear for my virtue." As if suddenly becoming aware of the impropriety of the situation, she smoothed her skirts down over her knees. "I should not even be speaking to you now."

"So do you mean to run away screaming?"

Her luminous eyes sparked with an appealing levity. "No. I have been a dutiful daughter all evening. And I am curious to know why you are speaking to *me*. Why are you here at my aunt's ball, my lord? What do you want?"

I want you, lovely lady, came the unbidden thought.

His fierce attraction boded ill for his plan to dislike her, Jack acknowledged, laughing inwardly at the irony, but all his possessive male instincts were now keenly awake.

Deciding the truth was his best defense, he fixed his gaze on her luscious mouth. "I am here because I promised my cousin I would kiss you."